THE DREAMS IN THE PEARL HOUSE

THE NORTHWEST TRILOGY PART 2

CRAIG RANDALL

switchboard
PUBLISHING

DEDICATION

To H.P. Lovecraft, Mike Mignola, John Arcudi, and Neil Gaiman, for showing me the way.

To my wife, my children, and friends and family for your unrelenting support.

To all those who fed my inspiration: Anne Druse, Andy West, Emma Bascom, MJ Carstarphen, MY STUDENTS, Kevin Randall, Jamie-Lee Kelly, and so many more!

Most importantly, to those who've lived their lives marginalized by the weight of their own pain. To those whose minds have been trained to work against yourself. May a path to brighter days open to you, and may you find hope and healing.

(And to Brian J. Lynch — for helping me weed out all those pesky little errors!)

Trigger Warning

This book contains graphic scenes of panic, anxiety, depression, and violence that some might find disturbing and/or triggering to past feelings and/or experiences. Read at your discretion.

"For in this sleep of death what dreams may come..."

— William Shakespeare, *Hamlet*

"Whether the dreams brought on the fever or the fever brought on the dreams, [he] did not know."

— H.P. Lovecraft, *The Dreams in the Witch House*

PROLOGUE

Shadows crept across the almost frozen asphalt, enveloping the jagged, worn-down street that cut underneath the West Side overpass of Portland's Burnside Bridge. A hustle of scraping steps and pounding boots coming down on the ice-cold concrete echoed as men scurried back and forth, going about each task as assigned.

A hand reached out. The older of the two detectives lifted a yellow string of police tape for his partner to step under.

"Thank you," she said, in a quiet but sturdy voice.

The man nodded but gave no reply.

Their footsteps echoed across the night, colliding with the chaos and flurry of noise collecting beneath the overpass. They joined an already gathered group of officers.

He took the lead again.

"So, what've we got?"

A uniformed police officer ran through the facts for them—a sergeant who had been holding down the command until a higher-ranking officer arrived.

He walked them through what they'd found, what they'd collected so far, as well as anything else they noticed about the scene that might seem relevant. As he spoke, he spared no detail about the crime scene his men had set up, about their efficiency and adherence to protocol. He was proud.

The detectives listened with attentive patience before asking for a few moments alone at the scene.

Everyone dispersed and faded into the cold, dark corners of the night, shivering from their lack of movement.

"So, what do you think, rookie?"

He only said it because they were alone, but it made her smile. She understood what it meant, that he was handing it over to her. When she spoke, her voice sounded collected, confident. It filled the senior detective with pride.

"It's definitely ours," she said.

The man nodded once more.

"Single body. Male."

He nodded again.

The rookie crouched down, wanting a closer look at the victim's arm and torso. "The same strange bruising covering the entire victim." She stood up again and looked around. "No evidence how the body got here. Who the victim is? Where he's from? Nothing."

Annoyance draped itself over her like a cold blanket in the already frigid night.

Her partner smiled. *It's getting to her*, he thought.

"Yup..." he agreed. "And?"

She rounded on him.

"And...we got nothing, Scott. Again."

Feeling her frustration even before the words spilled out of her, he smiled, patient and kind.

This did little more than frustrate her more.

"*And...*" he paused again. "... our job is to...?"

She grinned then, though with some reluctance. Rolling her eyes, she mocked something he had forced her to repeat a thousand times before.

"Our job is to collect data and make what connections we can through the information available."

He nodded to his partner, but before he could speak, she broke in again, saying, "But we don't have *enough* data." Her frustration only grew, especially given the stark contrast to the steadiness of her partner. "We *need*–"

"We need to be patient, Cait. The data will come, and we will break this case. In the meantime, we–"

"And in the meantime, people are d–" Cait Lane couldn't bring herself to even finish the word, though she pointed down to the grotesque and maligned corpse lying between them on the cold ground with the pen in her hand.

Her partner paused, contemplating his words. He recognized Cait's propensity for impatience, knowing his patience with her would be the best reminder. He leaned it, making sure not to push her too hard.

"All the more reason to be patient..."

She looked up.

"... and thoughtful."

He was right, and she backed down, breathing deep. She just got so frustrated.

The aged man smiled at his younger partner. Her drive pushed her forward, but her understanding and willingness to be coached kept her steady. There was room to grow; but she was adaptable. That was one of the many reasons he'd chosen her as his new partner the year before. She showed greater restraint and aptitude for awareness than any of the other candidates. Besides, he loved the fire she carried around in herself. Over time, she would learn to wield it.

After his gentle reminder, he waited. She was smart. She knew.

"You're right. I'm–I'm sorry, Scott. It just–"

She let out another exasperated gasp.

"I get it," he said, his words carrying the perfect dose of consolation and encouragement. "I get it, rook—"

"We need more to go on!"

Taking in a deep breath, her partner waited before responding. Forcing her to slow down with him.

"Sometimes, we have enough to work with. Other times, we don't."

She let her fury collapse. He was right, again. And like he'd taught her, getting angry wouldn't help.

She nodded to him as she understood.

"Alright, now let's go over the scene ourselves, huh?"

She looked up, allowing a slight smile through.

"See if we can't find anything Portland's *finest* might have missed."

Her smile widened at his smirk. He always had the right words. Knew how to calm her. to reset her focus.

"Okay, okay." She took a deep breath.

"Where do we start, boss?"

Her eyes narrowed.

"I want to canvas each logical exit point. Look for signs of anyone else. Or anything. Work our way to the body." She looked up at him. "Alright?"

He smirked and nodded.

"You guide me, rook—I mean, boss. Let's go."

The glimmer returned to Cait's eyes, and she strode off toward the far end of the scene.

As she left, her partner took a moment to recognize and appreciate how she'd recovered from her frustration. He beamed with pride, knowing how much sharper she was when she calmed herself. How much more controlled. She was getting better. A lot better. Her temper was the only thing that disrupted her, but she was learning to balance it. To cut out the noise and get to the rational conclusions quicker.

She would get there; he felt that. He had to remind

himself he wasn't all that different when he was younger. Raw, impatient, and hungry for progress. He, too, had had to learn restraint and the slow art of letting the puzzle put itself together.

"You coming, Scott?"

Cait's words rang with a taunting pull.

He smiled again.

"Coming, boss."

He followed behind her, ensuring she was in the lead. They stopped right at the crime scene's edge, ready to begin.

ONE

I t had been months since Charlie West had been able to focus on what he would've considered a rational thought. As the night spilled into its early hours, like so many nights before, he lay in his cot twisting and turning in the shallows of an uneven, ill-tempered sleep. To say it had disrupted his life fell short of the complete picture, unless you added disturbed, displaced, and disenfranchised to it as well.

He was trying to sleep. Desperate for it. It'd been months since he'd had a decent night's sleep. He couldn't even remember the last one; something he chose not to think about.

His new rooms didn't help. A dark, dank hamlet of a room in the forgotten basement hall beneath the Portland Rescue Mission.

Charlie had been living there about four months. Oscar, The Mission's manager, offered him a room in exchange for help around the building. Miscellaneous cleaning and tidying, which didn't bother Charlie. Nor Oscar. Oscar just wanted him around. He'd never seen someone care for other people the way Charlie did. Charlie was incredible with the residents

—the homeless patrons. He understood *them*. Who they were. Their stories. He always managed *something* out of them. Oscar had never seen anything like it.

He'd give anything to keep someone like that around.

And he did.

Charlie wouldn't open up to others, though. It bothered some of the other workers. Oscar ignored it, choosing only to see the best in people. The best in Charlie.

Charlie is diligent, he would tell people. *There's a purity to him, you know? He just wants people to be alright.*

Oscar always spoke to others about Charlie with the greatest pride; Charlie might as well have been family. But no matter what happened, Charlie wouldn't allow that to sink in. He kept his distance from everyone. Everyone else who worked there noticed it, but Oscar always defended it.

That boy's been through hell, you know? Can't ya feel it? Give him some damn room, is what I say. Leave him be.

The same as anyone else, Oscar saw the pain which Charlie carried. There was a weight to Charlie's posture—a burden, a need for absolution—but he didn't dare approach the subject with him. He knew better.

Let other people come to you when they're ready, he'd say.

The cot springs squeaked and rang with every shift of Charlie's body. Each a plea to the confiding shadows. Pleas the shadows continued to ignore until once again their screams slipped into silence. He wasn't sure if the squeaking or the unnerving silence were worse.

His body made one rough turn after another, crying out into the dark. The empty, callous space hung over him, indifferent to it all.

Next to his cot sat an old furnace. It no longer worked. And a series of pipes fed back and forth through the old building's dizzying under-structure. Who knew if they worked? Or what they were for?

Charlie ignored them, as he did many things. They were nothing more than features of a world he found himself fading from.

Shifting again, this time almost violently, the cot screamed out once more, but Charlie's own cries outweighed their burst. His reach was much longer and more practiced.

The dreams were settling themselves in with a swift fury; not to be ignored.

They started right after Charlie's return to Portland. Not too long after he'd found his mother.

After the first one struck, a week passed before the next. Then another week elapsed before the next. By the end of a month, it was happening every third or fourth day, and Charlie developed a stifled pattern of sleep. And once one's sleep becomes infected, that's when fear can settle itself in.

The fear all but destroyed Charlie's rhythm of sleep; Like an eager ocean lapping at an unprotected beach, they eroded into nothing.

After three months, the dreams visited him every night, preying upon these growing fears. They settled into every crack and crevice of his past, all those heel-set bunkers past traumas had left behind.

In his state, Charlie never stood a chance.

He tried everything he knew to maintain those restful nights, but nothing seemed to help him. No matter what he tried, these thoughts kept bleeding through.

No amount of mental exercises worked. He just couldn't concentrate for sustained periods of time anymore; so he gave up. He tried sleeping medications, weaker and stronger, but something within him seemed bent on fighting back against their lull, leaving him agitated and restless far into the morning. When he'd at last fall asleep, the dreams were more vivid—vicious. He abandoned this because of the quick surge of fear. He tried listening to music, loud and quiet, reading, blasting talk radio, and anything he could think of until odd hours of the night, but nothing worked. Nothing he found quelled the fearful and frantic back and forth of his mind, keeping him from sleep. It was only when physical exhaustion settled in, he would find sleep; even then, his mind was busy.

It was anything but restful.

He tried a stiff drink before bed. The whiskey would warm his insides and numb his mind for a short time, but as always, the warmth would fade, and his worries would return tenfold as the alcohol affected his brain.

There were entire weeks on end where, whether it was sleeping pills or whiskey, he overindulged. This too only made his dreams more visceral and real, increasing his terror and fear; thus, he abandoned this remedy before long.

He took melatonin every night before bed; more out of habit than the fact it worked.

Because nothing worked anymore.

Life became a hollow existence, made bearable only by his intention to forget.

No matter what he did, sleep evaded him. If it came, whispering its sweet melodies, so would the dreams.

They always started with his mother, her body lying there, still and lifeless. It was his reactions he regretted most when these thoughts permeated his well-constructed barrier.

He ran.

He didn't want to see it. Or process it or deal with it at all. In any capacity. The confusion was too great. Facing it only added to the crushing burden he already carried.

So, he left. And he didn't stop. He still hadn't stopped.

This brought about many complications to his life, both emotional and practical. The most obvious became visible. Pain, which he'd learned to hide all those years, he'd found himself unable to conceal. That tightness in his chest, how it hunched his shoulders. He walked half-concave inward. His skin wore an almost translucent winter sheen. His face sagged with his posture.

All the while he clung to hopes that everything, his pain, even his memories, would just fade and disappear. This unrealistic hope cinched around him, suffocating his grip on reality. Any light feeling at all became impossible to cultivate. If he dwelled on them long enough, they grew into agony.

This is where the dreams always began. Fighting for room; battling over the line which despair and hope clashed at arms. Thoughts of his mother dwelled there, too. He could not push these thoughts away. Instead, he would linger there in the guilt until they took root. Then, the thoughts would take control. They'd run in whatever direction they wished to go.

Though, always ending in the *same* place.

Charlie's hands gripped the sweat-soaked blankets. Damp, they gripped him right back. His grasp, fierce and defensive. Fending off the imaginary attacks that were coming.

His body let out an involuntary yelp, flailing into the lonely dark. His legs kicked out from under the cover of his blankets. A soft sweat clung to him, but the air pressed in, making him cold.

Charlie would slip then; out of the real world and into his mind's darker corners where no sanctuary existed.

He was standing over his mother's still and lifeless corpse once more. Pits of fear and regret building and wrapping itself around him. Then, lightning struck and claps of thunder peeled their way across an expansive sky; it felt to him he was being transported through his memories, which raced past as he flew; images of his journey over the pass, of meeting pleasant towns-folk in Astoria—Trent's face flew by, and various men and women he had met—slight images of shops he'd stopped by, meals he'd eaten, the sunsets he'd watched from afar. Then there was Ellie. It always went to Ellie. And his stomach lurched and churned—it always made him feel sick. Booming pangs rang in the background and Charlie would find himself standing before a towering house; a house he thought he'd never seen, but felt so real, so vivid; deep down, he recognized it; how could he have made it up?

Aching laughter cracked off the house's interior, as if they had made the woodworking to redirect it all to Charlie's fears. Fires burned and men in dark suits loomed around him; their shadows grew. Towering high above and breaking through the ceiling; the laughter died, as always. A man with wild, ghost-white hair led him down a long, mysterious path. He wore matching wild eyes.

Same as always, Charlie's stomach turned as he met Ellie's face, and thunder ruptured across his mind.

Time sped up, and Charlie found himself underneath the ignited skyline. Lightning tore across a broken sky, swirling together in the mixture of a series of screams, of shrill wails that accompanied the constancy of a horrid chant, all to the rhythm of the cool, steel rain. Always present was the thunder's periodic pulse, stringing the night together, counting down the seconds until what Charlie most dreaded came.

"EKK-ELDERETH-AMMON-EDA-EDA!" went the haunting chant as it faded upward into the chaos of the vast and tumultuous sky.

"EKK-ELDERETH-AMMON-EDA-EDA!"

Charlie's whole body shook—the body in his dream and the one trying to sleep atop his cot.

He couldn't understand where the images came from; when he thought about them, they were impossible. Nothing like this had happened. Could happen. Yet there they were, so real.

The man with wild hair would present himself again; bathed in bright crimson.

Charlie's panic rose. His shaking grew wilder and more uncontrolled. He knew to fear what would come.

A voice would chime; something he thought he recognized. It would fade again beneath an echoing chant.

"I'm sorry, Charlie!" it would say. His heart both swelled and calmed.

He wanted nothing more than to fight against it, everything; but no matter what he did; no matter where he looked; no matter where he ran, hid, or whatever else; he ended up in the same place.

The chanting grew louder and louder; lightning struck; thunder erupted through the river vale.

"No!"

Charlie screamed in his dream and the room both, but it was no use. The scene propelled itself forward.

From there, it all happened so fast. He sped upward in the sky with a terrifying quickness; he fought and fought, but it was no use—it had overcome gravity; he flew higher and higher over one tumultuous rush of wind, then another; his eyes clenched shut tight, and he screamed the entire way until he came to one harsh and abrupt halt.

Then all the world became still.

Oh, no, *he thought. Whatever lay beyond this point of the dream was blank, but he knew it was terrible, whatever it was. Alarms blared. Whatever alarms were going off in him showed it wasn't good.*

His heart raced; sweat poured from every part of him; a fear and panic that he'd never known before—gripped him. His whole body would explode at any second... then he heard it... that voice.

Charlie, *it said.*

No... *Charlie tried to push it off, his attempts feeble.*

Charlie West, *it said again.*

N-no... no! Leave me alone!

Charlie West, *it said once more,* it is time.

This made no sense to Charlie.

For several seconds, there was silence except for a few gentle gusts of wind.

Then the voice returned.

As you wish, it roared—and as it did, several bursts of lightning shot across the sky, which was torn in two; from the void, something *had ruptured through; something terrible; something Charlie dared not describe and erased from his mind.*

When he'd waken, he'd have lost any memory of what he saw. Far too terrible to face, his consciousness would wipe it clean.

Some things are too terrible to understand.

Charlie shot up from the cot, screaming. Shrill terror flooded from him and spilled out into the empty room. In his panic, he stumbled around the room, gathering what clothes he'd need—his pants and coat and boots and hat—and before he could exhale, he'd tear himself free. Having left the room's door wide open, Charlie was already halfway down the winding hall that led toward the outside, where he would try to bury these thoughts, these memories, in step after aimless step. Like every night when he woke in terror, he'd flee from the building and march until his legs gave out. He walked for the motion. He walked to forget. His future, gone, as far as he could see. And the past, charging toward him, fuelled his pain. If he could forget it, maybe he wouldn't feel its sting.

Most years, September was the nicest month of the year in Portland, weather-wise. But not this year. And that's when Charlie had returned, vowing not to settle anywhere near his old life.

There wasn't much left for him to claim, anyway.

He'd spent most days that first month marching back and forth between the East and West Side. Nights too.

With nowhere else to go, before the dreams came, he found refuge sleeping in various parks. He found food where and when he could and occupied his time meandering the city he'd loved so much. He did what he could to stay away from others; his goal, disappearing.

He never thought of himself as homeless. That came later, too. He took every day as he could. Keeping his head down and his heart at bay. Doing what he could to avoid the creeping feelings that seemed hell-bent on freeing themselves.

As it does, the weather turned. September shrivelled, the temperature dropped, and October withered away into November, and so on.

That's when Charlie followed the flow of homeless crowds into the various shelters. He'd already found them for their readiness to feed him and pass on other basic needs he had. But it wasn't until late-fall that he found reason to sleep there, if sleep you could call it.

It was the Portland City Mission he gravitated to the most for the warmth of its workers. It was here that Charlie found himself first able to trust again. First with some patrons. Next with Oscar, the manager. He'd taken a liking to Charlie right away.

Without thinking, Charlie fell into helping whenever he could, always without being asked.

He found a strange peace in tidying up. In the monotony of certain tasks. One could put their mind on pause and escape their thoughts.

Oscar watched how it always settles Charlie. Brought him calm, which was not Charlie's typical affect. In time, Oscar had offered Charlie a permanent bed for his continued help around the building and grounds, and it thrilled him when Charlie accepted.

For months now, even Oscar had watched in pain as Charlie seemed to crumble from bad to worse—especially as winter set in—and Charlie lost his form and became a wreck. Jumpy and frail, even his pigment seemed to have abandoned him.

"Damn you, you ungrateful—I've–I've indulged this fantasy of yours far too long already. Do you hear me, Blackwell? It's over!" wailed an angry, almost frantic voice over the phone.

"But sir?"

"Do not interrupt me, god dammit–"

"But we're so close, sir!"

"I don't care how close you think you are! Your own man said it: without the *boy*, it would prove impossible. And *he*— I'll add—along with the other miscreants who followed that madman Wilkes, is nothing more than dust now! You hear? Mixed into what's left of those god-forsaken towns. They're gone. He's gone, dammit! Wiped clean off the face of this accursed rock."

The man spoke with such ferocity; the man in the penthouse couldn't help but sense a coming fear.

"But *sir*, if you'll just–"

"No!" the voice blasted again. "No *buts*. No *sirs*. Nothing, dammit! Not anymore. You've been at this for six months, and where has it gotten you? Or *us*? You will cease this *now. Do you understand me?*" Before even giving the man a chance to respond, he continued. "We've wasted enough time and resources on this ridiculous notion of yours. It's time to prioritize and redistribute our means elsewhere, to more promising leads. Things we *know* will work."

Holding the phone farther away from his ear, the man stood there, taken aback, gritting his teeth, working hard to hold back the many plausible arguments that flooded his brain. It was clear he would make no more headway with his superior.

We're so close, he thought as desperation wrapped itself around him. *We just need...* He trembled. *I just need a bit more time.*

His body tensed as he stood up straighter, clenching his other fist. His mind churned over every possibility of what he could do.

He couldn't stop thinking about the miracle of how far they'd come. The Inner Circle only agreed to give him this time because he, Weyland Blackwell, was the head of Portland's sect of The Order. It was his men who retrieved the surviving artifacts from Astoria's wasteland.

It was they, The Order's *precious* Inner Circle—whom he loathed—who'd convinced The Head to allow them this time. But *he* was taking it away. And for what?

He'd always known it would be a matter of time before they pulled the plug on him, which was why he'd been working with such tenacity, having teams at it round the clock, searching for their breakthrough. And they were so close, as he reminded himself often.

So close!

What was this *other* plan, anyway? It's not like The Order's higher ups would ever tell *him* what was happening. It was infuriating.

In that way, he understood the merit of Wilkes breaking away. He had no one above him, overseeing his actions. Interfering with everything. Look what he'd been able to achieve.

"Blackwell!"

Blackwell took a step back, his ability to hold back his fear faltered.

"Dammit, Blackwell, do you hear me?"

"Yes, sir," he said, making sure his response was slow and void of any trace of rebellion.

"Do I make myself clear, then? I want all activities halted. I want those texts sent up here today! Back to our secured facility! I want *all* pertaining research and artifacts in route *here* by tomorrow! Along with you and the heads of all your teams! Is that clear?"

A severe crease formed across the man's forehead as a bitter anger fuelled him, but given the voice with which he responded, one never would have guessed.

"Yes, sir." His answered was quick and short. "Right away, sir."

"Good."

Blackwell's short and sharp tone Grenier felt lined with the same joy a predator would exude for coming upon an injured prey.

"Will that be all, sir?" Mr. Blackwell hid his nervousness well. At least in his voice; his opposite hand twitched at his side, giving him away. "Many preparations await us if I am to accomplish all this in a week."

Silence hung in the air a moment, carried back and forth between the miles and miles of phone lines, before his superior responded.

"Yes, that will be all."

Then, the phone line went dead.

Mr. Blackwell stood there, holding the phone out before him. The line was dead, yet still he stared down at it, allowing it to fuel his growing contempt.

They've never understood, he thought again. It had become his mantra over the past few months. He couldn't understand why they couldn't see how close they were. If *he* succeeded, *they* succeeded.

The Inner Circle understood that, at least, so why couldn't he, The Head of their Order? He was the *supposed* visionary and would bring about the beautiful and triumphant shift in human history—in existence itself.

For years, Mr. Blackwell had thought the entire lot of them were so lost. It had even pushed him to accept that Wilkes had been right. About *that*, at least.

It didn't help that everybody, including Mr. Blackwell

himself, had learned that the boy, and even his father, had been hiding at the heart of his own territory.

How had they not found him? And how had Wilkes' people found them? That irked him the most. Outdone by that dried up maniac.

"Damn!"

He slammed his hands, palm down, onto the table before him. The phone clattered away, falling to the floor where it laid still, its dial tone continuing to pulse.

He looked around his room again, gathering himself. Surrounded by the posh niceties of a Pearl District high rise suite, something struck him.

This plan was years in the making. He couldn't give up on it now. Not after they'd come so far.

"They'll understand in the end." At least, that's what he always told himself. Often in a whisper so no one would hear. His voice had returned to its normal sense of confidence and strength. "Once they all see, they'll beg for my forgiveness." His eye flickered as he spoke, like lightning cutting across a dark and menacing sky. A strange twinge tugged at him. Something beginning to unravel. As if his superior's commands had unhinged something.

Reaching into his pocket, he picked up his cell phone and pressed the number at the top of his recent call list. A man picked up.

"Sir?"

"Dr. Grenier, are you prepping the latest subject for testing?"

"As we speak, sir."

"Good."

"Is everything alright, sir?"

Mr. Blackwell waited a moment before he responded. He contemplated telling the good doctor about his most recent exchange with their higher up, but decided against it. He lied.

"Yes. Yes, all is well. I just wanted to check up on our progress. Keep at it, Doctor."

"Will do, sir. It will be difficult without subject zero, but we are close–"

But before he could finish, Mr. Blackwell broke in again.

"I want us to double our efforts, Doctor. Do you understand?"

"Sir?"

"I want us to make a big push. With *everything*. Get the retrieval team out there immediately. We need to gather more subjects. Up the number of tests. Start prepping a new subject *as* the others are being tested. I want to up the number of variable shifts. We need to home in on what we're missing. Increase everything. Is that clear?"

"Um... yes, sir, but–"

Mr. Blackwell grew even more uncharacteristically impatient. His eyes grew wide again, and reckless.

"No!" He exploded. "No excuses, Dr. Grenier! Is that clear? Nothing will hold us back. We are going to see this through. Do you hear me? No matter what! Nothing, and I mean *nothing*, is going to stop us."

Dr. Grenier gave no response. This sudden upheaval shocked him. Mr. Blackwell had always been driven. He had always pushed them hard, but he was always reasonable.

"Do you understand, Doctor?"

The doctor's words fumbled out.

"Yes, sir. We'll... we'll get on it right away, sir."

"Good."

This relieved Mr. Blackwell, leaving him more confident; thus, satisfied for the moment.

Without warning, he hung up on the doctor, leaving him to follow his given directives, confident of their implementation.

Mr. Blackwell turned to face the windows overlooking the

city. For the past several days, an oppressive blanket of high-forming gray clouds had overrun it. They pressed themselves down against the cityscape, smothering it in its crisp winter chill.

He imagined what the city would look like after their victory. A quiet shadow of what was. Ruins. An epicenter of devastation wrought without mercy, it would shake the very foundations of creation. It would reach out beyond the veils of time. Beyond the veils of night. Such destruction, they'd read, would call forth the only beings powerful enough to lay this crumbling world to waste. And it would be him, Weyland Blackwell, whose finger was on the trigger. He would stir the heavens, causing the great *recreation*, ushering in the new race of man. Not Wilkes. Not The Head nor the witless Inner circle.

Looking out over an unsuspecting city, he considered it all. The Head's phone call didn't need to mean anything.

The world deserves better. A wicked grin formed itself beneath his two eyes as they glared. *Take care world, for the* Nameless *are coming.*

———

Charlie couldn't walk fast enough to keep his feet in front of his thoughts. They seemed compelled forward with an indifferent fury. Still, he trudged on. He scraped his way up and down the freezing, raw pavement, desperate for the impossible. To *not* think.

Like everything else, as of late, it was something he wasn't finding much success in.

His steps were quick and frantic, and his movements erratic. Anyone watching him would have known right away that something was wrong.

His only comfort was the sharp and numbing cold. It

assisted him in his hopes that he would feel nothing at all. If he focused on his cheeks and nose's finite irritation, he would no longer be thinking about where his mind seemed bent to go.

It was the closest thing he had to freedom, and he clung to it with an ugly, fumbling grip. He continued his forward progress to the rhythm of his frantic steps, as he did so often, and let them carry him forward in what he would hope was a mindless bliss.

He'd walked these streets so often. They'd grown accustomed to his presence. Welcomed him with a dull embrace, and he welcomed them right back in turn. It was there in this gritty maze he felt as if he belonged. His only respite from the constant ebb and flow of a guilt he did not understand.

As soon as his boots hit the concrete, the *pull* would come. Some strange, unknown force. Somehow within him, connected to something out beyond his little world. Like gravity, it tugged at him, desiring him to give into its pulsing current.

For whatever reason, Charlie associated it with the guilt and fought it, but at night when exhaustion was at its peak, the pull seemed only to strengthen, and Charlie didn't think he'd be able to hold out forever.

Like a lighthouse, it beckoned him; and he so desired to be free from this rocky and maligned estuary. He yearned to come to shore. To rest. To breathe easy. For the fight to be over.

Still, it called to him, and the louder it blared, the less he trusted it and would often turn on heel and speed off in the opposite direction whence it came. Thus, his night-time wanderings weighed him down, defined by the strange and weary tension that added weight to his already weary shoulders.

Most nights, he'd duck his head lower yet and let his feet carry him further and further away.

His mind and all its many threads were far beyond frayed.

He felt always just on the verge of panic, of complete break-down. Somehow, his body kept going. If he stopped for a moment, the fear would catch him. It always did. Then what could he do? Where could he run to? Where could he be free? Nowhere, he always told himself, and he kept going. Moving forward but making no progress. He only hoped to *not* feel. To *not* engage. As far strung out as Charlie felt, his greatest hope was escape. At his darkest moments, he wondered whether being *in* the world anymore was even worth it. This thought came to him more often than he cared to admit.

So, each night, he kept putting one foot in front of the next, hoping only to forget. He'd become a phantom to this world. A ghost. Unattached to anyone. To anything at all. A meandering specter, tethered to existence by a frail, icy grip; a grasp that stung and grew tighter as each week seemed to slip away.

That night, Charlie found his steps leading him down Portland's Waterfront—what had become his usual haunt. He passed by empty benches and fields which, in the spring, bustled with picnicking patrons, frisbees, and barking dogs. On that dead night, it looked like an aged photo. Black and white and stained with gray. Abandoned. Void of both light and life.

It was a few blocks before he came upon his first sign of life. Three, to be exact. Three people underneath the Morrison bridge. Dressed in tattered rags, torn and old. Piecemealed together. They draped ripped blankets around themselves. The three huddled together around a dying fire.

Their voices softened as Charlie drew closer to them and, though he was unaware of it, his steps quickened.

Months before, Charlie would have stopped and spoken with them. He would've sat with them for hours and listened to their stories. He would've found out if they were hungry or if they needed anything.

But that was then.

He was well beyond the place to help these days, concerned only with himself. Charlie had joined the ranks of all those who just kept walking. Even after he'd watched so many others pass him by when he lived on the streets. Without so much as a second thought. His own brash, numbing pain made him indifferent.

Not when he was so close. Off in the distance, the outline of his destination came into view. Once again, though he was aware this time, his pace quickened.

Charlie kept walking, and without even looking up, made it to his destination. The base of the Hawthorne Bridge was recognizable by the landmarks next to his feet. Reaching out with his un-gloved hand, he gripped the railing as he turned to walk up a set of stairs.

He never considered what drew him there. Though he knew something about it that brought him a certain amount of peace. For reasons unknown even to Charlie, it allowed him the luxury to let go. He'd always loved the twin retractable trusses that stood tall, jetting upwards of day—and especially their silhouettes against the cityscape at night. They were beacons to Charlie, like the bumpy, metal grating that was the bridge's road and the act of walking. The rhythmic treads of tires rolling over each link as they zoomed past. Charlie loved to look down through the grates as he walked and watch the river flow on by beneath him.

The Hawthorne Bridge was one of this city's monuments. It brought comfort to more than just the city's restless loners who walk the streets at night. Most Portlanders who saw it would stop and swoon and smile, knowing they were home.

Charlie hit every switchback of stone stairs and ascended through the night to the bridge's surface; where it stretched out over the cold chasm, the river flowed.

At last, he reached the bridge's surface and turned.

The wind, then unobstructed, brushed itself across his exposed skin.

His footsteps continued to carry him forward to the bridge's center. Moonlight flickered off the water's surface, keeping his attention removed from what he knew he'd rather ignore, anyway.

The water always spoke to Charlie. Its gentle lapping waves, whispering to the empty caverns within him. Its lonely song brought him as close to peace as he could go. There was a certain level of stillness that it brought. No matter how Charlie ever felt, no matter how shaky, this place maintained its steady stature, it seemed for him.

Standing there, Charlie never felt alone. Somehow, he felt connected there. To *something*. Whether it was the cold or the faint and distant light, he didn't know. Perhaps it was that standing there made him feel he was outside it all. Looking in. A spectator, off stage, observing. He felt on the periphery of everyone else's life. Here he was beyond the reach of others. Far from whatever pain they might cause him. Here, existed a promise of safety. Though frail. At least that's how he felt.

There was one more peculiar aspect about that spot though. He felt it whenever he was there. That strange and leering pull. A sensation, tugging upon him; a violent whisper telling him there was some place he needed to be. Stemming from just beyond Union Station. He couldn't explain it. And he'd never had the nerve to investigate it, but it called to him. To *him*. He felt drawn to the triune towers that stood behind it. He would stare out at them; feeling they were always staring back.

Either way, here he felt safe. Protected.

For several long, drawn-out moments, Charlie willed his eyes to close and tried to listen to the wind and waves.

More peace came. The world around him shifted; at least in his mind it grew still.

Charlie always found himself quite taken by the gentle ripples of water's flow beneath him. It evoked a jealous tension in him. The river flowed. No matter the time of year. No matter the temperature. Sun or storm, it flowed. No obstruction could contain it. That filled him with a strange and fragile hope.

Even as his movements halted and his dreams and plaguing visions hung over him, ravenous to consume... here, Charlie felt free to *be*. Here, his mind was less susceptible. Though he still felt the heavy weight of the pressure that crushed him, as he listened to the river passing underneath him, he let his thoughts sink down far into its depths and join its flow.

In those moments, he could take control of his dreams; like his own hands held the reins. He would imagine himself stepping up onto the cold and icy railing and standing high over that tumbling depth. Dizziness would come again, which he welcomed, a break from his constant strain. Then it would take him. He'd let it take him, then he would fall. Down. Down. Cutting his way through the still air like a knife through soft fruit. Somehow, he imagined himself slowing down as he went. Somehow, the laws of physics ceased. The fall would last for days; and as the moments stretched out, he would be free. Unattached from any of the normal weight that fastened him to his crippling reality.

Then there was the plunge, or at least how he assumed it would feel. That sweet dip as his body splashed through the threshold of the water's surface. In his mental construct, breaking through the surface was always a crisp, clean break. Pure and instantaneous.

All his attachments, the chains he wore, faded, broke away, but without pain. The river's tender and icy touch would smooth over any blemish that he'd picked up from the surface world. What had happened above would fade. Down there, where the city lights wouldn't reach, safety existed. The water cocooned, protected.

Beneath the surface of the water, the gentle music of the river's sweeping grace would take him, of its arrangements and the rhythms of her welcoming arms.

In Charlie's mind, whatever had happened to him in his past could never reach him there. This was his safe place. If life became too much; if he became too tired, he could enter these waters and swim until his strength gave out. Then it would all be over. His struggle would be over. Finished. Done. No more weight or pain. Swept away. Gone.

If he'd had time to consider it, it was a mere illusion of peace. But, to him, it was peace, nonetheless. Charlie would settle for that.

Out of nowhere, a scream pierced the darkness. It echoed through the empty void of night, shaking Charlie from his false reverie. As he once more noticed his surroundings, he too realized the weight that settled itself back onto his world. Once again, that splitting pain made itself known to him within his gut, his chest, and his mind.

He leaned back and caught the weight of his body with his heels, his hands still gripping the rail, now keeping him from falling backwards into the street—a less than pleasant end. The fog returned and filled his mind with a mounting dread and regret. Both feelings he still did not understand.

And always, there was that phantom pull. That feeling that something was drawing him closer inward. But he didn't know where. All he knew was that he didn't trust it, and if he could help it, he would never go near where it led.

Another scream cried out in the distance. Again, coming from the West Side. Near Burnside, he thought. It rode on a chill, firm wind Charlie felt was most un-welcomed.

He did not bunch his shoulders or arms together. He welcomed the cold and took it in with an attempted deep breath, hoping to help remove what he had already been feeling.

Longingly, Charlie leaned back over the rail to stare into the dark water's surface, hoping to re-enter his escape. It was too late; the moment had passed. He would have to fight off these looming thoughts and memories himself.

His countenance collapsed, even more so than before, as disappointment overcame Charlie. Disillusioned by what he saw as his few remaining options, part of him felt it cowardly that he turned where he stood and, head down, continued his night-time march.

He did not know where he was going, nor did he care. He felt lost; like a boat capsized, whose wreckage had drifted far from the shores of his own soul. Tossed about by unforgiving waves and discarded.

Often in his waking dreams, visions of *this fall*, himself plunging into the river, went uninterrupted. He'd step out of the water and onto a shore. Far, far from anything he'd ever experienced, yet somehow he knew it well. His weary steps would lead him toward where gentle waves crashed and lapped down onto unsuspecting grains of sand. The beach stretched out on in both directions, infinite. Charlie would turn around and the river had disappeared; transformed into a vast and endless ocean. Its wild waves crashed down hard yet brought to him a certain corresponding comfort that he couldn't explain.

Just past the shore, there stood a towering wall built of immense, hand-carved stones. It stretched up high into the clouds as far as the ocean stretched itself toward the horizon. It stood, hiding something. Keeping it secret and safe. From what, he didn't know. He never bothered wondering about that. When he was there, he focused on the ethereal rhythmic crashing of the waves. This was his peace.

A voice would always call out. Haunting and terrible.

That was always his cue to leave. It echoed from somewhere far off behind him. He always felt like it stemmed from behind the wall; but this fact he didn't like to dwell on.

Charlie, it would whisper. Bringing no comfort, for he knew it meant returning to the real world. Back to the weary pavement. Back to the unforgiving harshness of his thoughts.

The loud burst of a car horn startled Charlie back into the conscious world. He hadn't realized how deep into his own thoughts he'd traveled.

Tiredness wrapped itself around him. Exhaustion, like giant bags of sand, hoisted itself over his shoulders and hung down, reaching for the ground with all its strength.

Charlie thought he might burst from all the pressure he felt. His guilt, ever eating away at him, and his shame. This led to lingering and strained thoughts of his mother. Forcing the entire process to start over.

His stomach turned and sank within him. It pulled against the weight of his own mind. He couldn't hold out much longer, but what choice did he have? None that he saw. So, instead, he just kept walking. He'd walk until he'd figure out what to do. Or until his mind grew numb. Most of the time, the latter.

The truth was Charlie was beyond lost, and unsure he wanted to be found.

Two

A thick, oppressive blanket of cloud hung itself over the city as the morning stretched itself overhead, readying itself to bring forth the day. It hadn't rained in weeks—a strange occurrence for Portland in January. The air felt heavy, yet somehow still biting.

Cait Lane stood in the corner near her apartment holding two paper cups. Steam wafted up from the little opening of their lids—warmth unable to sustain itself in the bleak winter chill.

Her expression was blank, a by-product of too many late nights followed by an equal number of early mornings without much of a break between.

She had little outside work. No friends. No hobbies to pass the time; despite that, her partner badgered her about it all the time. She told him she preferred it that way. It helped her stay focused. This was a comment that triggered Scott to shake his head at her.

It had, as she always defended, helped her achieve her long list of work-related goals.

Taking a sip of coffee, she played the latest iteration of this conversation over in her head. The day before, she'd had her first annual detective review. A day she'd been dreading given the pushback there'd been to her appointment.

But it was over; and a conversation she'd had with her partner, Scott, echoed in her mind.

Detective? At your age, Cait? He'd said then. *Forgive me for saying it, but as a woman, too. You've... you've done the impossible.*

As she'd cocked her head to refute him, he'd lifted his hands to plead.

Hey, you know me. Right? I believe in you. And yeah, there're women throughout the precinct, sure. But regardless of the year or the city, each occupation's progress varies. Right?

They'd both smiled at that; he snuck in what she saw as a usual encouraging gem.

I just want you to be proud of yourself.

Still, she'd called Scott out for not being more serious about the process. She'd wanted it to go by the book. She didn't need anyone questioning the process. Or her.

Scott kept skipping what she saw were the important details. Things that showcased her progress as an officer. Her skills. Her accolades. Accomplishments. Instead, he droned on about the lack of balance in her life. A not-uncommon topic of conversation, but in between stops on the street. Not in a review meeting. He already knew that and told her such. He'd take care of that. Over again, he'd tried to impress upon her how important understanding *this* was.

That she didn't need to kill herself for anyone else.

She understood it, and she knew why he did it. He was just trying to encourage her. Even though he believed in her, it didn't always seem like he understood all she fought against. Most men didn't.

As always, Scott, I appreciate your concern, but can we please take this more seriously? I mean, you know the Chief would love to find the smallest reason to get rid of me.

You let me and the Captain handle Gilman. He's an asshole. An archetype of a dying world.

She never had the heart to explain that him fighting her battle was part of the problem.

She then remembered his last words, and as always, found comfort in them.

The people who matter believe in you, Cait. Besides, the paperwork here is on me. I write your review. Captain Sykes processes it further. We're here to protect you, and ain't nothing gonna happen while we're around. You hear?

The thought brought her immense comfort.

And I only have one piece of feedback that I'm going to be reporting your progress on, starting tonight.

She remembered looking up, somewhat astonished.

Stacey's making a special dinner tonight for the anniversary of you making detective, so you have to come over and let us celebrate you. Tommy and Hannah are already expecting you, so you can't say no.

Scott was always pushing her to build a life outside of work. Inviting her to spend time with his own family whenever she could.

She took another sip of coffee. It warmed her against the constant barrage of whipping wind.

Scott had always believed in her. He was the reason she made it; she knew. His encouragement and patience and direction. She could always vent to him when overlooked for certain tasks. Or they side-lined her for work more fitting to *her* disposition. Her life was a constant bombardment of jabs. Of lewd remarks made by other officers. Some direct. Intentional. The others were the usual indirect fare, comments that cut like a knife but passed as acceptable in most circles.

Scott saw her for who she was, looked past the precinct's

abject gender bias and noted her police skills. She was a good cop. *Damn good*, he always told her. Her record as a uniformed police officer had been near perfect. There was always more pressure on her. Pressure to be perfect. For as long as she could remember.

Everyone else seemed allowed to screw up any time. They ebbed from case to case and day to day, lackadaisical, coasting. Cait had to excel, always.

Since she'd started, everyone was watching her; waiting for her to fail, waiting for a justification to let her go. Or at least slide her into a lane more suited for her.

There were other women in the department. Sure. But no allies. No one she trusted. They'd fought and staked their claim. The mindset was to cleave out whatever space you could and keep it. Portland is a progressive city, but like all cities, many corners get overlooked. They'd taken ground, but the fight was far from over.

Nobody rose to *Detective* as quickly as she did. She knew she should feel pride in that, but the constancy of proving herself drained her.

She'd often wondered if that was something Scott didn't understand. He could afford to make mistakes. After choosing her as his partner, Scott maintained the respect of everyone at the precinct, while her battle was near vertical. So, she shrugged off his comments of developing a social life as mere distractions from her ability to continue to prove herself. She would never let herself become what they expected of her. Never.

She'd lucked out the night before. Scott had invited her to family dinner, only to have it canceled again by another body turning up. It almost made her feel guilty, but she leaned into the relief. Working a case always put her mind at ease.

It wasn't that she didn't want *that*. She did. She just didn't know how he cultivated it. *How could he play both parts?* she often wondered. She spent so much of her life holding lines against who others expected her to be. At home, she wanted to be alone. Be herself. There was such safety in that.

She'd never learned the art of interacting with people. Her mother had passed when she was very little, and her father had retreated into one bottle after the next, avoiding grief. Since then, humans were always better understood at a distance to Cait. She could wrap her head around crime scenes. Forensics and discarded bodies. The pathology or need some felt to commit heinous acts. There was a distance to those cold facts she understood. It was in the warmth of company she felt unsafe. This was something she assumed Scott would never understand.

Just then, Scott's navy Camry pulled around the corner. Both a calm and a tension settled over her. She knew she could be herself; but still that orbiting need to prove herself lingered; something Scott reminded her over and over was not true.

The car pulled up and the passenger door flung open, revealing her eager and smiling partner.

"Morning, boss."

Cait nodded, feigning a grin.

"Still brooding, I see."

Scott never missed a chance to chide her, always in jest.

"Ha-ha-ha."

Cait over-enunciating each vowel. She slid into her seat, handing Scott his coffee and taking a sip of hers.

"Ah, fuel for the early morning. Thank you."

"Don't mention it. What do we got?"

He let a wide smile linger.

"All business, eh? We'll—Oh, before we get to that, the important stuff first. Stacey is rescheduling your celebration for tomorrow night, okay?"

Cait let her head fall back, but knew enough to act thankful.

"Scott–"

"Hey, don't look at me, alright? I get the loner thing. Okay? You don't wanna be around people. Put yourself in the center of anything…"

She appreciated the way he could skate—not around an issue—but through it. Head first.

"… but remember, there're *some* who really care about you. Like really, really, really care. And want to show you."

He stopped and let the quiet settle. It helped things sink in.

"You don't have to go it alone. Ever. You hear?"

Her insides squirmed. She wanted to wave it all away, but deep down, she appreciated it.

"Thanks, Scott."

"Always, but look…" He paused, turning to her. "… we're gonna keep asking. Again and again and again. You know? Stacey's worried about you. I've explained it as best I can, but she knows you don't have many people and… and she sees you as family."

Cait trembled at the word.

"We *all* do."

Her eyes welled a bit, catching her off guard. A strange pressure grew beneath her lungs, making it harder to breathe. She couldn't shake the sentiments away fast enough to speak, so looked away.

He knew it was difficult for her, but everyone needed sanctuaries. Places to turn off, to stop and re-connect. To just let go and decompress. Places a person could be themselves. He hoped she knew to find that in them.

Steadying herself, she turned back to face him.

"Thank you, Scott. I know, and I'm grateful, but—"

He grinned and dropped his chin just low enough to cut her off, causing them both to chuckle.

"Knock it off!" she said, elbowing him in the arm, knowing he wouldn't.

Scott just shook his head smiling as Cait broke in again, shifting to a more serious tone.

"Look, we have this *big* case and I…" She stopped, realizing something for herself. "*I* want to keep things simple. So nothing gets in the way."

The car quieted.

Scott stared at her, taking that in. He understood it, but as always, saw a bigger picture. His eyes sharpened. They carried no danger, no threat or reason to worry. There was a shine to them, Cait noticed. She knew she should listen, so she prepared herself to hear.

"You're an incredible cop, Cait Lane, but we're no good on the job if we're no good *off* the job, right? And remember, I *get* to monitor your *work/life balance*."

He raised his hands, shaking them in a contrived, strange way; that, combined with a mocking tone—the one reserved for when he made fun of her eye rolls—told her he was trying to keep the peace.

"Scott!"

They laughed together, each used to these strange deviations in their conversations. Most of which were caused by Scott.

Yet Cait appreciated them nonetheless.

"Look, for Stacey's sake, promise you'll come to dinner tomorrow night and I won't mention it for the rest of the day, okay?" His smile grew wider yet. "And I promise we can spend the rest of the day thinking about horrible mayhem and death. Whaddaya say?"

Cait pondered this while Scott mouthed three words: *mayhem and death*. Even she couldn't help but laugh. She never understood how he could be so carefree yet so perceptive. It didn't compute with her.

She lamented.

"Okay."

"Great. I'll tell Stacey and the kids. They can't wait to see you."

Though she would never admit it, a comforting warmth bubbled up inside her—a longing she didn't quite grasp.

"Now." He cleared his throat. "For your daily dose of horror."

He tossed the new case file into her lap and put the car in drive. His tone caught her off guard, laced with a ring of warning.

"It's ugly. Weirder than any of the scenes before."

Cait began flipping through pages and notes and photos.

"And the body?"

"Bodies."

He corrected, still holding to the grim reality presented.

Cait hesitated, taking that in. Eyebrows upturned, she sifted more quickly through the file's pages as she continued her questions.

"Underneath Burnside?"

"Yeah, the West Side overpass. Right up from Union Station."

"But the bodies have the same—"

"The same strange bruising everywhere, but that's not everything."

"What is it?"

"You're gonna wanna see for yourself."

Cait looked up as they pulled up and parked outside the scene. One look at him told her all she needed to know. He knew how she preferred approaching a scene without preconceived notions. In fact, he was counting on her sharpness right then. They got out of the car. Walked over and crossed beneath under the police tape to the heart of the crime scene, taking it all in.

"Well, what d'ya think?"

Cait took a minute to gather herself.

"I guess the question is whether there are two crime scenes or if they're linked."

Scott nodded in agreement and pushed her to the next conclusion.

"Right. And you think?"

Cait walked over to the *first* scene, where the bodies lay piled.

Scott knew to let her think. He knew the fact that she hadn't answered his question was the reality of her working her way to her conclusion, which was the correct one more often than not.

She forced on a pair of rubber gloves and crouched for a better look. They were just like the others before; except there were more. Circling the pile, she canvased every detail, collecting every piece of data she could; intoning, making involuntary noises all the time.

Scott smiled at this.

The bodies were each stripped bare and covered from head to foot in bruising. Cait still couldn't imagine what had caused it; like whatever *had* caused it had struck the victim's whole body at once. All of it. At the same time. In one blunt burst.

She pulled out her notebook and scribbled something down, then reached out and picked up one arm, lifted it, and looked underneath before she set it back down.

"Well, boss?"

Cait took another several seconds before she stood and at last responded to her patient partner.

"There's more of them..."

Scott nodded.

"... we still don't know who they are or where they're coming from; but there's more of them. Whatever's going on, and *whoever's* doing it? They're worried."

Scott cocked one eyebrow, growing intrigued by Cait's estimation.

She kept going.

"I mean, look at this. This is sloppy, isn't it? The last several drops, it's only ever been one body and laid out. Almost neat. With intention? Each scene was careful." She looked over to Scott, catching his glean of admiration, and her cheeks flushed, encouraged. She continued on. "Three bodies this time, just piled up."

At this, she sidestepped the bodies and focused her attention on the nearby road and sidewalk.

"They must have been in a hurry. Must've gotten spooked and left—that's it!"

As the revelation struck her, she broke away, almost running to the second scene.

Scott jogged to catch up.

"And these–"

"These?"

"Yeah, plural. The notes say they abducted one person from here, but the scene shows it was closer to three."

Scott's smile grew even wider now. He loved watching Cait's mind at work.

"Look." Her tone was matter of fact. "Burn barrel here in the center." She reached out and touched it. "Still warm." She pointed to various objects around the area. "Makeshift chairs. A couch. Boxes broken down to shelter from the wind. And check out these drag marks. They cut right through that muck."

Scott followed her finger as it pointed to where they'd dragged the victims through the mixture of dust, dirt, and rain that had built up underneath the bridge.

"There are three sets of marks. See? All leading back to the tire tracks. The paths each die away somewhere in the road, which gets more traffic."

"And to conclude?" Scott pressed.

"This is one scene, not two. These guys were dumping the bodies and didn't think to check for bystanders."

"And?"

"Couldn't leave the witnesses behind."

Scott canvased the scene while he considered it.

"Hm, well, per usual, you're able to outwit all my own conclusions and go well beyond in half the time. Good work, *boss*."

Cait couldn't help but blush. She never took compliments well, especially from someone who'd earned the right to give them.

Just then, something struck Cait.

"Scott?"

"Yeah?"

"The bodies–" she started.

"Yeah?"

"We can't I.D. them, right?"

"Yeah. Can't find a thing on–"

"What if we're looking in the wrong places?"

Scott's smile widened further yet as he realized what Cait was getting at.

They both looked over toward the burn barrel.

"Why not just eliminate the witnesses? Leave them with the dumped bodies. Why take them?"

Scott nodded, excited at her thoughtful direction.

"Has anyone been checking the local shelters? There's half a dozen right around this neighborhood alone."

"That's good. That's real good, Cait. I'll call it in. Get people canvassing right away."

Detective Cait Lane couldn't help but beam. She loved this part of the job and Scott always gave her the room to stretch her legs and test herself. She was proud of her abilities. If she could only make similar connections with the living.

———

Charlie walked beneath the canopy of a sky at war. He had no idea of the time; nor of how long he'd been walking. Given the dizzying buzz that drove him, he only knew he needed to get back to The Mission. He could sneak in a few hours of restless sleep before the terrors returned.

Exhausted legs, like stilts or unmanned machines, worked to carry him back to bed.

The morning dared to stretch itself forward into day, and Charlie kept his pace as he walked underneath the still-oppressive ceiling of heavy clouds. There was no wind that night, nor the morning, either. No one could even remember the last time it rained. Beyond unusual for a Portland winter.

Per the norm, Charlie found himself somewhat lost to the moment, trying to lean into the fuzziness and his inability to think. It brought him glimmers of hope; it was a chance at rest. But somewhere as he approached the Burnside Bridge, the streaming echoes of a bustling crowd—it seemed to grow —stole away his attention. He felt surprised at the intrigue.

Upon drawing closer, he saw the threads of police tape stretching out and both marked and unmarked cars, indicating something big had happened.

He'd never been one for crowds, but this spot, being a common haunt for the homeless crowd he found himself a part of, steered him to take a peek. Just a quick one. Then he'd keep going.

Charlie pressed forward; each shoulder that brushed against him further strained his nerves. He said excuse me over and over. His guilt grew heavier, but at last he could see. Officers bustled from one place to the next. Several stood gathered together beneath a tent put up to block the expected wind and rain. Charlie found his attention drawn to them; the looks of grave concern written across their faces. Something bad had happened. That much he could tell.

Frantic, Charlie glanced back and forth, surveying the scene. He saw several police markings, things he didn't quite understand. Must've been evidence markers or something; things important to the case.

He thought of the many people he'd met beneath that bridge. The community he'd found as summer waned. They hadn't judged. Asked questions. Anything. His stomach sank with grief.

As it did, the same strange stirrings from before tugged in his gut. They pulled back and forth, unsettling him all the more; he felt the edges of his mind continue to fray; worn and beaten down—he just wanted to sleep; he wanted rest; he needed the space to—but his heart fluttered; he felt his thoughts getting away from him.

Shit!

He couldn't help but hold his breath. Though unaware, Charlie's whole body tensed and he tapped the end of his fingers upon the edges of his thumbs.

His body was still in charge, and he was at its mercy.

Charlie backed up as quickly as he could. He fumbled, bumping into several people on the way: stepping onto one set of toes.

People near him threw out complaints, shoving him, but Charlie neither heard nor felt them; immersed in the revolving spin taking over his mind. Catching several people's attention beyond him, a few of the nearby officers walked over.

One of them called as he approached; one hand out in front of him, the other hovering back toward his hip.

"Hey."

Charlie just kept backing up. "Excuse me..." The words came out more frantic than he would've liked.

The crowd dispersed, though Charlie would have sworn that it was growing based on the pounding roar in his ears.

The cop yelled again.

"Hey, you!"

Tightening strings of guilt and shame tugged deep into Charlie's gut; he needed to get out of there.

Another angry person in the crowd grabbed Charlie's jacket sleeve and pulled him.

"Hey! What's the—"

Charlie pulled away, then froze. Stricken and worried, he wouldn't dare look up.

"I-I'm sorry..." Each syllable bumbled out over the one before. "I-I j-just... I'm just t-trying to get outta here."

The officer looked at him, along with everyone else in the crowd. For a moment, no one spoke; this only allowed Charlie's dread to expand out.

The officer glared at him, each half-squinted eye boring deep into his defenses.

"Alright." The cop said in a slow, methodical manner. "Get outta here then, alright?"

Charlie shook his head up and down, the damage done.

"And just watch it, everyone." The officer addressed the crowd this time. "None of you should even be here. Let's just keep our distance, will ya?"

The crowd said nothing, feigning stunned silence, hungry for understanding of what happened.

The moment's tension loosened, and Charlie could wiggle his way back out, doing what he could to keep his breathing slow. He stumbled a bit as he stepped up onto the sidewalk and caught himself scraping his boot against the harsh concrete edge.

One of the lead detectives looked over, catching sight of someone she took for a weary, nervous bystander. As he shuffled away from the scene, the distracting noise he'd caused frustrated her.

As Charlie disappeared beyond the crowd, she turned her attention back to her partner, back to the case at hand.

You're fine, Charlie! You're fine! You're fine! You're fine, Charlie! he said to himself, over and over, hoping it to be true.

But he was anything but fine. He had worked so hard to numb himself. To walk until his mind slipped into a state of rest. It hadn't worked.

Why hadn't he gone right back? He was wondering. Why did he always do this? Get sidetracked when what he needed was so apparent. Something always got in the way.

Calm yourself, Charlie. You... you can still get some rest. You can still fall asleep, he tried to tell himself, but he didn't believe it. Not a single part of himself believed it, but he couldn't acknowledge that either. He had to keep pushing forward.

As he drew closer to the Mission, he thought of the eventuality of running into Oscar or Janet, the receptionist. It made his stomach crawl even worse than it already was.

The back entrance, he thought. He needed to stay away from people.

Without even waiting for the rebuttal from any other part of his mind, Charlie let his body continue to carry himself forward. Almost on its own, it rounded onto 3rd Street, turning into the back alley behind The Mission.

His hands shook from exhaustion and cold; Charlie turned the handle of the door and disappeared into the dark, winding halls.

On the streets above, life emerged with the morning, bustling about, unaware of what threatened it.

THREE

Aman walked down the hall from the outer elevator on the highest floor of the Pearl District high rise. He was nervous and short of breath. His legs scurried forward in frantic bursts, wanting to move with swiftness without being perceived as rushing.

Coming to the massive, pearl-white twin doors, he stopped to catch his breath. Upon wiping the sweat from his palm onto his pant legs, he turned the handle and entered the office with his usual trepidation and panic.

A sullen Mr. Blackwell groaned upon the man's entry, not removing his eyes from what he'd been reading.

"What is it?"

The assistant hurried in and fumbled his way toward his superior, the way a mouse would skitter up toward a cat. He searched for words that wouldn't come, distracted by the piles scattered over the desk.

A series of ancient and priceless-looking books, massive stacks of papers, old and new, littered with strange symbols and incarnated script. Mr. Blackwell had scribbled his personal notes all over each of them. A calendar of a more modern make sat amongst everything. Its days were being crossed out one by one, like a child tiptoeing between excitement and impatience.

After a quick glance, the man knew he'd seen too much. He noticed a date from days before, with two words underlined and circled. It read: *must begin.* He'd crossed them out as well.

Mr. Blackwell sat back in his chair, hunched and downtrodden—the equivocal look of a man caught in desperation.

Dreading his purpose there, the man decided to wait to be addressed before speaking.

Silence reigned for some time.

At last, Mr. Blackwell spoke up.

"What is it? Can't you see I am busy?" His voice held to a strong tenor, one that always kept the underlings in line. "Time's short and we've much to do!"

The man squirmed.

"Yes, sir. I understand, sir, and my apologies—I just thought you ought to know—"

"Know what, god dammit!"

The messenger jumped, startled at the burst.

"A... a man... sir... Uh, one of *our* men... from the police force... Um... called..."

Mr. Blackwell's interest piqued, but he'd yet to look up from his desk.

"And?"

"He said he just left a certain.... crime scene... under the Burnside Bridge."

Mr. Blackwell took in a deep and firm breath.

"And... well, sir... he said that it concerns... it concerns *our* project."

Mr. Blackwell's gaze shot up, his glaring look piercing right through the man across from him.

"What? How? How dammit? What else did he say?"

Filled with a rising fear, the man couldn't help but stumble more.

"Well... it appears there are two detectives... uh, causing..." He stuttered, hesitating to gather himself. "... *trouble*."

"What trouble?"

The man stepped back, holding his glance to the floor before the desk.

"It appears they're... they're getting... *close*, Sir."

His jaw clamping shut and grinding, Mr. Blackwell gritted his whole body and slammed a fist down onto the table, disturbing everything in sight.

"Damn!"

The other man's whole body twitched and jumped again.

"What else? What else did he say? What do they know? How did—I told them to be careful, dammit! I told them— ugh. Get Reggie in here right away. This can't be happening now."

"Very well, sir." The assistants calmed somewhat, knowing the anger wasn't channeled directly at them.

Mr. Blackwell looked at the man, disgusted by his cowering presence.

"What did he say they knew?"

"Um... he said they're getting close to knowing the demographic of where we get our subjects and that the last drop was, and I quote, 'sloppy.'"

Though on the verge of erupting, Mr. Blackwell said nothing.

The assistant waited for directions, his hands fidgeting.

Mr. Blackwell mumbled to himself, in strange inarticulate bursts. His eyes widened, flashing fiery bolts of anger.

"Not now... This can't be happening..."

A painful quiet set in. The air strained.

The man looked up, coughing so Mr. Blackwell would remember his presence. Mr. Blackwell snapped.

"What?"

"Aside from collecting your head of security, is there anything else I can assist you with, sir?"

"No. Just get him here, now. As soon as possible. Do you hear? We need to fix this. And I... I need to think."

Mr. Blackwell's hand was half raised to send the man away when something else struck him. A thought that filled him with fear he worked hard to mask.

"One more thing."

"Yes, Sir?"

"Has... has the Head called. Or anyone from up north?"

"No, sir."

The man's voice didn't falter; there was little reason for concern yet.

"Good. If anyone calls, they only speak to me. Is that clear?"

"Yes, sir."

"And if they call, just tell them I'll call them back, understood?"

"Okay, sir." The man's tone shifted towards alarm.

"This is vital!" Mr. Blackwell slapped his hand down onto his desk. "*We* are in a delicate phase of the project, and they're going to want updates, but it's instrumental that we're not interrupted. At all."

Mr. Blackwell knew his assistant wouldn't like this directive, and his stomach grew tense, untrusting.

"I need to know you understand *this*."

He drew the last word out; forcing them both to endure the moment's long discomfort.

The assistant back-pedaled again.

"Of course. Of course, sir, but if the Head—"

But Mr. Blackwell cut him off.

"*An-y-one*... Is that *clear*?"

So definite was the question the assistant gave no response.

He just shook his head in subservient agreement. Then, feeling dismissed, he gave a slight bow and scurried off to exit through the same towering doors he'd crossed to enter the room. Within seconds, was gone. Mr. Blackwell didn't even notice. His eyes grew wide and distant; focused on what needed to get done. His grip on this world, loosening.

After a time of quiet contemplation, Mr. Blackwell reached forward and pressed the call button marked *Lab* on the intercom before him. A voice called out, having expected the call.

"Yes, sir?"

"Get me Dr. Grenier. Now."

"Very well, sir. One moment."

As Mr. Blackwell waited, a stark pressure built itself within him, clogging ventricles and airways alike. It caused a great deal of discomfort, a fogginess in his mind, and slight sharp pains in his extremities.

So much was falling apart. All the more reason to stay resolute. He needed to hold it all together. He alone could accomplish this, that he knew. Who else could he trust? The Head and the higher ups wanted to shut him down. How could their connections at the police force allow anyone to make any headway? Why were his men giving them that chance? What did he pay them for? Didn't they understand what was at stake? Why couldn't everyone see the purpose? The finality of it? With every question he asked himself, his anger grew. It wasn't until Dr. Grenier's voice called out to him, whole universes away, that he released the tension that had gripped him. He loosened his clenched fist to respond.

"Dr. Grenier?"

"Yes, sir. What can I do for you?"

Mr. Blackwell cleared his throat and gathering himself once again. It was imperative his men saw him as the absolute apex of their strength.

"Where are we now? Any closer to our goal?"

Dr. Grenier stayed quiet for a moment.

"Um... sir, I'm sorry but–"

"God dammit, Grenier! I don't want excuses. I want results!" When the eruption came, Mr. Blackwell didn't hold back. He showed none of his usual restraint.

After several seconds of Mr. Blackwell's angry panting, the doctor still hadn't answered.

"If you had even the remotest sense of the pressure, we're under right now, I mean–" The frustration reached a height where even his thoughts fizzled out.

Dr. Grenier stood aghast. Few men there understood the pressures he faced. As lead researcher, he'd made the majority, if not all, of the discoveries. And it was he, not his superior's tight leash, who kept his mouth shut when the credit passed right over him, eluding his grasp.

That aside, he was used to Mr. Blackwell pushing him—he pushed all of them—but this burst? He'd seen nothing like it. Something must have happened, but what? There was no way to tell.

At last, Dr. Grenier garnered the courage to speak.

"Sir, I assure you that–"

"I don't want your assurances, Grenier! I want results! I want success! The Head–" he began, but grew flustered once again and shifted directions. "We must see this through! *I* must see this through!"

"But, sir, without the boy?"

Veins emerged in both Mr. Blackwell's neck and forehead at the doctor's words.

Mr. Blackwell paused, collecting himself, before he spoke again. "We don't have the boy, do we, Doctor? Therefore, you *will* make it work! Do you hear me? Or I'm–"

"Sir, we're doing our absolute–"

"Do better!" Mr. Blackwell screamed. "No excuses,

dammit! After everything we've done? Everything... *I've* accomplished? To have it crumbled now because... Ineptitude... We just... You need to..."

Dr. Grenier grew more concerned at each syllable of his leader's mumbling babble.

"Figure it out, Doctor! Now!"

With that, a shaking Mr. Blackwell slammed his hand down, knocking the speaker off his desk. It shattered on the floor and the buzz went dead. He couldn't remember feeling such anger, ever in his life. He shot up from his chair where he paced back and forth from wall to wall, following the line made by the floor to ceiling double-paned windows overlooking the cold street below.

As each footfall touched down on the carpet, cruel thoughts of unfairness fueled his anger. Thoughts of Charlie entered; the boy, who'd lived right in *his own* backyard for years; yet that crackpot *Wilkes* had found him! Not only that, but he'd figured out *how* to use him. Almost to success! And he was bitter. Bitter that The Order's higher ups didn't see the merits of his plan. That they didn't see or understand the perfect timing of everything. Maybe it was because *they* wouldn't share their plans with *him*. The so-called *fool proof* plan. For years now, they'd kept him out. And why? He didn't know.

He saw the lot of them as nothing more than pillars of a past long dead, making mindless decisions without the remotest understanding of a bigger picture, a clearer picture.

Staring out over the city then, it looked like a distant painting. A frozen landscape, embossed in time. He gritted his teeth and sucked in a hard breath. Both fists clenched at his sides and his thoughts circled around his mind, never slowing or stopping, and always moving in one singular direction: *I will show them all.*

More than anything, he, Weyland Blackwell, wanted to

stand above them. To be his own man. He wanted to be free. Free of taking witless orders. Free of the burdens of his past failures. He wanted to be free of the taunting ghosts of his past. Of Wilkes and The Head. Of what was.

Wilkes! He thought. *You began this, but I, and not you, will achieve our mission. You'll see...*

———

The day disappeared as the bleak afternoon faded into an early and somehow even bleaker dusk. The sunlight struggled, finding itself too weak to break through the cloud cover.

Detectives Donovan and Lane had regrouped back at the station and were overseeing the team of uniforms, canvassing and calling all the local shelters.

Cait busied herself looking into the calls from the local shelters at the precinct. There weren't many in the past month, anyway. She chased up what she could and grew more impatient by the second.

"So, what'd'you want for dinner tomorrow?"

"Scott, I don't—"

"What? If there's a connection, it'll come in. Cait, remember to pace yourself. There will always be an emergency. Kick back for a moment. Take a breather."

"The victims didn't get any extra moments, Scott. You know that. You–" she stopped herself. She was getting riled up. "I'm sorry. You don't need me telling you—"

"It's okay, Cait. *Really*. Just trust me when I say you'll save yourself a lot of trouble if you can learn to be patient and accept the things you can't force now. That took me a while to learn. What d'ya think made me go bald?"

He could never keep himself serious for too long.

"Look, Cait. We just have to wait. Our guys have already made their first mistake. It's coming our way, right?"

"You're–"

"Detectives?"

Cait and Scott each turned to find one of the uniformed officers walking towards them. They answered in unison.

"Yeah?"

"We've got something. It's not much, but it's something."

Cait couldn't help but let several questions spill out of her; the excitement was too great.

"Where? What is it? What do you have?"

Scott looked at her, grinning, then back to the officer. He loved her enthusiasm.

"A few weeks back, some shelters started noticing absences from some of their regulars. There's been talk of strange things happening."

Scott and Cait looked at each other. Cait spoke first.

"What are we waiting for?"

"Be ready in five?"

"How about ready *now*?"

She was halfway out the door before she'd finished speaking, her jacket already on.

Scott shot up after her, somewhat surprised but also fueled by her tenacity.

"Alright.." He scrambled to put his own coat on and catch up, calling out to her. "Cait!"

But she didn't slow down.

"Cait?"

He stumbled out of the office, following her, only to find she'd already left the building. Smiling, he jogged to catch up, pulling his own jacket on as he went.

———

The Portland Rescue Mission stood on the prominent corner of 3rd Street and Burnside Avenue, beneath the weight of a heavy winter sky.

Scott let the door swing shut as he and Cait stepped in. It slammed behind them, kicking up dust, startling them both.

An unassuming voice broke in.

"Sorry about that. I'm afraid it's an old building, and the wind pulls at it with quite a force."

Scott and Cait turned to face the speaker, whose soft tones reach out again.

"And you are?"

Scott cleared his throat and put out his hand to shake.

"Hi there. I'm Detective Scott Donovan, Portland P.D., and this is my partner, Detective Cait Lane."

"Detectives! Of course, of course. I'm sorry. I knew you were coming, but I just assumed you'd be late…"

The man lifted his hand to greet both detectives.

It didn't appear the man had meant for his comment to be offensive, but Scott found it strange.

The man continued.

"Thank you for coming and on such short notice. I… ah, I'm Oscar Barrera. I manage the Mission here."

"Wonderful." Scott took the man's hand, giving him a sincere nod. "Thanks for seeing us. We understand you might have some insights into the—"

"The *strange happenings* going on."

Oscar cut in, trying to be helpful more than rude.

Scott hesitated at the eeriness in which the man spoke.

Cait maintained a cool demeanor but thought it strange as well.

Oscar looked worried, unsure of what to make of everything. But his smile broke soon enough.

"We're very thankful to have you." Oscar appeared to be

catching on to the awkwardness in the air. "And, uh, beg your pardon, but we're all a bit surprised to see your interest."

Part of Scott saw this comment as a personal jab. But he knew better. He sensed Cait's defenses rise, but understood all too well what was happening. The city's view of the homeless had changed over the years. Portland used to be a haven for them. Loved by the city and its citizens alike. But that had shifted. They'd become burdens, overlooked and seen as worth discarding. That change was enough to sour anyone who'd dedicated their lives to helping them. It was incredible, Scott thought, that this man was still smiling as he spoke.

Scott offered a gracious smile, forgiving any unintended offense as he spoke.

"That's understandable, sir."

"Please, call me Oscar."

"Well Oscar, I can't speak on behalf of the entire department, and won't make excuses, but we'll do our best here. We go wherever the case takes us and push for unilateral justice."

Oscar brightened at the sentiment.

"Very understandable." He exhaled, then turned to lead them away. "Shall we? I thought we could talk in our conference room."

Clapping his hands together, Scott looked at Cait.

"Sounds good?"

Cait nodded, seeing no reason to interject.

As they walked, Scott looked around the building.

"So, how long have you managed the Mission here, Oscar?"

Scott was incredible at defusing tension. It was always something that left Cait in awe, his ability to articulate a question that would calm someone, making them more comfortable and reassured.

Oscar's smile grew and his shoulders relaxed as he carried himself with more ease.

"Oh, I took over as manager in 2013." The excitement increasing in his voice. "But I've worked here since well before. Even before the Pearl District was the Pearl District."

"You don't say?"

Scott opened the door for comfortable small talk. A door Oscar walked through with gladness. It never ceased to amaze Cait, watching Scott work. All the while her own frustration boiled at the man's comment. She supposed a certain sense exited in it; she felt the same way herself sometimes.

Scott offered his own anecdotal tidbits.

"I had just started as a uniformed officer when they started remodeling the Pearl."

"A different world back then, right?"

"Yeah, it was. Grittier. A bit more bleak."

"A lot more crime, if memory serves me right."

"That is true. I've probably chased crooks through every one of the old warehouses. Before they tore most of 'm down. You name it, I was there."

"Yeah, it's a different world now, that's for sure. Things are better, most places. I think that's why we're all a little spooked. Here, come on in."

Oscar held the door to the conference room while Scott and Cait stepped inside.

Cait didn't think it much of a conference room. A couch and a few old chairs scattered around a coffee table.

"Spooked how?"

A gleam welled up in Cait's eyes; followed by amazement and wonder at the way Scott could turn a conversation around.

"Well, truth to tell, I'm not the one to ask."

Both Cait and Scott couldn't help but turn their heads at this.

"But–"

"I can attest to feeling some weird things from people. You know? An odd energy from everyone. More so at night, but..."

Cait leaned in, intrigued.

"... but I'd better let Charlie tell you about that."

"Charlie?"

"Yeah, he works here, sort of. He was the one that first noticed anything, brought it to my attention. That's when I called you guys, about a month ago."

Again, Oscar didn't mean for the comment about timing to sting, but Cait felt it anyway. Looking over at Scott, she assumed he somehow let it roll off his back, if he felt it at all.

"Can we speak to him?"

"Yeah, I asked Janet, our receptionist, to check on him." Oscar paused at this. A grave look fell upon his face, as if a great weight had laid itself upon him. "Ah, let me go see if he's ready."

Oscar turned to go, but he stopped, holding the door.

Cait could sense something gnawing at him.

"Say, before he comes? There's something you should know."

Both Scott and Cait looked up, their interests piqued.

"Yeah?"

"Well, the kid, especially as of late, can come off a bit strung out—he's been through hell, you see—he's fragile."

The detectives stared at Oscar, waiting for more. Scott's stare was one of compassion, while Cait was more confused.

Scott ventured a question.

"What happened to him?"

"That's the thing. We're not sure. He was away for a bit. And when he came back, his mom had passed. Tragic, really. And he... he carries a lot of weight around with him. You'll sense it. You can feel it when he walks in. But he's an incredible kid, Charlie. A real help around here. He was one of *our* regulars before we noticed how people took to him–"

"Wait. He was *homeless*?"

It was the first time Cait had spoken since they'd entered. She couldn't help the outburst; it hadn't been what she expected.

Scott lifted his arm toward her, a gentle reminder.

She could hear his words in her head: *It's not our job to make judgements on people or things. It's our job to collect facts.*

She felt a little foolish.

"*Sorry.*"

"It's okay. Comes with the territory. But yeah. Like so many others, he sort of just lost his way, I guess. He's still trying to find it, I suppose."

Scott and Cait listened, feeling like they were learning something.

Oscar rolled right along.

"He's so good with the people."

"Excuse me?"

"Charlie. He's incredible with people. You wouldn't guess it by looking at him, but he just has this natural empathy about him. He gets them, their pain and whatnot. I told him he could live here in exchange for work. It took some prodding, and the threat of winter, but he agreed."

Oscar cut himself off. His cheeks flushed, as he knew he'd shared too much.

"Um—look, sorry. He's a bit shy, so—I don't think you guys need his life story, but I didn't want you to be surprised when he walks in here, you know? I wanted you to take his information seriously."

"We can't *wait* to speak with him. We're looking for anything and everything that might help with our investigation."

Scott hoped his tone would console the worried man.

"Right. And you think there's a link?"

"Maybe. We'll have to talk to Charlie first."

"Of course, of course. Um, let me go get him."

Scott nodded, and Oscar opened the door and called down the hall.

"Hey, Janet, is Charlie back yet?"

"I didn't see him last I checked, but I'll call down."

"Thanks."

Oscar stepped back into the room.

Scott looked at his watch. It was still early morning.

"Where's he been to this early?"

Oscar looked up, his face no less concerned than before.

"Things started going worse for Charlie about a month ago."

The detective's interest was only growing.

"He started losing sleep and, as you know, things always go downhill from there. These days, he spends most of his nights going on these long walks. Trying to exhaust himself, I think. Nothing's really working, you know?"

Scott's face grew grave with concern.

Even Cait felt for him, thinking about how isolated he must feel.

Just then, the doorknob turned. Oscar stepped back for the door to swing open.

Silence hung in the pregnant pause as Cait and Scott stared up in anticipation.

A young man stood in the doorway. A shadow of him, more like it. At least, Cait thought. Hunched and brittle. He carried a colossal weight on his shoulders.

It was Charlie.

Scott and Cait saw it right away, his frailty. He was a shell of a person; almost all sense of life siphoned out.

Charlie, un-showered and un-shaved, stood there himself. He recognized the detectives right away as the two from the crime scene earlier. Distraught and irrational waves of guilt passed through him as he remembered.

"Charlie?" Scott put his hand out as a way of introduction, his diffusing and compassionate smile attempting to breach Charlie's protective facade. "I'm Detective Donovan of the Portland P.D."

Cait felt him right away. It shook her, the immensity of the pain he carried. He might collapse at any moment; she wondered how he was even there, let alone speaking with them. To her, it seemed a marvel.

Charlie shook Scott's hand.

"And this is my partner, Detective Lane."

Charlie turned and shook Cait's hand. He didn't so much as open his mouth to greet either of them, but nodded in accordance to using the littlest amount of energy possible.

Nobody held their breath more than Oscar, who waited, watching for how Charlie would react.

"Why don't we all sit down?"

He motioned to the couch for the detectives. And to the chair next to them for Charlie. It was the most comfortable. He himself took the folding chair next to it.

Scott eased into the questioning.

"Charlie, we understand you were one of the first to notice some strange things happening. Is that right?"

Charlie felt something lodge itself in his throat. Words or emotion. It didn't matter. He tried swallowing but found he couldn't.

With no other options he gave a weak nod before a single syllable escaped from him.

"*Yeah.*"

"And when was that, would you say?"

Scott and Cait each had their notepad out.

"About two months ago. A little after I started here."

For no explicable reason that Charlie could fathom, he felt the rising tension within him. It tugged those same old strings of guilt, filling him with shame. They were mere baseless thoughts, but Charlie couldn't help but assume he was the one at fault; that he caused what was happening. He was desperate to be released from this burden and would've confessed to it with certainty if he thought it would bring him peace.

Noticing the detective's glances, he tried to push the thoughts away and hold himself together as best he could.

"Interesting," Scott said, stealing a glance at Cait. They both jotted something down. "And what was it—at first, I mean—that you noticed?"

"Um... I..." Charlie began, coughing to clear his throat "... noticed a few... um... of the regulars stopped coming around... and..." Hit by a sudden and strange wave, Charlie trailed off. Peering over at Oscar, he pressed on with the encouraging nod he had received. "Then more people..." He gulped. "P-people I hadn't... gotten to know yet..." He looked away. "Just stopped coming in..."

Scott sat before Charlie, his arms resting on his knees. He was leaning forward, interested and disarming.

Cait seemed skeptical and unsure of Charlie's story. Something didn't add up. He was too jittery, too at odds with himself, but she followed her partner's lead.

"And then?" Scott prompted Charlie. Sure to keep his voice calm.

"*Sorry.*" Charlie said, his words fumbling out as he struggled to think. "That's when I started asking around. When I realized *how* scared people were. How scared people *are.*"

Scott and Cait exchanged looks again.

"What do you mean, scared?"

Charlie began again. The words seemed to come easier.

"There was already this *feeling*. I felt it. Just an odd atmosphere." Charlie paused again; acknowledging these nudges to anyone but Oscar felt strange. It gave credence to the pulls he felt at night and the layered weight of fear he felt.

Charlie noticed the piercing look in Cait's eyes. Both intent and impatience. It filled him with shame.

Sensing things going the wrong way, Scott interjected.

"And these *feelings*, others reported them too?"

Charlie looked up, sensing both the security and the distance in Scott's tone.

He nodded yes.

"People, they're scared. People who've already lost everything. Abandoned by everyone they've known. With little trust left. Even in each other." It was the most fluid thought he'd yet spoken. "In *this* world, people stick to routines. The same paths and people. You don't change. But now? People are sticking together with whomever. It's... strange."

"Sticking together? How do you mean?"

Scott's tone never left the soft space of understanding.

"The usual spots that people go? The territories? It changed the whole hierarchy of the community. Something —" Charlie paused again and took a deep breath. He could feel his heart rate on the rise. "*Something's* after them."

"Something?" Scott pressed for a gentle clarification. "But what? Who?"

Even if Charlie had an answer, he couldn't answer that.

Tension gripped him as the pull he always felt crept back in. His jaw trembled, and he could feel tears building.

Unable to speak, he just shook his head back and forth, quick, that he didn't know.

Scott and Cait both could feel Charlie's growing agitation.

Oscar looked as if he were about to cut the meeting short.

Having felt they'd increased the probability of his assumptions, Scott pushed a little further.

"Did you get anything specific from anyone? What they saw? Anything concrete?"

Charlie looked up at him again, somewhat frightened and more unsure.

"Just strange sounds... *rumors...*"

"Rumors?" Cait shot in at last, causing Charlie to jump.

"What sort of rumors?" came the gentle calm of Scott's voice again.

Charlie attempted another deep breath. He looked strained.

"That the streets weren't safe anymore. That people were being snatched. *Taken.*"

At that, Charlie's hands shook, an involuntary tremor.

Oscar wouldn't stand for it much longer.

"I think that about does it. Huh?"

Charlie and the detectives looked up.

"I mean..." Oscar cleared his throat, pushing his presence out into the room. "That's all Charlie shared with me even before, so I think we're done. No?"

He looked down at Charlie. His eyes heavy and empathic.

The boy's suffered enough, he thought. He then looked back to the detectives.

"I'd say he's earned his rest."

Scott and Cait both looked up—even Scott seemed a bit taken aback.

"Um... yeah..." Scott looked back and forth between Cait, Oscar, and Charlie. "... yeah, this has been helpful. Just–" He looked from Oscar to Charlie, understanding the display of protection he was witnessing. "Is there anything, Charlie, anything else you think you can tell us? It would be a real help."

Charlie looked away, considering it. He shook his head there wasn't anything else to tell. Or so he thought.

Scott looked to Cait.

"Cait, anything else?"

She feigned thinking about it for a moment before shaking her head.

"I don't think so."

Then Scott closed the conversation.

"Thank you both for your time. We appreciate it very much."

Both men nodded. Afterwards, Oscar maintained eye contact with the detectives. Charlie's glance fell to the stained carpet by the coffee table.

Oscar reached out in the quiet.

"Can I just have a word with you both before you leave? Outside?"

"Of course," said Scott.

"Thanks."

"Wait for me in here, Charlie?"

"Sure."

Charlie felt in trouble then. More so even than before. Something had gone wrong, but he couldn't tell what.

"Goodbye, Charlie, and thanks," Scott said in parting.

Charlie stood and shook both his and Cait's hands, nodding to them both.

Oscar led the detectives out into the hall where the bustle of activity echoed.

"Look, I'm sorry for cutting it short, but Charlie seemed a little agitated. I-I'm worried about him."

"It's okay, Mr. Barrera. Quite understandable, too. Seems he's been through quite the ordeal."

Oscar nodded but did not speak. He seemed to appreciate the understanding he'd received.

"And I feel you both could help us a great deal, so thank you. Will you let us know if anything else comes up? If either of you hear or remember anything?"

"Of course, of course. And thank you. I didn't... I want the boy to get better. That's all."

Cait and Scott exchanged understanding looks and nodded in unison. It was Scott who responded.

"We understand."

"Thank you." Oscar forced a half-grin. "Thank you very much. Uh, if you don't mind seeing yourselves out, I'd like to check on Charlie real quick."

"Of course. We'd be happy to oblige. And, again, thank you for your time."

Oscar nodded once more, and Scott looked to Cait.

"Ready?"

She turned to him, breathing in and nodded herself.

"Yeah. Let's go.

Scott turned to leave as Oscar watched, but Cait, feeling a nudge of her own, looked back to steal a quick glance at Charlie. He intrigued her. She wondered what did that to someone? What could've splintered him so much? She felt only a fraction of the weight he carried, as if it emanated off him; it was a burden she couldn't fathom. In the brief moments he thought he was alone, she sensed him letting himself down and something in her shifted. Whereas before she'd seen him through a lens of annoyed confusion, after speaking with him, she couldn't help but feel admiration. To bear the weight and wounds he did but keep going? That was strength. A strength she couldn't quite believe. It was something else. She felt for him and wished she could help him.

Scott's voice called to her from down the hall.

"Cait?"

She looked up.

"You coming?"

His smile illuminated the dark and weary hall.

Cait looked up.

"Yeah?" She said, then forced her own smile. "Yeah, I'm coming."

Distracted, she followed Scott through the foyer and out into the cold gray.

Oscar took several deep breaths and went back in to sit next to Charlie. He couldn't shake the worry from his voice.

"Hey, kid?"

Charlie noted Oscar's warm voice, its understanding weight. Which he appreciated as he felt on the verge of tears. He looked the other way; daring to speak but not betray himself.

"Thanks, Oscar."

The older man's head nodded back and forth with vigor.

"Don't mention it. I thought enough'd been enough."

Charlie shook his head that Oscar had been right but let his chin fall to his chest.

"Hey, you okay?"

Charlie sniffled.

"Good enough."

Oscar knew he wasn't.

"You know, the offer still stands?"

Charlie looked up at last. Toward his friend and mentor.

"Only if you want it, though. But look, Charlie, I... I get it if... if you don't."

A month back, Oscar had offered to let Charlie meet with the state psychologist who worked with the local clinics and shelters. He wouldn't need to worry about any of the paperwork or financial burdens. The Mission would take care of it. Charlie kept putting it off. He knew from previous experiences that route would force him to experience those wounds again. Something he felt he lacked the strength to endure.

"Thanks again, Oscar, but–"

"Hey, look..." Oscar hesitated, taking care to choose his words. "... I know it's not my place, but..." He paused again, unsure whether to finish the thought. "You don't have to go it alone."

Charlie's legs shifted beneath him, squirming.

"What you carry, Charlie? What you feel? You... You're such an asset to us. To so many, and we..." He hesitated again. "*I* just want to see you happy. You know? *Well.*"

The tears came even stronger; confusion flared through Charlie. Without thinking, he fought off Oscar's encouragement; it being at odds with his ability to hold back the coming storm. If he accepted it, he would've crumbled even faster.

Letting the light in then would bring it all crashing down. Of that, he was sure.

The tears emerged. He couldn't help it. Instead of saying anything, he just nodded his head up and down.

"You get any sleep last night, Charlie?"

He shook his head. "Nah."

"Why don't you get downstairs and try to get some rest, huh? Don't worry about any of the projects you were working on. You just take it easy, okay? Until you're feeling better."

Still, Charlie found it difficult to speak without bursting into tears. He nodded he understood. Overwhelmed with a strange combination of thankfulness and guilt, Charlie fought for stillness.

After several long, quiet moments, Oscar said, "I'll just give you a bit," and he turned to walk away.

Charlie reached out.

"Oscar, wait—"

Oscar turned.

"I-I'm sorry—"

The dam burst and tears flooded now.

"No, no, no…" Oscar cut him off, predicting what Charlie would say. "You have nothing to be sorry about, Charlie. You rest. You take the time you need. You'll be back up soon, I know it. Until then, come here."

Oscar reached out and lifted Charlie into a deep embrace.

It was the steadiest Charlie had felt in longer than he could remember, but he didn't trust it either. He held a loose grip on Oscar, tears streaming from his eyes. He held more tightly to the feeling in his gut he saw as his protection. Those fleeting glimpses of safety. The distance between him and the world.

Getting closer to anyone right now, he thought, would only bring him more pain.

All Charlie could think about was escaping. About getting out. Leaving. To get downstairs or back outside. He would take the bleak and heavy winter air over this path to pain.

"Oscar–" he said, his words spilling out in a frantic burst. He pushed his would-be friend away.

Oscar stood back.

"What is it, Charlie?"

"Thanks, but... I... I gotta go."

Charlie turned and ran.

Oscar stood there gaping amid a fallout that he couldn't understand. Instinct told him to go after Charlie, but he also knew he needed space. Charlie needed time to heal. He hoped Charlie knew he could always come to him. And that it wasn't too late. Most of all, he hoped Charlie still believed he could return at all.

―――――

Scott and Cait were halfway to the car when Scott stopped, letting an excited smile form across his face. He turned to Cait.

"So?"

Taking this as her cue to celebrate, Cait turned, almost leaping.

"This is it! Right? I mean, this has to be it. I knew it!" She let herself get carried away.

Scott laughed.

"Remember, we still need something more conclusive, but this confirms our suspicions. It gives us—"

"The direction we've been dying for!"

Unfazed by her interruption, Scott smiled at Cait's enthusiasm. He knew she was about to rupture with excitement.

"Yes, but remember: *patience.* We still have much to consider. *Much* to do."

Cait brought her excitement down to a more reasonable level; she knew Scott wouldn't begrudge her celebration.

As her mind worked to thread its way through where the case would lead next, she found herself distracted with thoughts of Charlie.

She looked up at her partner who said nothing about what *she* considered being her unprofessional interruption during their interview.

"Hey Scott?"

Her tone caught his attention more than her words.

"I'm sorry I couldn't keep that reaction to myself in there. It was just..." Somehow, the words escaped her. "Wasn't that a little strange?"

Scott shook his head, acknowledging that it was.

"Yeah, that was a *strange* experience."

Cait couldn't get Charlie's blank expression out of her mind.

Scott sensed he needed to bring her back.

"This entire case is strange though, isn't it?"

She looked up at him.

"I mean, look what we're dealing with. No better a reaction than any other."

Cait thought about it. Scott always knew how to frame things. It allowed him to keep his mind clear and focused.

"Sorry for slipping. I'll, uh–"

"Hey..."

He used that voice again. The encouraging one she knew to listen to.

"... you're great at what you do. When I had a full head of hair, my passions and instincts drove me, too. Believe it or not.

Cait nodded, holding back her grin. The sincerity of his words made her feel better.

"I'm not worried about you or your progress. Otherwise, I would've said something myself."

She cocked her head at this.

"Two things, though."

"Which are?" She looked up, more concerned.

"*You* can't beat yourself up so much. If you make a mistake, acknowledge it and move on. Let yourself do better next time. Never strive for it."

She shook her head she understood, which made Scott smile.

"And you still haven't told me what you want for dinner tomorrow."

Cait rolled her eyes and feigned a scowl. Turning, she began walking to the car again.

"What?" Scott pandered, his arms stretched out. "Stacey needs to know so she can go grocery shopping. Depending on what you want, she might fix the kids something else. Don't let that sway your decision, though."

Cait grinned and kept walking.

"Cait? This is important stuff, okay?" He jogged to catch up. "You're going to get me in trouble with the boss."

Without looking, Cait prodded.

"I thought I was the boss."

Scott stopped dead, appreciating her levity and mocking tone.

"Well-played, rook. Well-played."

She looked up him at last.

"You mean *boss*."

Grinning, Scott unlocked the car, and they both got in.

"Well, what now, *boss*?"

"We get back to the station. Get more officers out there. Though in street clothes. We place lookouts at all the local haunts, increase our patrols in the usual sheltered communities, keep all our ears to the ground."

Scott's smile showed he approved.

"We need to get feelers out there. As many as possible. Get the word out. You know? See what comes forward. Do you think the cap'll let us take Mitchell and Dornman as well? Widen our efforts?"

"Good question. Leave that to me. You get whatever messages we need to the dispatchers, and we'll get moving."

"Sounds good."

"Good plan, *rook*."

"Thanks, *partner*."

Scott's grin widened, further yet. He turned the keys, and the engine roared to life. Crisp plumes of warm steam flushed upward in the cold, and they sped off toward the station. Continuing the investigation.

FOUR

Weakened by the constant struggle to shine, the evening sun still fought with vigor to break through the thick and icy layers of cloud cover. In a few lucky places, gentle rays of light touched down. Never long enough, though, to maintain warmth.

Mr. Blackwell stood behind his desk, hunched over. He was a virtual statue, stricken by the suffocating situation he found himself trapped in. There had to be a way. He knew it.

A single desk lamp illuminated the large space. The light couldn't quite reach across the room. Its tepid, sickly glow fell upon the series of texts and ancient books strewn across his desk. One in particular, at the very center, had countless post-it and pages marked with wide fanning papers covered in his own scrawl. It was imperative to The Head they found this book. Next to it lay a hefty notepad—its pages worn and used, littered with the scribbles of someone else's hand.

His body spun around with a swift burst and picked up the notepad.

"Damn *you*, Professor Lake! There must be something

we've missed! Something you stumbled upon that would guide..."

When in solitude, he couldn't help but let his thoughts slip toward despair. He hadn't the strength to keep the egotism alive when it wasn't necessary to command.

Flipping through the pages, he scoured for anything he might have missed; only finding the same cryptic references to some northern outpost. It tugged upon the threads of his anger, assuming The Order's move in that geographical location was most likely a direct result of these discoveries.

Their *final* plan, he would mock.

But within these texts and within Professor Lake's translations, he had discovered the breadcrumbs to achieving his own goals. When alone, he too believed—deep down—they had no chance without Charlie.

His hands shook at the thought. Anger was the only way to keep himself together.

"Dammit! There must be something here!"

He took a deep breath, but not to calm down. His aim was to sharpen his frustration, to redirect it.

"You studied this pre-human culture your whole life, Lake. You must know something! You must have—"

Unable to control his temper at that point, his words collapsed into a wail, raw and primal.

He needed to speak with Lake. The man who'd made the discoveries. The one responsible for their breakthroughs. Their progress so far. Though that was impossible, he knew.

He looked around his empty office in desperate hope of conjuring the man they needed out of the hollowness of the surrounding space.

"Where did you disappear to, Lake?" The question lingered several moments as he stood there thinking. "How did you get away?"

Lake himself was a professor of anthropology. The discoverer of a race pre-dating modern man by millennia. They lived all along the northern rim of the world before the continents separated. He discovered the remnants of their civilization, cracked their language, and discovered the secrets of their religion that he was sure would radicalize the notions of the modern world. That's when The Order found him, years ago. But he'd since slipped from their grasp and disappeared.

While ruminating on these despairing thoughts, the phone rang, startling Mr. Blackwell back to the world.

"What?" He didn't hide his fury. "What do you mean, *it* failed again?" His forehead creased and fold with the news. "God dammit, *Doctor*, prep the next subject, immediately, and run it again! Then prep the next one and the next one and the next, do you hear me? We will continue to run tests until we accomplish our goal! Don't interrupt me, dammit! And yes, we will procure however many subjects we need; whenever we need and, however, we want; for as long as we need." He waited for the desired response before responding; again, holding nothing back. "Yes! The next time I hear from you, *Doctor*, I expect you'll have different results for me. Is that clear?"

Not waiting for an answer, he hung up. He slammed the phone down and crashed both hands down onto the tabletop. Its echo fired across the room in all directions.

"Damn!" he screamed, and his jaw shook from the immensity of all he felt. "Damn it, *Lake*! You—" His eyes glared as if embers of faint fire burned at every word. "If this doesn't work, I'll use everything at my disposal to find you! And when I do, you'll wish to the gods you'd never made this discovery!"

———

He could feel the chemicals coursing through his brain. Charlie had always been hyper-aware of how he felt. An important survival instinct he'd developed. In an escalated state, though, it always intensified.

Charlie lay for a long time, tossing and turning on his cot. He was doing his best to calm himself, hoping beyond reason for sleep to come, but his heart was pounding, pressure was building in him everywhere, and somehow, he was even more desperate and exhausted than before.

Though his overhead lights were off, a pale glint of sunlight shined itself into Charlie's room. It stretched, almost sick and weak, across his legs.

Charlie's body was still, but he was so gripped by crippling doubt and such deep-seated guilt that he gripped himself. He was causing himself to slip further and further into a heightened negative state. The walls in his mind weakened. Eroding at a slow pace, as the minutes passed. Revealing what he already knew lay just beyond the other side.

The longer he lay there and the more he tried not thinking about the images that plagued his sleepless nights, the more harshly they seemed to attack, creating a strange and chaotic war zone in his expansive mind.

Shit! Shit! Shit!

Panic gripped him. He struggled against it, trying to hold himself still; it didn't work. Nothing helped. The nightmares only came on stronger; ensuring sleep would never come. Flashes of an ominous forest, lit up by a blinding blue light, and the accompanying chants that hung beneath the sky.

Charlie would twitch and his face would scrunch together; he knew he wouldn't be able to hold out there much longer.

Worried that these visions were now creeping into the daylight hours, fists clenched and stricken by his lack of options, Charlie shot up from the bed, swearing. With an angry whimper, Charlie grabbed his thick coat and hat, slid on his boots, and burst out into the shadowed hallway once more. He did not know where to go. So, with his body shaking, he scurried forth. Coming to a door, he missed the handle several times before opening it at last. Then he spilled out into the abrasive light of day. He only hoped that he could lose himself in the monotony of a brainless march. He would give himself over to the unforgiving and bitter winter winds. They could numb him, he hoped. Then he could continue ignoring the world around him. At least until everything passed, if it *could*. Whatever he did anymore, it came with that rotting feeling in his gut, that feeling that, regardless of his choices, the morning would never really come.

———

A man in a worn out and tattered lab coat stood—despondent —holding the phone in his hand. Only a dial tone sounded until someone with a clipboard across from him ventured to speak.

"Sir?"

Dr. Grenier waited a moment before giving the order. "Prep the next subject." His voice hung, drenched in reluctance.

The other man said nothing in return. No one did. No one in the whole crowded room. Everyone's head either hung where they stood as they tried to save face from their presumed failure or drooped, as if accepting defeat.

Dr. Grenier looked out over the men; men he had trained and led. Cultivated and coached. They'd come so far. Accomplished so much. His heart wrenched, thinking of it all crumbling because one man was unraveling. A man they all, including Dr. Grenier himself, once trusted. But that man was much changed.

He didn't like it himself, but wouldn't dare say anything.

The higher ups had given this project the go ahead. Who was he to interfere with that? He was no one. A groundling to follow orders. And follow orders he would. There was a certain safety in that.

He knew morale must be boosted. Looking out over his despondent men, something struck him.

The men looked up when he spoke; he struggled for the words, but they came at last.

"Look, this hasn't gone how we expected it would. And *we* know the data. What it shows. We know what *can* happen, but—"

He paused for a moment, watching the surrounding faces wonder what he was getting at.

"But orders are orders," he said, a painful fact. Each man's shoulders leveled, rose in unison. "And it's clear to *him* what must be done." At the mention of their superior, the man went rigid. Not out of respect, though. The doctor's irreverent omission of the man's name surprised the room. A sign of disrespect never perpetrated. If word got back to Mr. Blackwell, the repercussions would be severe.

But each man stood a little taller.

He looked down as he spoke.

"In the end, we're not doing this for any single man." He smiled at this point; his expression grew warm. He felt something igniting in him, a certain passion returning. "We're not even doing this for ourselves. We are so much larger than that, aren't we? The Order. We stretch out across the world for one singular purpose. And *this*, gentlemen, could bring us *that* much closer to our purpose being realized. Yes, it's moving quickly. Too quickly, some have said. And though it appears a dead end, we must press on. For everything we each signed up for. For everything we believe in! We must find the breakthrough and persevere! This is for the Nameless themselves! For *their* return! For the tearing down *this* world! And rebuilding the new! Men, we will triumph!"

The heartbeat of the room shifted as their collective spirit showed signs of life; shoulders relaxed, and smiles returned. The very air itself felt thinner, easier to carry and step through.

He looked forward, away from the men.

"So..." He paused for himself as much as them. "... who's with me? For the *new world*!"

A collective burst followed him, harmonious and deep.

"For the *new world*!"

The doctor couldn't believe the shift, nor could he fathom the fact that he half believed what he'd said. He saw no genuine hope in their purpose, but felt he owed the men some boost for their sacrifices.

"Are we ready?"

The unified, collective voice echoed again.

"Yes!"

"Then bring in the next subject."

Everyone turned back to their stations and readied themselves for the next experiment.

Dr. Grenier, too, turned his attention back to the task ahead, maintaining his feigned assurance. Waiting for the go-ahead from the technician next to him, who gave him a nod, the doctor wrapped his hand around the lever before him, which stemmed up from the control panel at his station. It clicked out of position, then slid upwards and, with a slight amount of resistance, he could push it in the other direction; back into a locked position, setting the procedure in motion.

The lab, buried several floors beneath the city's street level, had plenty of room to reach out in every direction. All you could see on this floor was a series of workstations and office spaces along a singular glass-walled corridor. At its terminus was a control room for observation. Opposite the control room was a vast open space, white-walled, like the rest of the facility. Eerie and uninviting. From the left wall ran two industrial-grade hoses; they stemmed from the wall and snaked across the floor to a smaller chamber, set into the center of the rear wall. By appearance, this chamber looked like a strange show, invasive in its placement. Enclosed and built from floor to ceiling. It looked sturdy, though, like it could withstand a significant amount of pressure. Two ducts extended out of this smaller chamber, connected by the hoses to whatever lay beyond that far wall. Few knew what did. Mr. Blackwell and Dr. Grenier were among those few.

Behind the walls, gears came to life. Mechanical components, bringing about a hollow and strange false sense of life. Components switched, shifted, turned, and triggered, all to a slow-building hum.

A sudden noise, a sort of grinding slide, shot itself across the space surrounding the smaller chamber. The wall behind it opened up—to no one's surprise—revealing only the shadowy darkness beyond. A man fell—flung really—forward, slamming against the chamber glass. He grunted and collapsed to the floor. The wall jarred to a close behind, trapping him once again.

Scrambling to stand up, he beat his fists against the then-closed wall and screamed.

"Wait! Please! Stop! Let me out of–"

The man stopped, giving a helpless turn. His body hung, pleading, feeling the dozen sets of piercing eyes on him, sharpening the painful awareness of his lack of cover. Bare and exposed, he just stood before this group of men, open and vulnerable. Unable to think of anything.

Still covering himself with one hand, he smacked his other against the glass in pleading jabs, as if it would help get their attention or maybe their sympathy. It didn't work.

His helpless voice trickled out again.

"Please! You–You have to help me! What are you—Why am I—"

It cut out. Stopping as a despairing realization settled in, *these men would not help him.* They were holding him. Therefore, would remain deaf to his pleas?

Falling backward where the side of the chamber met the wall, his body relaxed. Not that he was calmer. The mind copes in strange ways. It accepts that there's nothing one can do but give in.

There is no real peace in despair, but strife is often absent. Along with hope. As if one has given up their need to struggle.

It was then he looked down and realized he was wearing one thing: a bronze chain with a heavy medallion. Something he was unfamiliar with. He couldn't fathom its purpose.

The invisible machines churned their gears out of sight. One technician turned a wheel hanging on the wall next to him. A sharp and piercing hiss cut through the air, emanating from the far wall.

Everyone's eyes were on the unsuspecting subject, their collective breath held tight in reserved anticipation.

A murky fume built and rose. It grew with every passing moment and plumed at the chamber's base.

Right on cue, thought Dr. Grenier.

The man in question, their subject, continued to moan and wail. Tears fell. Slow at first, like the gentle rising of fumes from the ground. Not to be held back. That's when he first noticed the rising gas. A plume of sickly green, putrid-looking gas built up around him. He panicked; his whimpers erupted into sustained and violent shrieks. The drive for self-preservation overcame embarrassment as he pounded on the glass with both hands, leaving himself exposed.

The horrid and toxic hues continued to waft, aiming to surround the man in his entirety. They spread to each corner and consumed whatever space they could.

"Vitals?" asked the doctor. His voice was low and calm.

The man nearest him answered.

"Steady, sir."

"Good."

Even so, the fumes continued to rise. When they could go no further, they thickened, consolidating their strength.

Before long, the subject in question became obscured. A shadow in the building cloud. Yet his coughs and frantic bursts and wails broke through, reminding each technician that a man stood there.

"W-wha-what!" he coughed out. "W-w-wha-at… is… t-th-hi–is? W-wh-ha-at—w-why?"

No one answered. Each man stood still, observing, cold to the distant reality that they were witness to a human burdened by terrible suffering.

Dr. Grenier looked down at his workstation's clock, counting down the seconds.

"He's made it longer than the last two."

Something in him dared to hope but not to breathe; he would wait 'til it felt safe to exhale.

"Are we recording this?"

The man next to him answered in a weak whisper.

"Yes, sir."

"His vitals?"

"Rising, but still stable."

Dr. Grenier's eyes widened; his brow un-furrowed, as if worry was being lifted off his shoulders.

"Nothing abnormal?" he asked again.

"No, sir. Wait—" The man's tone turned. Red emergency lights blinked, along with a series of warning sirens.

The test subject gave way to several almost inhuman screams.

"What! What is it?" Dr. Grenier's muscles tensed. "Why—"

"I don't know, sir. He just spiked."

"It's starting! It's–"

The screams grew sharper, more pained. With every burst, the decibel rose. It was unlike anything they'd heard before. Any of them. Ever.

Bones cracked and the sounds of flesh being ripped echoed their way outside the glass.

Several men turned away—just hearing the sounds gave way for their minds to fill in their lack of visibility.

"The–the *transformation*... it's actual–"

"Vitals are topping out, sir! We're losing it!"

"Keep going, god dammit! We must press on!"

"But sir!"

"Keep going!"

"But–"

A violent growl ripped through the commotion, stopping everyone dead. Visibility was still zero. Suddenly, a hand—or forearm—slammed itself against the glass. Deep, gnarled and widespread bruises stretching across it; the collective group of technicians all jumped at once.

Fear tightened its grip on the room.

Feverish screams tore through the silence. Whatever lay behind that glass chamber was in anguish; and it couldn't be human anymore.

One more thud. Then another. And another. Crashing against the glass. Whatever it was, lashed out.

Following the course of the momentum, it built and built and built before collapsing, cutting off.

The alarm bells blared and rose to dominate the room as the feverish sounds of the subject died down, eliminating any competition.

"What? What happened?"

Frantic, the doctor couldn't help but feel his hopes melting away before him again.

"I-I don't know, sir. Its vitals, they've dropped off. Its—We're losing it!"

"Well, do something, dammit! Flood that chamber with—"

But it was too late. Whatever was behind that curtain of fumes wouldn't make it. Its screams had faded and disappeared behind the machinery's hum and the hissing of the gas. All became silent and still until Dr. Grenier spoke up. The single word crept out in a whisper. Almost nonexistent.

"Vitals?"

Sometime preceded the response.

"It's gone, sir. It didn't survive the... the..."

Dr. Grenier finished the thought for him. For everyone.

"... the transformation..."

The technician nearest him looked up, and dredging the depths of their collective uncertainty, ventured an encouragement. A welcome remark, but out of place.

"It made it longer than the last six subjects... sir."

The doctor's whole countenance sank, but he couldn't let it fall in front of the men. He turned, forced a smile, and nodded in agreement. He had to remind himself that he knew it'd never work, but still he'd hoped.

"We'll keep getting closer, Doctor. We'll keep trying."

Each man wore the same expressed conviction. It was a collective look that told Dr. Grenier that, in that regard, he'd accomplished his goal. Still, he felt no victory. But they had to move forward.

"You're right..."

That's all he said. That's all he *could* say. Then, looking at the men nearest him, he forced a thin smile.

"We come closer and closer, and we *must* keep at it."

With every word, his insides tightened. All his research, everything he knew about the procedures, the rituals, everything they learned from Astoria and Lake's translations on the ancient texts told him that this would never work without Charlie West. But Charlie was lost to them forever. Ensuring their hopeless labor would never bear fruit.

Yet, without this illusion, he knew his men wouldn't carry on. He had to allow that lie to live or else they'd grow purposeless.

Looking back to the chamber beneath the pooling smoke, something lay. Something—it was no man.

He gave the next order, his voice gruff and unsure.

"Reset everything."

He tried to sound strong but couldn't pull himself above an insecure drawl.

"Remove the body. Prep the machines again. And the next subject. Change nothing. We came close that time. Let's see if we can at least recreate that. Then we'll make what adjustments we think we need."

It moved the men, and with renewed vigor each set out to accomplish their given task.

Dr. Grenier stood there amid all the scurrying, a man trapped between two paths. Both led to a failure of sorts. He stood there like a statue in the cold; desperate to reason which path he'd prefer. More than anything else, he wondered which would lead him toward the hope he wished he could cling to.

FIVE

The wind's harsh and bitter sting eased his nerves, and Charlie could finally take a deep breath. At last, without thinking, he could settle into a default state and just walk. He again let his steps carry him forward, only somewhat conscious of the feeling that was pulling him in the other direction to whatever sat beyond Union Station.

As always, he walked the other way.

He let his head drop low, chin to his chest, shoulders slumped, and allowed one foot to touch down in front of the other and carry him away from every thought he hoped to avoid.

Charlie was somewhere beyond strength now, beyond what he thought he could endure. He only hoped to disappear into that sea of city streets. Surrounded by people scurrying about their day. Filled with hopes and destinations. All the while, his mind was a vast mass of ocean waves, rising high and crashing down over him, hard. Associated with this vision was a singular revolving thought. That one day, his striving would cease. That he would, one day, find rest and peace. That one day this would end. Until then, he'd put one foot in front of the other. Trying to forget.

By midday his mind became mush, unsure even where he was.

Somewhere just east of 20th on the West Side near Couch Street, he'd walked north, wrapping all the way around where the 405 ended and back. Zig-zagging up and down streets, turning one way, then another, always keeping his momentum up.

He'd bumped into several pedestrians as he went; so far removed from his surroundings. A few spoke up. Most didn't. They'd looked up at him and, weary, let it go. Charlie would say nothing in return. Just continued walking, lost even to himself.

The world wasn't tangible to him anymore. There was only the distance he hoped to put between himself and his growing fear.

The longer he walked, the more pronounced the pull within him grew, intensifying the need for him to keep walking.

He had very little rationality left. His body felt fuzzy, not just his mind. Like it triggered some inflatable device within him, something designed to save one from drowning, but ended up causing him some sort of severe allergic reaction.

His face grew gaunt and hollow, and his body ached for food and water, neither of which he had awareness enough to give it.

At one moment, several children ran by, playing. They'd come up behind Charlie and startled him. He yelled—a hoarse screech—and the children screamed. Two ran to their mother nearby, who held them close, a reassuring and protective grasp, and she glared at Charlie as he stumbled off.

Onward he walked as he grew less aware of everything.

Somewhere off Lovejoy Street, unknown to himself, Charlie stopped and leaned against a lamppost.

"Hey!" boomed a raggedy voice as it flitted through the cold. Its echo muffled, carrying with it a toothless burden of heavy loss.

Startled, Charlie jumped, letting out a quick yelp; then looked up once more.

"You gonna throw up, you best fin' yoself a corna or a can." The man's order was strict and straightforward. Coming from both experience and authority, it appeared.

Charlie gaped at him, attempting to discern whether he was real when the man erupted into a wheezing bout of laughter.

"I jus mess'n wit you." The broken words came out in a slurred mumbled. Followed by a strange, stunted laugh. "You can go throw'p where ya want."

The man laughed again, but Charlie didn't notice. He grew dizzier and dizzier as the laughter seemed to echo all around him, surrounding and attacking him on all sides.

"What hap'n to you?" The man's voice struck a harsher tone. "Ya look like hell!"

Laughter thundered out again as the man pointed to his own clothes. Charlie looked at him before peering down at himself. Shame washed over him.

He focused on the wreck of a man before him. He was someone Charlie would have wanted to help before. Someone he'd have seen as one who'd slipped through the city's cracks. Someone he would've empathized with. And identified.

His mind couldn't connect with anything as the man's laughter cackled on.

Then, he feared he'd stopped for too long; and the worries returned, stronger. He hadn't even realized they'd softened.

He took a step back.

"Hey! Wh're yous go'n?" The man yelled out, laughing still.

Charlie took another two steps away from him, that piercing guilt rising through his gut.

"Wh're yous go'n, son! Look'n like dat!"

It was too much for Charlie; and images he'd worked so hard to hold back came crashing back in on him. He turned and ran; the cackling laughter of the toothless man echoing down the street behind his steps.

"Wh're yous go'n, son!" Charlie heard the man belt again.

Each time, his stomach cinched tighter. The words etched themselves into the walls of his already fragile mind.

As fast as he could, Charlie sprinted; several blocks, bumping into more people as he went.

As he ran, his lungs constricted and all the events of the day reached their apex. Unable to keep going, Charlie stumbled into the nearest alley where he collapsed onto a pile of trash and damp boxes. His body erupted into a series of erratic convulsions; Charlie felt trapped once again; in that all-too-familiar prison of induced panic, his mind and body stuck in flex.

All Charlie could do was wait.

As always, this attack would end, and with a weary sense of cathartic reprieve. But the fear, too, would return. It never felt far away. He couldn't think about that then. What consumed him was every image that flashed itself across his mind. They flooded, bombarding him; with his defenses laid waste, this only added to the heaviness he carried.

When it passed, Charlie's strength had almost given out and. Not knowing what else to do, he just laid there half conscious. He laid atop that pile of trash for some time before the thoughts meandered their way back toward him.

Until they did, Charlie would lay there on those restless and unconscious shores, dreaming, always, of crashing waves.

———

When Scott and Cait left The Mission, Cait incorrectly assumed that each step would start falling into place. Things would start to move. And fast.

Nothing could have been further from her reality.

She'd been staring at her computer for the better part of three hours and was on the verge of falling asleep when Scott appeared in her doorway. She didn't notice him. Her mind was busy going over the list of everything she'd already done; desperate to figure out if there was something she'd missed. She was at a loss.

Scott's grin grew wide as a thought struck him. It wasn't often that he found her so unguarded.

She still hadn't seen him. He hollered.

"Cait!"

Cait leaped up, yelping. Scott burst out laughing behind her, buckling over himself in the hall.

"Dammit, Scott."

"I'm–I'm sorry, but wow! I couldn't help myself. You were really in the zone there."

She shook her head at him, unable to help from grinning herself.

"I'm just so bored. I wanna get out *there*, Scott! Do something."

"I know. Which is good because we got something."

"What?" She shot up.

"A call just came in."

"What is it?"

"A strange story. Some guy called it in up north of the Pearl. Something about a struggle, followed by several screams, then the witness says he saw three guys carrying *something* big into a big van."

"A van?"

"That's what he said."

"It could be–"

"It could. So let's—"

But before he could finish, Cait had popped up; sliding her coat on, she moved toward the door.

"Cait?" he turned to find her already well down the hall-way. "Cait? Let me grab my coat." But she had already left. Gone.

He ran to grab his thick winter coat and catch up.

———

"Mr. Brennen, is it?"

A man looked up from the shop counter he occupied, eyeing both Cait and Scott with an air of suspicion and discomfort as they walked into his shop. He took a step back, keeping his distance as they came to the counter.

"Yes?"

"I'm Detective Donovan, Mr. Brennen. This is my part-ner, Detective Lane."

Scott and Cait each held out their badge and stood tall.

Mr. Brennen's back straightened as Scott worked to disarm him.

"We're here about a call you made this morning? You saw something *strange*? We were wondering if you could elaborate."

The old man gave a slow nod. Acknowledging he had some idea what Scott was talking about.

"I told them everything I knew on the phone already."

Cait's burned red in a frustrated flare. So tired of the distance and mistrust they received. It ate away at her.

Scott always seemed able to brush resistance off. In doing so, winning people over.

"Right..." Scott bobbed his head up and down as he

spoke. "... I understand that. I do, but we think there's a possible connection to our case." He leaned in closer and lowered his voice; the old man took another step back. "We have a..." he slowed, considering his words with care. "... different agenda compared to most officers you speak with, *sir*."

The man looked up, considering this; Scott stepped to the side.

"And—with all due respect—we keep hearing about how spooked people are. Around here, you know? Rumors and what-not. Pretty strange stuff. We just want things to slide back toward normalcy, if you will. Really, we were hoping you wouldn't mind showing us where you saw what you saw. Sort of walk us through it?"

Cait again stood, amazed at how most people's resistance caved with Scott. How his sincerity melted them. But it was genuine. Not false. Incredible how their walls collapsed.

The man eyed the detectives, still somewhat unsure.

Cait held her breath, but knew it would work.

Scott stood there with that same disarming grin.

The man gave in. He *caved* and turned.

"Follow me."

He led the detectives through the shop, toward a back door, into an alley.

Cait shot Scott a glance and rolled her eyes. His grin widened, and together they followed Mr. Brennen out into the cold.

"So, you think you could walk us through what you saw?"

The man looked put off.

"You don't believe what I told them on the phone?"

Scott's hands raised in the air to settle him.

"It's not that at all, sir. Not at all. It's just," he looked over to Cait, "It helps my partner a lot to visualize the scene. Often, she's good at catching what others miss."

The man grew more skeptical.

Scott followed it up with, "We just want to keep the streets safe, sir."

The man nodded, showing he would comply.

"I came out with the cardboard. Same as any other day." He pointed to the large green dumpster along the alley wall, the sort it would take a truck to lift. "And as I was walking, I heard these weird noises."

Scott and Cait both listened with intent.

The man kept going, his delivery smoother, as if he were growing more comfortable sharing.

"I looked up, cardboard in hand, to a fist coming down against 'nother guy's skull. Coulda sworn I heard a crack b'fore he hit the ground."

The man shivered at this last thought as if the cold had crept its way down his spine.

"And what happened next?" Scott kept his cadence slow.

Cait did not.

"Did they see you?"

The man retracted a bit.

Scott lifted his hand. A request for patience.

"I sort of backed against the door. Here. Like so." He showed his shop's back door and leaned against it. It was around the corner from where they'd parked the van. "That's when I saw another body on the ground. Two men picked up the one and carried him off."

"To the van?"

"To the van. Then came back for the next. Never saw me, though." His head nodded up and down, more relieved than proud. "Then they just sped off."

The old man's cheeks flushed, and he started fidgeting. As if he feared someone catching wind of what he was sharing. Either that or his wish hadn't come true. That once he had passed on his story, its weight would leave him. He didn't know that it would never leave; but cling to him, adding to his existing weight and struggle.

"A van?" Cait shot in again, catching the already agitated man off guard.

"Yeah. That's what I said."

"And you saw this van? Clearly? And the men didn't see you?"

Cait couldn't help but leap on this potential step forward.

The man took two steps back, withdrawing.

"Woah, woah? First off—as I said—*yeah*. I saw it. And no, they didn't see me. Like I said, I just froze when I saw them." The man trembled at these words. "Look, I-I don't want any trouble here."

Cait opened her mouth to speak again, but Scott held up a slow and gentle hand to stave her off. She held back.

"No, no, sir. It's okay, really. You've been a real help." Scott paused, waiting until comfort returned to the man again. "So, these men? Did it look like a disagreement? Were they arguing about something?"

The man's brow furrowed as he grew somewhat confused, considering the questions.

"No. There wasn't any argument. None that I saw, anyway. Just looked like three guys kicking the shit outta two others. Easy targets, really. Picking out those in rags, you know? Those down on their luck. Never woulda happened in this city before."

Cait's stomach fluttered.

Scott could tell the pronouncement excited her and worked in tune to allow for continued progress.

"Would you say they were homeless? The victims?"

"If I had to guess, yeah. These days, people seem to take their kicks out on 'em."

"And the others?"

"Others?"

"The ones who took them? In the van? What did they look like?"

Cait didn't know when it occurred, but she saw the man's effect had changed. Something had come over him. A fear. His guard lowered as she watched him pour his thoughts out to her partner. It was a mystifying thing to watch Scott work sometimes.

"Oh, I dunno." Mr. Brennen looked down, fidgeting. "Middle of the row, I guess. Dark jackets. Just guys dressed for winter." He just kept talking after that. "Well off enough. For the life of me, I couldn't figure why they were doing it. You know, what they were doing. It all felt so wrong. Just *off*, you know? In my neighborhood... My wife and I've been here going on thirty years. Seen this city change. I called it in right away, not wanting trouble either way."

Scott nodded along, slow and empathetic.

"And you saw the van?"

The man nodded that he had.

"Could you describe it to us?"

Scott and Cait both held their notepads out.

"Sure thing." He grinned, proud this time. "But I could do you one better."

Scott and Cait stole glances at each other. Scott let his note pad fall to his side.

"How so?"

"*I* got their license number."

The old man's eyes gleamed; he knew he'd just given them far more than they had hoped for.

Scott stood, mouth agape, while Cait's excitement almost caused her to lift off the ground.

———

Cait squealed as she fell in the car and shut the door.

"This is it!"

Scott turned the ignition over. The car roared to life.

"Now hang on a second..." Though unable to hide his own smile, Scott lifted both hands to steady them. "It *looks* solid, but we still need to check everything out and make sure."

Cait knew he was right, but she was growing so impatient. She needed the case to break. And she knew this would. This would lead to something *big*.

"So..." Scott poised, almost playfully. "... what's next, boss?"

She had turned and started speaking even before Scott had finished.

"We call in the license number right away—flag it! Get people looking for that description; you and I keep canvasing the shelters. Right?" Her excitement bloomed. "Like the old man said. *They* were *homeless*. It fits, Scott! It all fits!" The pieces falling into place, Cait thought their big break was imminent. She *knew* it. "And then we... we—"

Cait could already hear the words in Scott's mind. She dreaded them, but knew they were coming and that he was right.

"*Then* we wait."

Scott's words brought her back to the ground. She looked up. She could see his appreciation for her, beaming. But she also knew that look. He was about to say something important. Impart some wisdom that was passed down to him.

"Remember, Cait. It's the patient detective that breaks the—"

"... the case."

Cait feigned annoyance, but she appreciated it. She knew she needed the reminder. "I know."

The pill was easier to swallow, knowing that they had a clearer direction now.

Scott smiled his usual smile, knowing full well how hard she was working to contain herself.

"But I think you're right, Cait."

She looked back at him, letting her own intrigued smile crack again.

"Everything's pointing that way. But we need to be patient now. Why don't you call it in?"

Cait's phone was already out of her pocket when Scott put the car in drive and pulled away from the curb.

———

Though the panic that gripped him had passed, the fear drove Charlie back to marching, and he'd been at it all afternoon. His nerves tensed, heightened. He wove through almost the entire West Side. Then he crossed the river once again and found himself near Mt. Tabor's base in the early evening.

Night fell. Turning around, Charlie looked down Division Street. He could see to the river, where both halves of the city met. Just before downtown. The tracing lights of cars working their way through traffic with plumes of heat and exhaust sifting upward from so many straining motors.

Cars fired past Charlie as he shuffled along. It was momentum at this point that carried him along, and no real volition of his own. If he were to stop, he would collapse; just cease to be, which sounded restful. He longed for something deeper than sleep. Something he felt had become forever out of his reach. So, instead, he dreamed of lapping currents carrying him on where he could get away with using no strength of his own.

He passed through Laurelhurst, then Belmont on his way.

Keep going, was his only thought. *Just one more step.*

He felt done. Fried. On the edge of a faint hope, to get back and crash. Sleep.

Keep going, he heard himself say again, and he kept going.

One step in front of the next; cutting through a city that no longer seemed familiar; daring not to even consider his hope of rest out of fear it would shatter and vanish in the cold.

All he could do was keep moving.

Six

A bitter and frigid wind slammed against the windows of the precinct. As if it too yearned for the inside warmth. For shelter from the haunting night. Something had somehow scared the normal winter rains away this season, leaving only the biting cold to creep and take every inch of ground it could.

The last two hours were hard. At least for Cait. It had been four in total since they'd got back from their interview with Mr. Brennen. They'd gotten the license number out. Officers all over town were looking. Canvasing every organization related to the homeless community they could think of. They'd found nothing. Not one lead had turned up.

Cait sat there on the edge of despondency. She'd been so sure they'd broken the case, and it would all fall, tumbling, into place.

But it hadn't.

Whatever hope had wound its way into their day faded; the cold of night triumphed, returning to reign once more.

Scott walked up and stood once again in the doorway of Cait's office. Once again, she was not aware of his presence.

He didn't have it in him to scare her again, though. Her disappointment hung too heavy in the room.

"Hey." He called out to her, his voice soft and gentle.

Cait looked up. Her expression was like a child's who'd woken early on Christmas morning only to find no gifts beneath the tree.

Like a parent, he wanted to console her.

"I'd say it's time to call it, okay?"

Cait sensed the experience in his words. Their truth. She knew he was right and nodded.

"But this was a big day, Cait. Mark that. A big day. Remember, we need to be patient."

He wanted to offer some something. Anything. Some sort of life raft for her to cling to in her disappointment.

He remembered how that ached. Scott couldn't even find it in him to crack a joke.

"Come by the house. It's past dinner already, but let Stacey throw something together for you? Build Legos with the kids? They miss you, you know?"

"But—"

Scott put his hand up. It wasn't forceful.

"I know there's tomorrow..." He hesitated. "But I think we could both use the distraction. What do'ya say?" He could see Cait's mind coming up with excuses. "You don't have to be alone."

A warmth kindled in Cait's heart. She was thankful for Scott and his family. They were something she'd never quite understood. She wasn't sure she could make him understand. That social interaction required more from her than loneliness. The mask she'd feel she had to wear... She couldn't let any of this weight, the hefty burden of this insane case, step foot inside that home. She didn't want that for Stacey. Or to Tommy or Hannah. She couldn't fathom how Scott managed it. Another miraculous phenomenon.

"Thanks, Scott, but let's stick to tomorrow, okay? I'm tired."

Through lips pursed with understanding, Scott gave a resigned nod that also spoke that he wouldn't push it any further.

"Okay. I'm heading out then. See you here in the morning."

"See you, Scott. Goodnight. Say hi to Stace and the kids for me. Tell them I can't wait to see them tomorrow."

Scott's usual smile reformed at this, but what was more shocking was how much Cait felt she meant it.

"Don't stay too late, okay?"

"I won't. I'm feeling worn out. I'm gonna go for a long walk in the cold, then hit it."

"Sounds nice." Scott went to turn around but stopped himself. "Hey." He smiled at her, sincere. "Good work today. We're getting there, okay? I know something will turn up tomorrow."

Cait's expression reshaped itself into a smile, and her shoulders relaxed a bit. She said something she knew she needed to hear.

"We just need to be patient."

"That's right. It'll come to us."

"Good night, Scott."

"Good night."

He turned to walk away, ready for the warmth waiting for him at home.

Scott took the elevator downstairs to the garage. Most days he took the stairs, but he felt more tired than usual. Exhaustion crept its way up through him with every step, weighing on him. The day had worn him down. It descended, and his mind mulled over the day's occurrences. Mostly, he thought of Cait. How proud he was of what she was becoming. Of *who* she was becoming. He saw the long road before her; but also that she'd find her way to its end.

He recognized the realities she'd face. The hard way, not unlike himself, had given her tenacity.

Someday, he hoped she'd learn to let people in. She'd need allies in a profession like this. And he wouldn't always be around.

Making it to the bottom floor, he stepped out of the elevator and took what tired strides he could to his car, unlocked it, got in, put on his seatbelt, and started the engine. He pulled through the parking lot and, as he came to the main road, he shifted his thoughts to home. He thought of the smiles waiting for him, the bedtime stories, and the glass of wine he'd share with his wife. These thoughts filled Scott with the peace and hope he hoped Cait would find one day. She was an outstanding police officer. But when she was fighting for something? Something specific and intrinsic? She was another force altogether. A wonder, unmatched.

Scott shook these thoughts from his mind and pulled out into Portland's nighttime traffic. Despite how late it was, cars lined up. Scott would have to fight his way home.

———

Cait's eyes burned; she desired progress but couldn't stare at a screen any longer. Nor did she stay long after Scott left.

After taking the stairs, she left through the front doors of the precinct. The night met her with a biting wind. Cait tucked her shoulders up to brace herself against its continuous barrage and walked with a fierce intention through the dark.

A few blocks away, she went to check her phone, and realized it was almost dead.

Shit, she thought, remembered she'd left her charger plugged into the power strip under her desk.

For several brief moments, Cait fought to convince herself to turn around and go back. She'd need her phone charged. Right? What if something happened? What if something came in? Something she could jump on?

Then she heard Scott's voice.

Patience, Rook. Let the case come to you.

She could hear his past lectures coming back to her; how important it was to build a life beyond work.

The cold cut in, harsh, and Cait decided it wasn't worth going back. She'd get it tomorrow. She was sure she had another phone charger at home, anyway.

Proud of her decision to leave the job behind, Cait turned and continued her intended steps towards her apartment—the stars far above her, covered by thick clouds, illuminated by the sickly city lights.

———

He'd been in traffic for ten minutes without moving when he turned on the radio. He switched it to an oldies station and kept the volume low. Singing along, he let his thoughts drift from each sound in the night's current—the honks, cars speeding up and braking. The usual chorus carried forward with the same old pageantry.

No matter where his mind wandered, it always came back to Cait. He knew that in the end, she'd be okay. He just wished she could be now.

Scott flipped on his blinker and nudged his way to the right. He wasn't far from the intersection and the car ahead of him pulled forward to let him squeeze by. He smiled. Another defiant example proving there was goodness in the world. At least to Scott. He believed in the goodness of people, despite his years as a cop. He saw people's circumstances as what undermined both hope and goodness.

Having just pulled onto Burnside now and headed west, Scott's lane came to an abrupt halt. About to release an uncharacteristic exhale of frustration, something caught his eye.

He shot glances up in every direction he could to see if his brain would register it again. It had come and gone. He couldn't even remember what it was. It felt important, though.

On the verge of letting it go, the traffic a lane over shifted.

Scott's stomach tightened.

Holy hell, he thought as he blinked, double checking he was correctly taking in what he saw.

Still not moving, Scott reached over, grabbing his notebook. Shuffling through the pages, he stopped on the latest page of notes.

Large grey van.

Paint peeling.

Large dents down the right side.

A big dent on the back bumper.

L#: BVN 283.

Scott looked up again. His heartbeat quickened.

Several cars up ahead, a large, grey work van idled. Dents lined its back-right side and bumper.

A string of alarm to rattle through Scott. He reminded himself it might not be the right one; he couldn't help but grip the wheel with both hands, eager to see.

The lane to his left picked up and inched forward again.

No! he thought—his lane still hadn't moved.

The light turned green and each brake light in front of him flickered.

Scott leaned forward in anticipation; the concept of patience lost on him.

The left lane crept forward faster, as the lane he was in had cars peeling off onto side streets.

Frustration mounted while he waited.

But the car in front of him moved at last.

Yes!

He stepped on the gas, making sure no one would cut him off.

He gained on the van, which was still visible over all the smaller cars. Street and head lights glittered and lit up the scene. Scott couldn't remember the last time he'd been this excited.

He wished Cait was there and wanted to call her; but he would make sure it was *their* van before he did.

He gained one car length after another until, at last, he was close.

Still unable to see the whole license plate, he'd made out its last two digits. And a large dent in the bumper.

The numbers were *8* and *3*.

"Holy shit!" The words spilled out. "Holy, holy shit!"

The light turned red, forcing Scott to a stop again.

Behind the van, but a lane over.

He inched forward; as close as possible to the car in front of him, but still the van's license plate hung out of sight.

Dammit!

Reaching for his notebook, he checked again. The last two digits had been *83*.

The brake lights flickered again as the streetlight once more turned green and everyone inched forward. Scott maintained a close distance to the car in front of him, and he caught a break. It was his lane that was pushing ahead faster.

Closing in, he set its sights on the back of the van; he needed to keep a clear view.

It inched and inched forward.

A space between two cars emerged, and there it was.

It came as a shock and took several moments to register.

He shook his head back to focus before reading the

numbers out, checking them with what'd he'd written in his notes.

"*B... V... N... 2... 8... 3.*"

Scott pulled his foot off the gas.

"Holy shit..." He paused, letting the revelation hang there in the cold air. "... it's them."

Without hesitation, he picked up his phone and called Cait. The phone didn't even ring.

The traffic continued its monotonous push forward up Burnside.

"Shit, shit, shit! Come on, Cait!"

He dialed her again.

———

A key turned over in its accompanying lock and the door slid open, revealing the silhouette of a woman putting her keys away before entering her apartment.

Shutting the door and flipping on the lights, Cait walked into her small living room, set down her purse and bag, and took a deep breath.

A strange sense came over her; it felt like her phone was vibrating.

Pulling it from her pocket, she found it was dead.

"Shit, gotta find my other charger."

She set the phone down on the coffee table, walked into her kitchen, and opened the fridge.

———

"Cait, where are you?"

Scott found the words coming out more frantically than he was used to.

They'd gone over the 405 overpass, passing by PGE Park,

and were making their way toward the edge of the West Side, when the van's blinker switched on and it pulled into the left turning lane.

Scott switched on his left blinker as well and eased into the next lane, making ready to follow. The further they moved from the center of the city, the more space that opened between cars. He was now worried about being seen.

"Breathe, Scott. Just breathe."

He felt a little like a rookie himself, coaching himself through it.

The van was heading up toward Washington Park—either that or to the ritzy neighborhoods of the West Hills, which were less likely.

Scott wondered if they were making another drop. He scrolled through his phone to call the desk sergeant at the precinct. When the number was on the screen before him, he decided against it. He didn't want to spook these guys. Might see what they're doing. Keep his distance, scope it out a bit, then call it in. Officers would wait at the park's entrance, blocking their exit.

The light turned green, and the van pulled itself across the intersection and began its ascent up the hill.

Taking his time off the line, Scott followed suit. He drove slowly to avoid suspicion. By the time he had pulled onto the hill, the van was making its turn at the next block.

Revving the engine more than he liked, Scott pulled himself to the same turn. As he made his way around it, he glimpsed the van disappearing behind a large hedge.

The park, he thought.

His insides twisted. Everything in him wanted nothing more than to call Cait. But her phone was off; he couldn't believe it.

Long as he'd known her, she'd always been there and picked up right when he needed her.

He had no choice but to pursue. He had to.

Scott kept his distance and followed the van into the park, winding around the reservoir. Taking each turn with slow ease, he kept as much distance as he could without losing them.

As the road straightened out, he saw their lights in the parking area up ahead. He switched his own lights off to ensure they wouldn't see someone coming and get spooked—since the park was closed and it was the middle of winter, no one else should be there.

As their headlights stretched further forward, echoing off the various treetops, Scott inched forward himself. He pulled up the last hill and into the lot, then stopped. The light from the van had stilled. The tires churned over the icy pavement, which crackled and gave beneath the weight.

His breathing quickening, Scott steered his car into the nearest parking spot and turned off the ignition.

The fog hung low, gathering itself just off the ground, collecting above the vast fields of grass—what winter had left of them.

Scott took several deep breaths, and with care, made sure he'd switched the cabin-light off before opening his door. The brittle crispness of the blinding cold invaded his car. With his other hand, he pulled out his pistol. Stepping outside the car, gravel crunching underneath his footsteps, he checked to make sure the safety was off.

Shutting the door with ease, he crept through the grass. Making as little noise as he could along the way.

The chill wrapped itself around him, increasing how unsettled he felt. Tugging on the fear surrounding what he was about to discover.

A voice whisper to him again; not to do this alone.

But what choice did he have? It could turn out to be nothing.

Scott felt like he could hear every blade of grass crunch and collapse beneath his footsteps. He was sure they knew he was coming. Still, he pursued where the light was stemming from.

The turf ended at a parking area. The road narrowed, wrapping itself around the other side of the hill. Tucked into the bend and right beneath the keeping wall, Scott was standing on a children's play area. It was zoo themed. The Portland Zoo sat just on the opposite side of the next hill. A picnic area stood at its edge, enveloped by a towering stone wall. There were Giraffes, elephants, lions and several monkeys etched into the wall, illuminated by the headlights.

Scott had brought his children here to play hundreds of times.

He dropped to his chest so as not to be seen. The season's cold reached up from the soil and gripped him.

All he needed was a glimpse of what they were doing; then sneak away and call it in.

Peering through the railing, Scott could see the van just sitting there. Steam wafted from its front. A bleak rumbling sign of life in the cold. They backed it up onto the bark chips; its brake lights casting an unsettling crimson glow upon the child-like scene.

A door slammed shut, making Scott jump. He hunkered back down.

"Over here?"

A whispered voice came, carrying itself over the scene in fog and moonlight. It was a man's voice, frail and unsure of itself.

A second voice broke in, more confident than the former.

"Good a place as any other."

Scott held his breath and, laying out as quietly as possible, listened, praying not to make any sort of noise or draw attention to himself.

"*He* said don't make a pattern. And we haven't done this yet. It'll throw 'em."

The nervous one shook his head but kept silent. A statue, frozen in the chilly night.

The second man's voice came again.

"Here. Get the door."

The first man opened the van's back doors.

"Climb in there." It was the stern voice again. "I'll get the feet."

After a brief hesitation, the other complied. A strong invisible force was trying to keep him from entering the van. Yet, against his will, he entered anyway.

A thought occurred to Scott, one that he pushed aside right away. Given the situation, he thought he could sneak down there and surprise them. If he played it right, he could do this alone. *Get* them. Be one step closer to putting an end to this madness.

Besides, there were only two of them; and he'd have a jump on them.

His years of experience blared. The more rational side of his brain told him this was stupid.

He would give anything for Cait to have been there. They could do it together.

No, he decided. He would wait until he saw the bodies. Wait until he was one hundred percent sure what he was up against. Then call it in. They could have officers at the park's exit in less than a minute, he knew.

He watched with intrepid closeness for the evidence he'd need so he could sneak away and call it in.

A boot scuffle echoed; someone stepped back out of the van. A pair of legs extended from his hands into the van; illuminated by the crimson glow of the brake lights.

Scott's stomach flinched; he couldn't help but hold his breath.

Next to emerge were the hips and backside, hanging lower because of their weight. Then the toro, followed by the presumed corpse's limp arms. The hands dragged, lifeless against the concrete. If it hadn't been for the previous bodies found, and the reports he'd read, the bruising would've appeared as nothing more than an unsettling trick of the brake lights.

The second man emerged. The look on his face was one of abject disgust. Near sickness. His gloved hands gripped beneath the dead man's shoulders.

Scott's insides stirred within him. His worries wrestled with each other. He'd seen the body.

He could leave then and call it in. But something in him wouldn't allow itself to be pulled away. He felt trapped.

Stuck.

Come on, Scott. He pushed himself. *Get moving.*

But his body didn't listen.

Once both men stood flat on the ground, they shimmied their way to a covered spot. The designated picnic spot just passed the playground. The body, all the while, hung between them, hands dragging against the rough and icy surface.

A crippling fear crept through Scott.

He wondered who these men were? What they were after? And *why?* Why would they do such a thing?

None of it made sense.

The thump of the body hitting the icy cement woke Scott up, bringing him back to the moment. Startled, he shot up and, backing away, his shoes scraped against the frozen bark chips beneath him. Several chunks near the edge of the keeping wall broke off, falling to the playground level below.

Scott froze as a startled voice shot through the air.

"Shhh! You hear that?"

"Huh?"

"Shut up! I heard something."

Scott dropped to the ground again, his chest flat against the frozen grass.

Both men's heads spun, searching. Looking for anything suspicious at all. Their attention landing on a spot right next to where Scott hid.

His insides squirmed with panic.

Get up, Scott. Get out of here.

One of them spoke.

"Get up there and check it out."

Scott froze.

The other man looked up.

"Huh? Wait, wh–"

"Go!"

The first man burst out; in a hushed but volatile whisper.

The second man threw his hands in the air and began walking.

Scott panicked, his mind trying to catch up. When it registered that someone was coming—he heard the huffing footsteps of the man walking up the sidewalk—he scrambled backward, making as little noise as possible. Once his head cleared, he remembered a back path to the play area.

Matching the approaching man's steps, Scott crept away, making his way down the backside of another path.

The man made it to the landing; but Scott was no longer there. It was empty. He'd found a new hiding spot; just beneath an arbor lined with constricting, leafless vines. To his shock and surprise, he was just opposite the wall where the body lay.

"Nah, there's no one up here, Jo–"

"Don't say my fuck'n name out loud, man! Right? Jus' get down here! Help with the next one!"

In shame, the man gave no response. He made his way back down the sidewalk, his feet scraping the pavement as he went.

Breathe, Scott, he told himself. *Just breathe.*

No longer able to see, Scott listened as someone hopped up into the van. He heard the scraping noise of the body sliding across the cold metal floor of the van. The scratchy exhales and heaves both men made carrying the second body echoed off the wall and beyond, disappearing into the darkness.

Scott knew they were close, and worry told him his opportunity might slip away. He wasn't sure another body was in the van. He looked down the path. To the moonlight stretching its feeble arms down from a heavy sky. He thought about sneaking away. Descending the hill and calling it in. That's what he should do.

Then came the second thump.

Scott's panic surged. He heard the raspy voice again.

"Let's get the last one."

Shit!

His gut told him there wasn't time to sneak away. It would be too late, and they would miss their chance.

Dammit!

Scott breathed in and out, working to calm himself.

The same scratching echo of footsteps on metal crept through the air. Obstructed only by the wall at Scott's back. Faint scuffles of boot on the icy path told him they'd reached the concrete again.

They were getting closer.

Scott was almost out of time.

Dammit, he thought again, reaching for the pistol at his side.

A second man's voice burst in.

"Hey, you're letting up."

"Sor—"

"Just keep going."

Scott released his pistol's safety and, holding it out before him, took a deep breath.

The voices echoed out again.

"Here, put it down over here."

"But, what about—"

Scott knew it was then or never. There wasn't anything else for it.

"Just shut up and—"

"Freeze!"

Scott called out, jumping out from behind, catching both men in complete surprise. "Nobody move!"

Both men stopped cold. One's eyes dripped worry from their edges; he looked scared, like a child caught out of bed at night. The other man's expression grew sharp—angry, even— as if he was calculating his next move.

"Bad luck tonight, boys." Scott side-stepped around the men to stand between them and the van. They stood there, still, holding the body.

The words Scott spoke caught even him off guard. He wasn't one to gloat, but the adrenaline was pumping through him fast. Cait was the rash one, he thought, never taking his eyes off either man. He couldn't wait to tell her, but she'd be sore from missing out. He also knew he'd never hear the end of it—given how much he pressed her on being cautious.

His confidence growing, he looked straight into their eyes. One at a time.

"Here's what's going to hap—" He started speaking, but watched a smirk grow on the man standing before him; then something caught his eye.

Scott turned, but it was too late. Something heavy and hard came slamming down onto his head, causing a blinding pain to fire through him. He collapsed.

A third voice chimed from behind the van, sniggering.

"Always need to check the field. Where'd this guy come from, anyway?"

The other two looked at each other.

"Who knows? You think there's more of 'em?"

"Shit, I dunno. You hear anything else?"

All three of them looked around, their expressions wending between worried and alert.

"What do we do now?"

"We hurry the fuck up, right? And we get outta here."

"We gotta do something about this guy? Right?"

"Yeah, but—Shit, what—"

"Let's just shoot him."

They were growing more frantic by the second.

"Up here, really? In the Hills? No way, man. Get cops crawling around everywhere."

"There're already cops here." The speaker pointed down at Scott's unconscious body.

The raspy, more confident voice broke in.

"Well, we can't leave him here either, can we? Not next to the bodies."

The other two nodded in agreement.

Exasperated that it fell to him, the authoritative one decided.

"Let's jus' put him in the van, okay? And get the fuck outta here."

Pleased the decision didn't rest on them, the others complied. They picked up Scott's limp body and hoisted him into the back of the open van. They let his body fall with a hard thud. Consciousness flickered within him as the thud almost rekindled it.

There was a vagueness to Scott's awareness. He grew confused, unsure where he was or who those voices belonged to. Their chorus cascaded over the throbbing pain he felt cutting through him.

"Hey, Mr. Black–"

The raspy voice cut in; a hand accompanying it, coming down hard across the man's face.

"Don't say his fucking name in public!"

"Jeez, sorry, alright?" The man rubbed the spot the man had struck him. "It's just—I don't think the boss'll like this."

"No shit. But you think he'd want us to leave the body?"

"We shouldn't of—"

"Shouldn't's got nothing to do with it. He came, so we dealt with it. We *can't* leave 'em!"

The other man gave no response.

A quiet stillness settled itself back over the scene beneath the serene moonlight.

"Let's get the hell outta here." The raspy voice chimed again. "It's fucking freezing."

The other two obeyed; they all piled into the van. The unconscious Scott lay behind them, strewn across the near-frozen floor. Only the pale light of the weak winter moon found itself able to shine down through the windows.

With that, the faint noise of the van shifting into drive clicked and faded off into the darkness, and it pulled away, taking Scott with them. As it left, the crimson brake lights traded space with the night, leaving the three bodies they'd dumped encased in shadow.

SEVEN

Charlie's legs didn't want to move. He could've been walking through a swamp. Each time he lifted his foot, it felt as if it had collected a few too many pounds of mud, making it almost impossible to lift his boot-sole from the ground. His body burned for sleep and his mind hovered just outside himself, still tethered but loose. It, and not he, hoped for what rest could come.

By that time, Charlie had been awake for thirty hours. Not a record by any means, but it brought him no comfort.

Worries crept in the closer he drew toward The Mission. Growing heavier, sinking deeper, and proving more potent.

So much that he missed something. Some he never would have missed before.

He had taken a different path home that night. One he'd never taken. He usually returned to the Westside via the Burnside or Hawthorne Bridge—or even before—*always*.

But tonight, perhaps a slip of the weary mind, he succumbed to the call of that strange and subtle inward pull. The one he'd fought so hard against.

With each step he took, it grew stronger within him.

Stronger and stronger, but so subtle he didn't notice. He was so far gone, it all felt so impossible to discern.

Even as the warning bells rang louder within him, Charlie let his steps continue to carry him forward, walking right toward the source of what had been calling him.

His body screamed at its need for rest.

At the bridge's midpoint, he looked up, managing a glance. Somewhere within him, something recognized his surroundings. The alarms blared, but he couldn't fathom why.

So, on he walked, unsuspecting of any danger that might lurk. A lone soldier, lost in a wide, weary war.

Each footstep echoed across the vast and empty expanse that surrounded him. This part of town was always empty late at night. The sounds reached out into the night, marking his progress across the bridge. Coming to its end, Charlie turned and took the stairs that led to the walking path underneath the bridge. If he kept going straight, he would hit Burnside in minutes before turning left towards the Mission and arriving home. But as his aimless steps led him on, something whispered to him from amidst the night. It whipped in on the cool, midnight chill.

He felt it. A call clear and brisk. Discomforting as much as familiar.

Come...

Charlie stopped and looked around, weary and afraid; but saw nothing and so continued forward in the confused dark.

It came again; and he felt it in his chest more than anything auditory.

Come...

He spun around, and still seeing nothing, quickened his footsteps through the lot to carry on. He needed to get back. Away from here.

Why had he gone this way? Why did he change the route? He didn't know.

It came again.

Come...

He jumped, and in his fumbling state, tried discerning the fastest route back to The Mission. To cut across the empty lot before him. A shortcut over to the next street. He'd cross over just past Union Station and its neighboring high rises. That would put him home in minutes.

On he walked, one step before the next. But still the call rang out. The further he went, the louder it grew; they would not ignore it.

It rang out again.

Charlie...

And again.

Charlie...

He'd wince and wrench his eyes shut, but always letting his steps carry him forward.

Keep going, he'd tell himself. *Just keep going.*

No matter what he did, it only seemed to grow stronger. And louder, eating away at what little assurance he'd been holding to.

Unsure what else to do, Charlie buried his head, and focusing on the asphalt before each step, he kept moving forward in the cold. Ignoring everything else he could. He knew not to stop. If he stopped, he might never start again.

Charlie made it to the end of that empty lot and scurried across the street, making it to the high rises just opposite Union Station, where he stumbled. He crossed the sidewalk and cut through its half-full lot, then stopped. Just for a moment. But it had been enough.

Reaching out to steady himself and catch his breath, he felt the call again. The strongest yet.

Charlie...

He froze.

Unable to explain it; Charlie just stopped and found it impossible to continue on.

No... he thought, shaking his head, but the call rang out again.

Charlie...

A strange and horrid familiarity crept it. Something he only felt when—

He worked to push it away, but the feeling interrupted him again.

Charlie...

No...

He felt it, all his defenses wearing down. If he didn't keep moving, he'd collapse.

———

Dr. Grenier strode back into the Lab's observation room.

"The next subject's ready?"

His voice was gruff and forced, but no one seemed to notice.

"Yes, sir."

He looked around, unsure how long he could keep his smile propped up; he'd do the best he could.

"Okay, everybody ready?" Everyone nodded. "Let's do this again."

Once more, he slid the lever into position, jumpstarting the unseen mechanical process. Destined to fail or not, it began.

The other technicians looked on, hopeful, while Dr. Grenier stood there, hollow. Each step forward in this left him emptier than the one before.

Gears turned and pistons fired behind the walls; strange otherworldly engines spurred to life. The fumes flowed, their piercing hiss digging its way forward.

Through the observation glass, the doctor and his men bore witness once again as the wall split open, resulting in yet another helpless man—screaming wild wails—to fall forward and collapse onto the chamber floor. Like all the others, they would watch as he collapsed, beat his feeble hands against the glass. They would watch as he cried and pleaded for help that would never come.

A tangible fear would set in. Measurable. Palpable. Something a person couldn't ignore forever. But out of fear, they forgot.

Each observer, save for Dr. Grenier himself, stood there watching with hungry eyes. *This is the one,* some told themselves. But the doctor didn't believe it. It was impossible, he reminded himself as the procedure took its effect. *Not without Charlie,* he said to himself. *We're doomed without the boy who triggered the breach.* So, instead, he stood there frozen to the spot, taking in the rising flood of muffled screams that spread throughout the room. He was numb to them anymore. Any shred of empathy he'd ever had drained from him. What did it matter anymore? What did any of it matter?

———

Even in that oppressive cold, Charlie's body poured sweat. His head swiveled back and forth, searching for anything he could ground himself to, but he couldn't remember ever noticing these buildings before.

Either way, he couldn't latch onto anything. His vision blurred. He squinted his eyes to see, but they strained. His chest grew heavy, his breathing stifled. Each muscle grew weaker, as if he wasn't strong enough to hold up his own weight.

An old involuntary tick returned as he took turns tapping

his thumb onto the tip of each finger five times before moving onto the next.

A mixture of dread and delirium flooded through him. Looking up his path back to The Mission was clear before him, but he lacked the autonomy to walk it.

He just wanted to sleep. To collapse. Nothing could have felt more impossible. His mind, a drained battery, racing on and on, but without the proper fuel.

Concentrating, he focused all of himself he could on taking one step.

Out of nowhere, the surrounding mysterious force seemed to loosen its grip.

Charlie breathed in, managing a slow step forward. That's when the first spike hit.

It was instantaneous.

It was like being struck by lightning, forced awake by a deep, unnatural stir. His mind and body torn in differing directions.

His feet rooted into the cement, imprisoned by some strange hypnotic current he could feel but could not see.

The longer he stood, the heavier the feeling became. Pressing and pulling down on him from all directions.

As his mind raced, the scenery spun, and the concrete threatened to break open.

In the night's silence, he'd never felt more lost or more alone.

The more he struggled to ignore the creeping feeling that griped him, the tighter its hold grew.

It built and built, his body flexing in defense as *it* infiltrated—crawling up his skin and clothes.

His head shook, back and forth; his mind reeled: *No-no-no-no!*

But the feeling kept moving upward.

To his knees, then his waist, then his chest, then his shoulders, until it reached his head. He held his breath and clenched his eyes shut as it passed over him, and Charlie felt consumed.

His breaths pulsed, nearing hyperventilation, his mind cast in shadow; yet something held him together—something distant; a strange, familiar terror he'd felt before.

No...!

His boots became like liquid and seeped down into the ground. Like tainted roots, they gripped the soil beneath the cement and continued digging further down; and something reached its way back up through his body; speaking his name again.

Charlie...

His head shook back and forth as he trembled.

Through each muscle, vessel, and bone, the presence came, until it had complete hold.

Charlie went rigid; half lost to himself; his more conscious thoughts pushed further back into his mind; a spectator in his own life; a passenger in his own car.

Terror took control; made scarier by its unknown origin.

But deep down, he knew. He'd known all along. But he tried to shove it all away, especially as his thoughts turned towards his dreams, and they spilled from his sleep into the waking day.

———

The screams tore themselves across whatever open space they could find, but still nothing could leave Dr. Grenier more unsettled than he already felt.

"Vitals?"

"Holding, sir. Steady."

In contrast to the man's muted enthusiasm, Dr. Grenier reminded himself that the last subject had made it well beyond this point.

He said nothing in response, but sensed something emerge within him. A seed of hope. That his work might come to fruition. And they might overcome the impossible. Their sacrifice, his many sacrifices, will have meaning.

He'd been desperate to be involved in whatever scheme would bring the Nameless forth and correct the infinite number of errors humanity had made. This would wipe the slate clean. The world would begin again. He'd be a father of that movement.

He wanted for his doubts to overwhelm him again; it was too much to hope, too painful, but he couldn't help it.

"Steady?"

"Yes, sir, steady!" Everyone's excitement stirred. "And we're about to make it to the *changing*. Any minute, sir."

The doctor's heart skipped and betrayed the forced facade he'd worked so hard to build. His eyes widened at the possibility his wild desires might find life at last.

It can't work, he reminded himself again. *It's... it's not possible... Right?*

The subject let out another unearthly scream, anything but human.

Charlie's synapses fired and crashed like dominos in the solar system of his thoughts; he held on for life; but each moment led him further and further into this strange sea of unconsciousness.

Image after image took shape; always interspersed with thunder-cracks of lightning, tearing the sky in two.

The images were nothing new.

The self-same occupants of the visions which haunted *all* his sleepless nights.

But this time, he was awake.

Images of his mother appeared before him, followed by a vast and varied array of other childhood memories, falling to the floor like shattered glass. He saw his father's grimacing face and heard short bursts of shouts and screams; he saw himself driving in his car; his grimy, dark rental room in the basement, he saw Trent's beaten, yellow truck and his heart sank; and Ellie; always Ellie's face, longing for what she'd never have; a highway road leading to the coast; the town of Astoria sitting on the water's edge; he saw the Riverwalk, the coffee stands and various little shops; he was eating fish and chips; he lay there, strung out on his bed, kicking, screaming, wailing out.

Lightning struck again within Charlie's mind; his feet planted firm, fastened to the cold, harsh concrete.

That same crooked house emerged in his mind once more; it sent shivers down his entire self—not within his dream but from without. He saw Trent and himself sprint into the house; he saw the front door close like a hungry mouth, swallowing them whole; he saw the men, the fireplace, the stone hall; he saw himself entrapped.

Charlie's whole body shook by this point, for he knew he should fear what he assumed would come.

Rain fell from the sky within his visions and thunder burst and rolled across his mind; Charlie could no longer move his mind or body; shrieking screams tore their way through him as he shook and convulsed; it was like a wave was reaching upward, looming, readying itself to crash down hard.

Charlie, though his feet stood, planted firm on the ground, felt himself rushing upward through the air; he held on tight and clenched his eyes shut, giving into the fear. Something was trying to burst through, trying to emerge. He fought to hold it in.

Still, the pull he'd felt centered itself underneath him, like it would erupt through the asphalt and wash him away. The force of it rushed up, firing through him like a conduit.

In his mind, he kept shooting up into the turgid skies of his dreams, screaming all the way, eyes shut and fear filled.

He just wanted it all to end; any way it could.

Charlie was still firing up into the air, flying further into the suffocating shadow. When the feelings flowing through him shifted, his visions grew even more bizarre. Visions of worlds he'd never seen before and sunless skies of a bleak eternity.

Just before it all went black, one more image burned into his mind; himself screaming; shadowed by the glimmer of a weak, crimson glow.

———

"Sir! It's wor—it's working, sir!"

The procedure hit its most crucial point. Fumes filled the small chamber, blocking any visibility of the subject inside.

The screaming occupied a space of its own; and it started getting to some technicians. They squirmed in discomfort and looked away.

The man nearest him reported.

"Sir! He—*it's*... its vitals are still steady. Still rising, but steady."

Dr. Grenier couldn't believe it. He was a man of science. A man of facts and numbers. And this just didn't check out.

"He's made it further than—"

"Any subject so far... *Sir*. And going strong."

"*Miraculous...*"

The doctor looked around to see if anyone had noticed his reaction. This was not a term he used often used. Not very scientific. It brought him discomfort.

Behind the cloud of gas, echoes of crunching bones emanated from behind the fumes—of flesh and muscles tearing, breaking down and reconfiguring themselves into some new terror.

Every few moments, they caught glimpses of the change.

"... It's magnificent..." Dr. Grenier couldn't help letting escape. "... beautiful..."

Everyone stood watching, holding their breath, holding to every scream and burst that came forth from this *Nameless* thing.

Still, the doctor wouldn't let himself believe it would work. His mind prompted him to expect that the procedure would fail at any moment. When the subject in question would reel itself back, flailing for whatever choking breath it could without ever finding its foothold in this world; he *knew* how this would end. It was only a matter of time. Of moments. He held his breath too, but for the failure he expected.

A voice near him spoke in almost complete chagrin.

"*Still* steady, sir..."

Dr. Grenier's shoulders rose as he took a deep breath, wondering whether to give in to hope.

———

Charlie's thoughts were cycling through strange visions of this other world, the scene of him hanging in the air, those swirling storm-tossed winds—a scene he felt he couldn't have known.

In this scene, the same strange presence lurked; any residual feelings of possible peace faded away.

He couldn't make out much, but *something* was coming towards him; he shook and cowered at its approach; it drew closer and closer, and as it did, Charlie's body gave way to greater and more violent shakes.

At last, the presence stopped expanding outward and Charlie heard a faint whisper in his mind.

Charlie... the voice called.

No, he thought, and shook his head.

Charlie.... it called once more.

His body clenched and shook.

The voice called to him again. Steady, sharp and fierce.

Charlie West!

It spoke to him, as if coaxing him to open up his eyes and see it plain.

He wouldn't dare.

Charlie West!

No! Stop... he heard himself say. *No—*

It wasn't up to him anymore.

His eyes wrenched open; hovering before him was *something* Charlie would've sworn he'd never seen before; some terrible, nameless horror his mind could neither understand, let alone something it wished to quantify.

He screamed; a shattering echo that burst across the sky.

And then he fell, or so he saw himself, careening downward back to the river shores below.

The visions swirled and took hold; he'd never felt such fear in all his life.

Screaming, his feet tore from where they'd felt rooted, and he took off through the parking lot. His mind was so poised and made alert, it burst through his exhaustion. Only one thought came to him: escape. Get away from *that* moment. To get away from *any* painful moment. *Forever.*

———

Well beneath the city's surface, in dangerous proximity to where Charlie stood, the new-formed creature let loose a lonely roar. The cry shook the hearts of every man who stood there shaking, struggling to look upon its fierce and inhuman form.

"It–It's worked, sir. It's–"

"*Alive...?* It made it?" The doctor's voice was one of both awe and triumph. "But... but *how*?" He hadn't meant to say it out loud. To show his lack of belief. "It... it makes little sense."

The surrounding men all shook their heads in agreement, not knowing what to think.

"And it's...?"

Dr. Grenier let his question linger.

"Stable, sir. Stable and..."

"And?"

"Well—ready, sir. It looks like we'll be moving forward with the plan. Shouldn't someone alert–"

The doctor cut him off as the bigger picture settled in once more.

"I'll call him immediately."

Staring back into the whirls of sifting gas, he decided

"Get that *thing* contained and prep everything for another test. We need to replicate this before we do anything else."

Everyone there looked up, alarmed—as if pulled from their reverie.

"Of course, sir," he said, in obedience. "Right away."

Everyone dispersed to go about their own tasks, but Dr. Grenier lingered there, staring through the sifting fumes. There he stood on the verge of triumph, yet plagued by insecurity. A lack of assurance brought on what he named cowardice. He couldn't understand it.

One thing was clear though: prolong the call to Mr. Blackwell while he could.

He watched the men scurry about the rooms, powering everything down before resetting it for the next procedure. Proud was how he felt. Proud of all the work they'd done. Proud of all they'd achieved.

He didn't want that to be taken from them.

———

Next thing Charlie knew, whatever had been holding him let go.

He collapsed onto the concrete, gasping for breath. All strength had flooded out of him. He didn't know what to do.

He knew he couldn't stay there, so he pulled himself up and ran.

As fast as his feet could allow, Charlie tore through the parking lot. Tripping several times as he struggled to make it to the street.

He couldn't keep up with his own momentum.

The bottoms of his boots scraped across the lighter, paved concrete that marked the entrance to the parking lot. He was so preoccupied he didn't notice a van making a sharp turn into the lot.

Neither had it seen Charlie.

It wasn't until he'd struck the concrete and shot up that he realized what had happened.

The van's brakes screeched, and before it even stopped, the passenger door swung open. A man jumped out.

"Holy shit, kid! Are you okay?"

Charlie's vision of the moment traced itself into a staggered view. Trying to stand up, he fell back down.

"Woah, woah, kid! Stay down. You're alright."

Charlie couldn't focus. Looking up, everything blurred. He remembered a trick he'd learned years ago: think small. Focus on one thing, and let that bring you back. Just before him was a set of numbers and letters; he struggled to make out every number and letter as he read.

B... he started. *B... N... V?*

He tried making sense of it as the man talked over him, worried. It made it hard.

"Seriously, kid, are you alright?"

He walked over to where Charlie lay with his hands out.

Like a wounded animal, Charlie scrambled away. He ripped his glance away from the numbers, which were then imbedded in his mind.

"Hey! Woah, kid. It's okay."

Still, Charlie wouldn't look up. His heart rate raised again, elevated the tension. Like every second, the voltage within him was being turned up, straining his awareness.

"I-I-I'm... alright," he said. His voice weak, he turned away to place his focus on something else. Nothing came.

The man resigned himself to stand up straight, unsure what to do. A second head popped out from the van's door.

"Hey, what the hell's going on?"

Afraid, the first man swiveled around.

"I don't know, okay. It's *this* kid. He doesn't seem well, but he–"

"But he *what*?"

The man swiveled back to assess Charlie before turning to respond.

"He doesn't look good."

All the while, Charlie sat there, focusing on the letters and numbers before him. His vision cleared.

V... 2... 8... 28...

The men kept talking, their conversation a distraction to Charlie.

"What should we do?"

"The hell should I know?"

...28... 3? Yeah, he thought, *3.*

That's it! Charlie thought. *It's a license number,* he realized. *BVN-283.*

Charlie's vision settled, and he looked up, taking in the surrounding scene.

The second man climbed out of the still running van.

He stood up.

"Kid? Shit," said the first man again. "You took quite a spill there. Is there anything we—"

"I'm fine."

The man fell silent.

Charlie was staring down at a spot on the concrete near his feet. He looked up for a moment, drawn by the van's exhaust wafting upward, the heat rising and dissipating into the frigid atmosphere. The van looked like it had seen some miles. Large dents littered its backside and bumper.

Sensing Charlie's discomfort, the first man tried acting concerned.

"Kid, I really feel you should get looked at."

The other man shot him a worried look, near panic, causing his partner to regret his comment.

But Charlie lied, remedying the man's mistake.

"I-I'm fine."

The flow of whatever was coursing through him took over. It was less harsh than before, but he still felt its grip. He wanted to leave. Right then.

"Well, let's just—"

Charlie cried out, cutting the man off.

"No!"

The man stopped and held his hands up, showing he meant no harm. His partner's looks grew more and more worried.

Charlie squinted his eyes and struggled to think. The world was spinning again.

"Just... please... I need to..."

But the thoughts wouldn't come.

BVN-283, he thought over and over. The mindless repetition kept him distracted.

At last, the second man spoke up.

"Hey, let's get the fuck outta here."

"We hit this kid with the van! What do you—"

"Hey, Blackwe–"

"Don't fucking use his name, dammit! We're in public!"

This was all lost on Charlie, who stood there preoccupied by his own instability.

A third voice chimed in from inside the van.

"What's taking so long?"

Charlie looked up, startled at this sudden and unexpected burst.

"Come on!" the third voice said again. "We gotta get this —we gotta get inside now!"

Charlie could not read the rising levels of anxiety in the men surrounding him; too taken by the rising levels of his own.

"Kid. Do you need anything from us?"

Charlie froze, unsure of what to say.

"I-I—uh... I don't... *No.*"

The words just wouldn't come. All Charlie knew was that he needed to leave. To get out of there and escape.

"Good." The second man looked from Charlie to his partner. "Let's get the hell outta here."

But his partner didn't move. He stood there, staring at Charlie, fidgeting in the cold.

The second man hit him on the shoulder.

"Huh?"

"Come on! Let's go!"

Startled, the man turned to follow his given orders. Scurrying over, he climbed up into the van. Before closing the door, he faced Charlie once more. Something about how Charlie stood caused him discomfort. He spoke loud enough for Charlie to hear him.

"Sorry, kid."

That's all he said; Charlie didn't even look up. He kept silent and watched them from his periphery, desperate to be alone.

As the van pulled away, Charlie saw his chance. He turned and ran as fast as he could toward the road, his mind concerned with only one thing: *getting away*. From those men; the gravity of that gripping feeling. All its confusing familiarity.

Images continued to flash through his mind at every step; refractions of moments he hoped were not real.

Shit! he thought; he had to get his mind to stop itself from rattling. Churning over and over within.

The further he traveled from the parking lot, the less fussed he felt by the torrents that had fueled him; but exhaustion crept up. Within two blocks he couldn't even jog. He was too tired.

That had been his primary goal. To exhaust himself into rest. But it was no use anymore. He felt too worried to find sleep. Too wired. Something he'd long fought to prevent had won out. It had planted a seed within him that there was more truth behind his visions than he cared to admit.

Not knowing what else to do, Charlie kept moving, as he always did. It was all that made sense to him anymore. He would go until his body gave out. He only wished that it was the cool, enveloping ocean waves that would take him. They could lift the weight from his shoulders and carry him forward, taking from him the struggle and what pain it caused.

He'd give anything for someone to take the weight away.

The man turned to catch one last glimpse of Charlie, but Charlie wasn't there. By then he was only a tracing shape crossing the street. Then, the shape turned and disappeared at the next block. Swallowed whole by the night.

"Hey, shut the door, god dammit. It's freezing. We gotta get this guy to Blackwell pronto."

The man obeyed. He climbed in and slammed the door shut, providing them what little protection it gave from the recesses of the chilly night sky.

Eight

Cait tossed and turned beneath the soft covers of her bed as she tried to sleep. Sleep wasn't a problem for her, but after today—restless thoughts, her perceived failure at completing the day's task—it all just sat there, prodding the edges of her mind, never allowing it to settle.

She couldn't turn it off.

The little lingering annoyances pulled at her. As well, an unexplainable, sinking feeling growing in her that something was wrong.

She shook off the irrationality of it and tried sticking to what she knew.

Even this didn't seem to help.

There were several moments she considered calling Scott just to bounce ideas off him, talk through holes together, but she didn't want to invade the castle. She knew how sacred it was. She didn't know how to construct it herself, but she understood why Scott pressed her so much to cultivate it.

Either way, she already knew what he would say.

Do you have your notepad at your bedside table? Have you separated the ideas from yourself?

This had been Scott's first lesson after she'd made detective.

Always have something to write on. Get the thoughts out of your head. Rest. Approach them later with a method. With a clear head.

After the second or third time convincing herself not to call, she sat up in bed, switched on the lamp, and picked up her notepad.

She emptied her thoughts into its pages.

Questions, theories, and hypotheses filled the paper as her pen scratched back and forth. Cait felt she could breathe again. With every sentence written, the weight lifted from her shoulders. Not twenty minutes later, she'd outlined several new directions for the case. The hour was of little consequence. Her mind had cleared, and she could operate off limited sleep.

Rejuvenated, filled with a new hope, Cait couldn't wait for morning to come. She wanted to get to work. Get in early. Have things lined up for Scott when he arrived.

He'd be in for a treat when next they met.

Her confidence returning, Cait put the pad down and switched off the lamp. Sliding back under the warm sheets, she closed her eyes. In minutes, she'd fallen off into a deep and restful sleep.

"What are we waiting for?" Came one man's voice among the rest, more in a whimper, stricken, fearful and nerve-wrecked.

"We're waiting for Blackwell."

This second voice was stronger, more assured.

"But when—"

"I don't know where he is. Jeez, will you shut the fuck up? I mean, we're just supposed to watch the guy until the boss gets here. Make sure he doesn't get out. Do anything stupid."

The other man said nothing.

Scott's shoulders throbbed as he woke up, head spinning, to fragments of this conversation. He heard the first man's voice.

"Well, still. I don't like this."

"What *do* you like? And what does it matter? We do what we're told. That's that."

"It's a cop."

"So?"

"Well, that's a lotta—"

"Look, Blackwell says it's fine. He said we did good bringing him here. And that we watch the guy and wait. What else is there to say?"

A long pause stretched out; then the first man spoke again.

"Well, I don't like it."

The other man scowled at him and shook his head.

Scott's splitting headache was the first thing he noticed when consciousness returned. That and the fact that they tied his arms behind him. The angle left his shoulder cocked. This position, besides the fact that he was lying on his side in an icy, shallow puddle, left him feeling a strange combination of numbness and intense pain.

He retraced the memories of what happened. The last thing he remembered was something heavy coming down at him.

His mind worked to put the pieces together, struggling.

His next thought was of his family, how worried his wife would be. He wondered what she'd told their children to keep them feeling safe and calm.

His eyes strained as he tried opening them. Desperate, they blinked beneath a fading fluorescent glow that cast itself over him. It spoke of somewhere underground or a basement... maybe a parking garage of some sort? The frigid and acrid scent of oil confirmed his suspicions.

Voices just outside the door interrupted his thoughts. The weak light stemming in from the door drew him toward the sounds; he strained to listen.

"How much longer we have to wait?"

"I don't know! Would you stop—just be patient for once, okay? It's getting annoying. It's bad enough being stuck down here in this—"

"That's what I mean. *This* is annoying. I just... I don't like it down here. It's spooky."

"Spooky? What are you, seven?"

"You hear the screams too, alright, so don't give me that shit."

The other man conceded, nodding his head.

"I'm telling ya, there's some weird shit going on in that lab. I mean–"

"Did you take the job or not? We were told not to ask questions, so we don't ask questions."

"Yeah, but these guys are... something else, aren't they?"

"Yes, they are. It's really fucking weird, but they're paying us a lot of money for some simple work. Drop something off here, something else there. The only complication so far is this cop, 'n the boss'll deal with him, so *it* won't be our problem anymore." The man thought for a moment. "So... will ya jus' shut up a sec?"

The other said nothing for a time.

"Yeah, but we're running outta places to dump these bodies. It was one every week. At first, right? Now, it's what? Three drops this week. What the fuck are they doing?"

"I don–"

But Scott could no longer hear their conversation. He heard the growing hum of something coming towards them, followed by the sound of a faint ding. He wondered at what it could be.

The two men outside were whispering. He could tell that much. Straining to listen, he still could make nothing out; his worry piqued.

Muffled words echoed out just beyond the door.

"Yes, sir. He's right in here."

Scott froze. His breath evaporated within him. He heard more whispering and then the door burst open.

Silhouetted in the faint light stood three men. Two wore unzipped winter coats, ready to brave the cold at a moment's notice. The third stood out, though. Dressed sharp, in a fine and very expensive suit. Even their outlines cut a wide contrast.

When he spoke, his voice came out in a smoother roll; yet a gruffness existed in it, as if he'd dragged each word through gravel before he used it.

"So, this is the man in question?"

"Yes, sir. H-he's the one that jumped us."

The man stepped into the room, creeping with a methodic intention. A thin shred of light stretched across him, revealing his face. Scott didn't recognize him, but he recognized the look he'd seen countless times before on the faces of men he'd spent his whole life hunting. His expression was void of reason or understanding. Alert. More aware. A foundational instability that often required little to push it past the edge. On average, this didn't scare Scott, but given the glare standing over him, he couldn't help but find himself flooded with unsettling nerves and feelings of terror.

"And he *is*?"

The man's voice sounded off again, a quick and unsteady burst.

"A cop, sir."

"I know that, but *who* is he? How did he catch on to us, dammit?"

The others shook their heads, fear-stricken by their leader's angry interjection.

"He–He's a detective," one man rattled off. "Detective Scott Donovan."

"And he found you *how*?"

His tone was more accusatory than questioning; both men's glances fell to the floor.

"What do you know, then? Huh?" The man unraveled somewhat.

Each of the other men stepped back. Then one held up Scott's wallet.

"He seems to have a nice little family."

The well-dressed man looked back, his interest piqued again.

"You stay away from them! You leave them out of this."

Scott glimpsed the man's gleaming smile.

"Interesting." The man focused on the concrete floor as he spoke. "Very interesting, indeed." He looked up at Scott again. "I seem to remember giving the order to keep everyone off *this* case."

Scott looked up, desperate to exert strength.

"Pity *you* didn't get the message. Eh, *detective*."

Scott looked up at the man, his eyes pleading despite his desire to appear unfazed.

"Just leave my family alone... *please*."

The man kneeled down near Scott, his face coming into better view.

"That remains to be seen. The greater pity is what we're going to do to you. You didn't need to be involved. You were to be spared. For the time being, until our task reached its terminus."

"What–What are you doing here?"

The man's smile broadened again, his eyes widened, crazed.

"I don't think you're in a position to be asking questions." He kneeled again. "Pity again, we don't even need you. Any knowledge you have, we can gain some other way. You at least will die knowing we will spare your family... a little while longer."

Scott's feet scrambled to the ground, struggling as he attempted to stand up. His head spun.

"No." The man grinned, shaking his head back and forth. "That won't do at all."

As he backed up, one of his lackey's stepped forward and kicked Scott hard in the stomach, leaving him reeling on the ground once more.

Scott flailed, moaning in pain as the man crouched before him.

"Shhh." He reached his hand out to the man behind him, who reached into his pocket and pulled out a pistol, handing it to his boss.

He looked Scott in the eyes with a feigned expression of sadness.

"I am truly sorry you had to get involved. We warned your people, but appears they require a harsher reminder."

Scott shook his head back and forth, though without much conviction; a somewhat feeble gesture.

The man stood again and aimed the pistol at Scott's head.

Scott flinched in frantic bursts.

"No. No! Please don't!"

"It's truly *nothing* personal. You should feel proud of how far you came. *Really.*"

With those last words of encouragement, he pulled the trigger. The blast rang round the empty room and clung to the damp cold that hung over every square inch of the surface.

Scott's body went limp and collapsed to the cold and dirty floor. His body came to an immediate, uncomfortable stillness.

Both men jumped back at the shot. They'd known it would come, but not with such abruptness.

Scott had left the world so fast, his final thoughts hadn't even taken root. They weren't of the case. They weren't about how close he'd come to solving it. Nor even of Cait. His last thoughts were memories. Images of his wife and kids. Those who'd kept him tethered to the world. People he would never see again. The images flashed and faded as fast as they had come. Gone. Forever.

Whatever tension the room had held collapsed. It fell to an oppressive silence that stretched itself out across the space. Though a strange and restless motion awoke.

Each man standing there felt it.

Mr. Blackwell handed the pistol back to its owner without the slightest look or turn, indifferent. His greatest concern was to check and make sure no blood had sprayed onto his suit. None had.

He looked down and wiped his hands together.

"Get rid of the body." He hesitated a moment. "Make a show of it. Talk to my assistant before you leave. He has instructions. Follow them."

Both men answered in unison.

"Yes, sir."

With that, Mr. Blackwell turned and left. He strolled away, passing through the fading light into the hall, and stopped to wait for the elevator. Within moments, he disappeared back upstairs.

The other men waited until they knew they were alone. Neither spoke as they went over and picked up Detective Donovan's body. Together, they dragged him down the hall.

Up one flight of stairs and down the next passage to the other garage.

Making it to the van, one man opened the back door. Together, they dropped Scott's body back inside with no concern for the blood that spilled out as he thumped down.

One man slammed the door shut and turned to his partner.

"You go talk to Blackwell's guy. I need a fucking cigarette."

The man said nothing. He looked at his partner and shook his head that he would. His face was pale and filled with uncertainty.

The other reached into his jacket, pulling out a pack of cigarettes. Sliding one out, he rested it on his lips and flicked a lighter. A gentle flame awakened. Breathing life into the darkness, illuminating the owner's face; which was stricken and filled with fear.

As his partner walked off to the facility's inner corridors, he took a long drag off the cigarette, perplexed. He wondered who these people were. And why they were working for them? It all seemed so strange. So surreal and out of place.

The cigarette burned; smoke rose, collecting itself around him in a cloud. It hovered, equal in its lack of assurance of what to do.

Charlie had walked right past the Mission once he got to it. There was no chance he'd be able to sleep, that much he knew. Plagued and agitated, his body shook from the mixture of cold and exhaustion. His mind was unraveled and in disarray; like a torn fabric that was once taut and whole. Stitched in place with care.

So Charlie continued on, cutting through the cold.

Moving against the flow of the world. A world intent on shoving back.

Looking up, he caught sight of the Hawthorne Bridge trusses. Something in him subsided. He felt no peace. Thinking it was beyond his reach then. And would remain so.

But something shifted; the amount of conflict in him had somehow lessened. He was at least thankful for that.

NINE

The next morning came quickly for Cait and hit harder than she'd expected. She had woken early with her plan, but felt distracted, wound, and restless.

Her first action, even before coffee, was to check if Scott responded. He hadn't, which started her on strange footing. Scott always woke early, and he responded right away.

Weird, she thought, struggling to push the unsettling feeling away. It lingered, clinging to the unused recesses of her thoughts.

Redirecting herself in a more productive direction than worrying, Cait readied herself for the day she'd planned and exited her apartment, eager for her chance to frame and bring order to an altogether chaotic situation.

The low temperatures lay in wait for her, fierce and cold. Cait wished she'd worn a heavier scarf, but she was thankful for the distraction.

She took the same route she always did when heading to the station—it saved her the burden of juggling multiple thoughts at once.

Every other step she took seemed to draw her back to thinking about Scott. She kept checking her phone to see if he'd messaged back. She even kept feeling phantom rings as she held her phone in her hand and expected the call. But he never responded.

Not one for irrationality. Her mind kept wanting to wonder at all the possibilities for him not messaging her back, continuing to ramp up her already unsettled state.

She kept telling herself it had to do with the kids and that everything was fine. He would call soon and explain everything.

Cait was looking at her phone when she rounded the corner to the station. It caught her quite off guard when she ran into someone and looked up to find a bustling crowd.

"I'm so sorry—" she began. "What the hell..."

Raising herself up on the tips of her toes, Cait struggled to see over the crowd.

The yellow police tape was clear enough, though.

Her stomach twisted and dropped within her. Her heart skipped as she clutched her phone and worked to keep herself from assuming the worst.

She pushed her way through the crowd, mumbling to herself.

"No... no... no..."

Her vision blurred the closer she got to the edge of the crowd; it faltered and slipped into a strange contrast of slow and fast motion. The clamor of the different bystanders ballooned around her as she reached for many thoughts, each of which seemed bent on escaping her grasp.

Making it to the police tape, she tried to go under it, but someone stopped her.

"Ma'am, you need to stay back!"

The man's voice was sharp and filled with worry.

Cait shook her head, which was foggy and heavy.

No, she thought, fumbling for her badge.

After showing it, the man lifted the tape for her, sheepish as he did, letting Cait enter the scene.

"What happened here?"

Cait's voice was softer than usual. More cautious.

"We're not entirely sure yet, detective."

"But who–"

Cait froze when she came to the white sheet that covered who she was talking about.

Before her, on the front steps of Portland's main precinct, lay a body, blood trickling on the sidewalk near where the head lay. An arm protruded from beneath the sheet. Cait recognized the sleeve right away and couldn't help but emit a haunting and constrained bellow.

The entire world seemed to give out; Cait lost a step.

"Detective?"

The uniformed officer reached out to grab her, but she steadied herself soon enough and pushed his hand away.

He stepped back.

The icy air smothered her; as if determined itself to freeze her in this moment forever; *willing* it to go on.

Cait stood up again, tall as she could. Her knees weakened and her gut pulsed with all the terse emotions flooding through her.

The uniformed officer leaned toward her.

"Detective?"

"Sco—"

But she couldn't finish even saying his name. She stopped. Everything stopped. Even her mind seemed too slow. It came to an abrupt halt when a hand came down upon her shoulder. She didn't notice it at first.

"Cait?"

The voice seemed muffled, distant. Cait still didn't notice.

"Cait?"

When she did not respond, it echoed again, though louder.

"Cait!"

Her body shook back awake, and she looked up. A man stood before her, someone she recognized but couldn't place. His expression was one of compassionate concern.

"Cait."

It echoed a fourth time. Still as if from a distance.

"I'm so sorry, Cait."

Cait stared back at the man, her expression blank, and at last, recognition came.

"C-captain?"

"Let's get you inside."

The world returned to its terrible pace.

Captain Sykes ushered her through the various other officers and the noise of the greater crowd grew in Cait's consciousness before the station doors came to a close behind her and cut it off.

The front entryway was no less frantic; less populated, though, and far less stimulating to the mind. The true gravity of the moment, its heavy weight, fell upon the unsuspecting Cait.

"It... It's Scott—it's–"

Cait's nerves spiked in a way she'd never experienced before. She'd never expected *this*.

Captain Sykes nodded his head.

"I know." His brow furrowed with a grim sadness. "I'm sorry, Cait. I feel—We shouldn't have been pursuing this."

"What do you mean? What–What happened?"

"We're still not sure exactly what happened, but I can't help but feel responsible. I should've been looking out. For both of you."

Cait's look grew sharper.

"What do you mean?"

The captain looked around. Back and forth, making sure no one was eavesdropping.

"There was a strange amount of pressure to drop this case —like, from on high—but I kept pushing it. I figured if anyone could put an end to this shit, it was you and—" He stopped short of saying his name. "And I think–" Choking up, the captain fell short of finishing his thought.

The sadness in Cait's expression faded as her inquisitive drive returned.

"What do you mean, pressure? From where? Why didn't you say anything?"

The captain grew more uncomfortable.

"Look, it didn't seem like a big deal. There was never anything official, just strained conversations and extra passive hints from the higher-ups." He hesitated again. Looking down, as if making eye contact with Cait would've added to his guilt. "I didn't want to distract either of you, but now..."

Strength returned to Cait. Her jaw tightened, and she stood taller. The world grew clearer.

"We must've gotten too close to something. Why would there've been pressure before? Unless some people were—"

She cut herself off as three other officers walked by, almost rubbing shoulders with her.

Captain Sykes looked up. Right into Cait's eyes.

"Cait, this thing here... it's fucked, okay?" He looked back and forth again. "I don't think I've ever felt *this* before. This case... it all just feels *so* wrong." Captain Sykes paused again.

"What is it?"

"We... we got a warning this morning. From the top..."

Cait took a deep breath, expectant of what she was about to hear.

"We're to cease all inquiries into these strange killings. And they assigned a special Task Force to Scott's death. Off our books."

"What?" It wasn't a question.

"It gets worse."

"How? What could be worse?"

The captain took a deep and painful gulp, showing how sick he felt by it all.

"There's something big going on here, Cait. Big. And it —" He hesitated again, waiting as more people walked by. "The Chief, Cait—hell, the Commissioner is bringing down executive pressure to–"

"To what? To look the other way? To fuckin' bury–"

Fury rose in Cait's voice. The tendons in her neck tightened in time with the bulging veins near her temples. Her temper had always been something Scott had warned her about.

"Cait, look, god dammit!" Captain Sykes' voice fell into a frustrated whisper. "I don't like it any more than you. 'Specially that Scott—" He stopped himself again and took a deep gulp. "I... I know what this is. I know what it looks like, but I—"

"Do we just keel over? Do what you're told? And what? Just let Scott–"

She knew she would regret those words later.

"I'm trying to save your job, Cait! And maybe your life, dammit!"

Cait stopped, struck by the force in his voice. Captain Sykes had always been one of the good guys in her book. An ally. It must've been a fear that caused him to talk like that. She figured at least.

"I'm trying to protect you, Cait." The captain's voice grew calmer. "It's no secret how much the Chief wants to let you go. You and I both know he's basically been looking for a reason."

Cait nodded. This time, it was her countenance that fell to the floor.

"He fought your appointment, remember? And Scott fought hard back. And I–"

"I know, I know. I'm sorry, Captain, it's just that I..." Cait's voice grew strained and weak.

"I know. We need to be careful here."

Cait nodded, as if in agreement.

Just as Captain Sykes was about to open his mouth again, a set of conference doors opened down the hall. They swung open wide and dozens of men spilled out into the hallway. At the group's center was none other than the Chief of Police. He looked back at Cait, a stricken, worrisome look on his face.

"You better get outta here."

But Cait made no move to leave. Her body turned toward the Chief, her muscles tightening, flickers of rage in her eyes.

"Cait? Cait, no! You need to keep it together right now! For your own—"

He tried halting her, but it was too late.

Cait was already storming off. Captain Sykes whispered to himself.

"*Fuck*."

Cait erupted. "This is bullshit!" It was something she'd dreamed of doing for a long time. Before, she'd always had reasons to keep quiet. Those reasons didn't seem relevant anymore.

The entire room froze, and the Chief turned on Cait, smiling.

Cait stood her ground.

"Ah, *Detective* Lane. I was wondering if we would see you today."

She did her best not to blink and let her glare bore into him.

"Letting our emotions get the better of us, are we?" His smile grew wider and more wicked. "Who would have thought?"

The fire flared within her and Captain Sykes came forward, grabbing her arm.

"Cait, let's go." He went to pull her away. "Sorry, Chief Gilman, it's been a shock–"

"No, *Captain*, let her speak."

Captain Sykes, in his place, let his shoulders shrivel and backed away.

"We're— No, *you're* just giving up on this? On *Scott*?"

"Detective Donovan died doing his duty. A tragic loss to us all, and a sure sign you're in over your head, *young lady*."

That did it.

Cait's hands reshaped themselves into fists. Her posture seemed to transform as her arms shook. Everyone else seemed to notice this, too. She said nothing.

Chief Gilman turned from Cait, who stood right before him. He spoke in a manner so all around them could hear. Bold and stern. His demeanor was one of a man used to being listened to.

"*Captain*." He hung on that word, letting the silence that followed draw everyone in. "One of your *officers* appears to need... time off. Time to recover from this... unfortunate tragedy. In need of a rest, perhaps?" It was only then he turned his attention to Cait. "Time to rethink things?"

The hall grew quiet. Cait's eyes flickered and sharpened as Chief Gilman gave a final order.

"Please take her badge and gun and remove her from the premises until we review her file. It needs to be decided whether she's fit for duty."

Captain Sykes looked up, desperate.

Cait's eyes never left her mark.

"We don't need anyone around here—*now*—who can't control themselves. Time to prune our ranks. Wouldn't you say? Not allow for any weakness to fester?" The chief turned back to Captain Sykes and grinned. "Is that clear, captain?"

Working to keep all emotion out of his expression, the captain managed a response.

"Yes, sir. Right away."

"Very good," said a smug and triumphant Chief Gilman.

Captain Sykes turned and faced Cait.

"I'm sorry, Cait. I... I never wanted this..."

His voice was soft. Caring, but heavy.

She fought to hold back a flood of angry tears and looked away.

"I'm... sorry..."

That's all she managed.

Captain Sykes nodded in understanding.

The Chief, and everyone else, stood there waiting. Intent on staying until satisfied by what they would witness.

Cait stared back, a growing despondence filing at her. She'd never wished for Scott's comforting presence more. With reluctance, she reached into her jacket and removed both her badge and her gun from her person. She placed them in the open and equally reluctant hands of her captain.

"Good," said Chief Gilman, looking more like a giddy child. "Now get her the hell outta here. I don't want to see her back here until I've given approval. Is that clear?"

Caged by the chain of command, Captain Sykes, never taking his eyes off Cait, said, "Yes, sir."

Saying nothing more, Chief Gilman turned and strode off. His sycophantic entourage followed, and within moments, the space was as quiet and clear as before.

The bustle died away. Leaving Cait and the Captain to themselves.

Captain Sykes looked at Cait. She was a mast's sheet, stripped of wind, hanging low with anger's weight. He knew that look and what she carried—he carried it too, but couldn't show it.

Then, something occurred to the captain. An idea struck

him, allowing him to stand taller. Taking a deep breath, he placed Cait's badge in his pocket but held her gun out before him.

It was Cait who spoke first.

"Captain," she said, "I'm sorry, but–"

"You had to do it, didn't you?"

She had expected a severe reprimand, but the Captain's broad smile caught her off guard.

Cait said nothing, nor did she look up.

"Yeah," he said, "you did. You do what you feel is right. That's what makes you so effective at your job."

Her worry and frustration subsided and Cait looked up, confused.

"But–"

"No. Don't start with me. Don't make me change my mind." His smile grew broader. "Don't waste your energy. You're gonna need that strength of yours."

She cocked her head in wonder.

"Way I see it, the *Chief* just did us a big favor."

Her mouth fell open, but she was at a loss for words.

"Come on, *rook*. Scott always said you were the best. Can't you figure it out?"

To Cait's absolute shock, Captain Sykes extended her pistol back out to her, showing for her to take it.

Cait hesitated.

"But I..."

"You're suspended." He leaned in, looking right at her. "And you're not allowed back onto our premises, yes. But... once you leave *this* building, I'm not in charge of you anymore. You could follow all nudges you feel so led to, unhindered by this failed structure."

Cait's shoulders straightened, and she met him eye to eye.

"I'm going to walk down toward my office, and I'd figure

you have about five minutes to gather anything you think you'll need before you get outta here."

Cait couldn't help but stand there, dumbfounded.

"You'll need something to do now. Right? Otherwise, you'll just lose yourself to grief. Might as well stick it to the—"

The Captain stopped himself, feeling himself getting carried away.

The first wave of relief she'd felt since she'd reached the station that morning settled itself over Cait. It swirled, inter-mixing itself with the other many fluctuating emotions she felt.

She looked up at Captain Sykes again, then down at her pistol. Hesitating before taking it.

"Thank you, John."

His smile flared, but then a look of concern formed on his face.

"Don't make me regret this."

She shook her head as she understood.

"But sir—" she started, but he cut her off, raising a hand.

"Cait, this whole thing is fucked, and something needs to be done. My hands are tied. Looks like you're the only one in a position to..." He paused again. "... to do *anything*."

She said nothing.

"Bring the whole thing down, Cait. The whole goddamned thing. For Scott."

Tears worked their way forward again.

"I will, sir."

At that, Captain Sykes placed his hands in his pockets and looked around.

"Alright, five minutes, *young lady*."

It was Cait's turn to crack a smile, and as Captain Sykes turned and walked away, she raced to her office to get what she thought she'd need. She would stop by Scott's desk, too. The morning had knocked the wind out of her, but she would let nothing deter her; if anything, it only strengthened her resolve to bring this heinous case to an end.

———

The sun made its weary way through the burdened sky. Still, Charlie trudged on. His nerves were shaky, somewhat shot. It was more the habit of walking that compelled him forward at this point; his body trying to outrun his mind.

He was crossing the river again; for the third time that night. The going was slow. His hope of proper rest still hovered out before him, just out of reach.

This time, he crossed over the Morrison Bridge, listening to the chorus of wind and lapping waves emanating from the river below.

Somewhat quelled by its weightless promise, Charlie once again gave himself over to those free-falling visions of escape.

Just as he could see his body cutting through the water, something near him stole his attention. A soft voice, forgiving, full of love, just a little way down. It reminded him of what his own had sounded like so many years ago.

"Mommy?"

"Yes, dear?"

"Is daddy coming to lunch today?"

Charlie looked up, taken by the staunch and airy openness between them. He could see the mother smiling, almost playing with her child. Then she stopped.

Charlie stopped too and turned, hoping not to be noticed.

"Guess what?" the mother played.

"What?"

"Daddy *is* going to meet us today!"

The boy cheered.

"He's been very busy at work this week, but he says he

needs a break and he needs to laugh with his little boy. Isn't that nice?"

Charlie could feel the tangible joy streaming back and forth between the two as they spoke. To him, it was a crushing blow. Driving him to continue onward but they stood—an obstacle—in his way.

Just when Charlie figured he would brush by them, the boy rang out again, "Now, mommy?"

"Soon, dear. Should we race home and meet him?"

"Yeah, let's go!"

They turned and walked away, their pace quickening with every step.

Charlie himself slowed, coming almost to a complete stop, just watching them until they faded entirely from sight.

His mental threads were just holding on. On the verge of tearing, he felt about to collapse. Part of him hoped, if he did, he'd topple right over the railing, ensuring his dream would come true.

Charlie followed this unsuspecting duo until they reached the stairwell leading down from the bridge. Though he tried to control it, he wasn't able to hold back the envy that had been unlocked. It joined the queue of other thoughts and feelings he'd chosen to ignore.

Reaching the base of the stairs, he found himself on the Riverwalk once more. That pull within him urged him north, so he went south and disappeared into the sparse and roaming winter crowd.

———

Time seemed static as Cait walked back to her apartment. Her mind raced as various threads and details fired back and forth. The shock of Scott's death shook her to her core. But it proved itself to be quite a propelling fuel to move her forward.

Somewhere within Cait, there was a recognition that this might appear heartless. That she should stop and grieve. Old adages would encourage her to feel the pain. To lean into it. Reach out to Stacey and the kids, check on them. Experience the empathy of remorse.

But she couldn't stop. If she stopped, she would collapse and perhaps not get up again. Something in her whispered she wouldn't be able to face Stacey, or Tommy, or Hannah until she'd brought them justice. For everything they'd done for her, it was the least she could do.

Maybe after I finish this, Cait thought, *I'll have earned that right.*

They needed peace, and Cait needed vengeance.

This, at least, is what she told herself as she reentered her apartment in mid-morning.

Even before taking her jacket off, Cait already began reconstructing her kitchen and dining space into a sort of workstation. It's not like she ever ate there, anyway.

She had repurposed her entire apartment to house the investigation. Every square inch of table and counter surface had been used to unravel case files, photos, notes, you name it. The entire wall next to her kitchen, which housed the peg board she put her meal plan, chore chart, and calendar on, now housed a map of the city with red pushpins, showing where they'd found each body, including the location at Washington Park, where they'd found Scott's car. They must've taken his body from there. Captain Sykes had called to fill her in. A gracious gesture that did little to lift her spirit.

Cait had poured over the map several times, making no sense or connection of any kind. There was no pattern. Nothing. She'd been over every file twice. She'd checked each note. Without access to the police records, she wasn't sure where to look next.

She went through her own case files and notebooks several

times. Scott's too. It was a last second grab she'd made on her way out. Walking by the staff sergeant's desk, she noticed Scott's effects—everything that was on him when they'd found him the night before. It was evidence, but when she saw his notebook, it had to be hers. For the notes he'd taken— maybe it would help her case—but, deep down, she knew it was to stick it to them... and it felt good.

And yet, Scott's notebook sat on the far end of the table, untouched. She hadn't the heart to look through it yet. Every so often, she imagined herself running into him. She'd see him standing in the doorway of her office, and her heart would seize and she'd cry.

To her own grace, she had built up a seasoned ability to stifle whatever tears dared come.

After concluding that she'd exhausted what lay before her, she at last picked up Scott's notebook. Even looking at it felt wrong. Like betrayal.

Just open the book, boss! he would have said as he laughed. She could hear his voice in her head.

Cait imagined him standing over her then, that sly smile cocked on his face. She realized he would never stand there over her like that again. He would never tease her again. Or sneak up and scare her as he always did. Nor would she hear his encouragement. His belief in her. Those words, *to hell with them,* when she needed a push to keep going.

She could use his encouragement right then.

At these thoughts, Cait felt herself sinking.

No! she thought. *I can't do this! Not now. Never.* She had to keep her thinking constructive or she wouldn't make it. She had to move forward.

Wiping away the encroaching sniffles, she cleared her mind. She focused on Scott; not in his absence but in the hope that his words still rang true. That everything he'd taught her was real. If she'd believed it in his presence, why not believe in his absence? That negated nothing he'd passed onto her, lessons *and* encouragements.

Her spirits lifted somewhat, and whatever had been obstructing her thoughts faded.

She wondered what Scott would tell her if he were standing there with her. After several seconds, memories of another case that stumped them came to her. She remembered what he'd said when she'd moved into the beyond-frustrated territory.

Go back to the breakthroughs.

Her excitement bloomed like a candle flame, given a little extra fuel.

Sometimes, she knew, revisiting the various dots that connected everything at a different time could lead you to a new conclusion.

She looked again down at the table where Scott's notebook rested. It stared back at her, taunting as it had before. This time, a confidence settled in; she knew what to do.

She picked it up and began thumbing through it with a hunger that would find no satisfaction until it reached its goal. A vague sense of what she was looking for existed. Nothing concrete though. She just hoped that anything would emerge.

Turning over page after page, discouragement built. Cait flew through the first few sections of the notebook.

No. No. She flipped through page after page. *No. Not that case.* She came to the most recent entries, near the end. Where he'd scribbled down his random thoughts regarding the strange, bruised bodies they'd found.

Her heart fluttered with hope.

She flipped through each one. The different days, the different scenes. Her eyes hung at the end of every word as she took her time trying to digest it all. Searching for something she they might've missed before.

Breakthrough... breakthrough... come on... when was the...

Her thoughts trailed off as she worked to stave off the coming disappointment.

Cait came to one of the last pages, littered with his scribbles. To their interview with Charlie.

The guy from the Mission, she thought. A feeling rose in her then. One she couldn't quite articulate. Nor could she explain the excitement that grew.

She scanned the page, only to find Scott's notes were almost identical to her own. The wind within her sails died down. Nearing the bottom of the page, her heart all but gave up. If it wasn't for one last phrase scribbled across the bottom of the page, she would've tossed the book aside. He'd scratched the words out, it looked, in frantic speed. They were almost illegible.

He had underlined the phrase and gone over it several times with frantic scratches of his pen, almost carving it into the paper.

Cait's mind warned her not to hope, but she squinted and leaning closer, struggling to make them out.

No... she thought. *It can't...*

She shook herself to clear her head, and blinking several times, she read the words again. Then was sure of what they said.

He knows more...

Cait stood there for a moment, unsure. She stared at the words. Consumed by what they could mean. Why hadn't Scott mentioned this to her? Maybe he didn't think it was important. Or it was a hunch he was unsure about.

Cait would never know.

Either way, it stopped Cait flat. What more could he know? Had he seen more? Did he know who was behind everything? Did he not say it all out of fear?

Too many questions came. Not a bad thing, considering her desperation for new leads. This provided just that.

Pausing for a moment, Cait remembered the interview. She remembered Charlie's state, and what the manager had shared about his life. How he'd been through something terrible. He'd looked like hell. Whatever he'd experienced, he'd come back damaged. She remembered the hopelessness that dripped from him.

As she thought about it, he knew he hadn't been completely forthright with them.

Her brain churned over what Scott assumed Charlie was holding back from them. She would have given anything to ask him, but that was impossible.

What did you mean, Scott? She heard the words shouting in her own head, feeling more alone than ever.

The only way to stop the rising feeling of doubt in her was action. That much she knew.

She couldn't ask Scott and was out of other ideas.

What else could she do?

Cait shot up from the chair, slammed the notebook shut, and picked up her jacket from the chair's back.

Hesitating a moment, she heard *his* voice again.

Take your time. Think it through. Gather what you need first.

Her stomach lurched as she realized again: he was not there. Nor would he ever be there to warn her again. Grief comes in waves, and this one hit her with full force. She did everything she could to shake it all away, to purge it from her heart and mind.

"Screw it," she said. The words tumbled out of her in a caustic whisper.

Cait marched to the apartment door. It swung open with her fiery assurance and slammed shut, marking an abrupt exit. There was one thing to do. She needed to find Charlie West. Somehow, he was the key to everything here. She didn't know how, but she wouldn't let that stop her.

Ten

Mr. Blackwell had yet to fall asleep as the sun crept over the horizon. A new day was upon him. He sat hunched over, staring at the handwritten note his assistant had taken down regarding the several calls that had come in from up north. The calls Mr. Blackwell was adamant he was no longer taking. They were demands of progress reports, completion dates of the various tasks assigned, along with an ultimatum to call back and the corresponding threat if Mr. Blackwell didn't comply. The foundations were shrinking away beneath him. Time was almost up.

He clung to his short and choppy breaths. His posture wouldn't allow any sort of depth for his lungs to expand.

He was still in this position when the phone on his desk rang. Watching him react was like watching something crafted out of marble come to life. He picked it up before the first ring finished sounding.

"Yes? Doctor?" The words came out in frantic bursts. "What's the— How was the latest test? A success?"

A difficult pause ensued while he listened, and his shoulders crumbled forward with the news.

"It failed again," he ventured at last. The words spilled out in a despairing whisper. Then, his free fist clenched, and he slammed it down onto the table, knocking over his stationery and pencils. "*You* failed me again, Dr. Grenier! God dammit! You know how important this is! How close we are! I thought I told you that failure wasn't acceptable—"

The doctor cut him off, something out of the norm. Mr. Blackwell's expression turned again; the man's face flashed back and forth between triumph and raged confusion. At last, it settled into fury.

"And *you* didn't inform me?"

Dr. Grenier went to defend himself, but Mr. Blackwell cut him off.

"How dare you, Doctor." Mr. Blackwell's voice was thundering, then. "I gave you the strictest orders to update me—on anything—right... right away! I don't care you wanted to be... *sure* first! God dammit—this... *this* is outrageous!"

Mr. Blackwell lost it once again, not even able to complete a sentence.

The doctor noted to himself that their leader *was* growing worse.

"You hear me, *Doctor*?" Mr. Blackwell's voice grew low and gruff. "I want you to have another subject ready within the hour. Do you hear me? I want everything ready, and I want to be present for the whole procedure. If I can't trust *you*, I'll have to oversee everything from now on. Questions?"

This time, he waited for a response. When it came, he blurted out a response. "*Good*!" And he hung up. He slammed the phone down against its base. A harsh echo flooded the dark room, followed by the clattering of the whole device tumbling to the floor.

He paid no mind to it as he stared forward. Nothing caught his glare. It was as if his thoughts were being carried somewhere beyond what he was seeing. Not to anywhere fantastical or otherworldly, just somewhere lost, beyond the confines of reality. The threads that held his typical self together loosened. He was becoming more reactive than his usual thoughtful self. In the more recent weeks, he'd allowed this path to dig deeper. Take more pronounced control over him. It grew worse and worse with every burst of rage. But nothing mattered more to him than the triumph of his success. He would let nothing stand in his way.

———

Cait stood out in front of the Mission, kicking herself. She should have called ahead, she knew. The thought of *moving* consumed her. Moving fast. She'd been dying for a reason to go; everything else just faded from her mind.

Her mind still raced, active in fighting off the gathering weight of despair, a feeling she was unused to.

She just stood there, unsure of everything. Unsettled by a growing sense of uncertainty.

By midday, Charlie's mind was a strained canvas; worn by the many iterative thoughts painting themselves over and over upon it. Wiping each preceding thought away, making way for the next. It, and *he*, was a mess. He still feared sleep wouldn't come; but was too tired to keep going. He resigned himself to return to the Mission to distract himself however he could.

Then, turning the corner from Burnside onto 3rd Street, he stopped in his tracks. Gripped by confusion, it took several moments to place who he saw. The person pacing back and forth at the base of The Mission's front steps.

It's that detective, he thought. *The one from the other day.* His brow furrowed. *What's she doing here?*

Charlie felt confused for multiple reasons. He couldn't fathom why she was there. He could fathom less why she was alone pacing back and forth the way she was.

He felt the tension pull upon the tiny strings within his mind and his own worry spiked. All he wanted was to be alone. He couldn't bear to be around another person then. Let alone someone who might need his help.

For a time, he just stood staring. He backed away, hiding himself around the corner of the building across the street.

She stood there pacing in front of the Mission, looking determined.

Shit...

He couldn't wait there all day; and going around seemed so burdensome.

Clouded mind and all, with strained and heavy steps, Charlie crossed the street and made his way toward the detective.

"Charlie? Charlie West?"

Cait's voice spilled out in excited but frantic bursts.

The force of it caught Charlie off guard. Something about her was different; he could feel it. A sort of added weight. A sharp and raw pain. Something had happened.

Even as he stood there, empathy flowed, instinctual in his desire to help.

Still exhausted and still worried, he couldn't help but feel intrigued by the urgency in Cait's posture. Without thinking, his inner thoughts moved themselves aside, making room for what Cait was about to share. It was as if her needs outweighed his own.

Besides, he wondered, maybe if he helped her, he'd at last earn the right to rest himself. Maybe it would help him let go.

Cait sized Charlie up as he approached her. A voice in her mind reprimanded her for coming to him. He looked even worse than before. Ragged and worn, as if he hadn't slept in months. He was a man nearing the end of himself.

Any reservation that came dissolved as Charlie spoke. His tone had a contrived, perky ring to it.

"What's up? Is everything alright—d-detective, was it?"

Cait feigned a smile to project strength, even as her stomach did somersaults within her.

"Cait," she said. "Please, just Cait."

Charlie nodded and for a moment they both stood there; each hoping the other wouldn't see past their weak facades.

"I'm sorry to come to you like this, but…"

Cait paused as Charlie looked up, intrigued. She wondered how honest she should be.

"I—I didn't know what else to do."

Charlie took a slight step back.

"Okay?"

"It's just that–"

Tears welled up in her eyes, along with a constricting flood of emotions—neither of which was common to Cait.

Charlie felt it all—as he always did—the entire on-rush of it. What coursed through her flowed into him, heavy and filled with pain—a sharp pain he preferred to his own. It was tangible, something he could understand and wrap his mind and hands around. It was not incongruous, like his own pain.

"It's okay," he said, reaching out to her as a gesture of steady calm. The more he pressed in, the more his own hurt faded. His own mind hungered for the continued reprieve.

Cait tried to speak again but found she couldn't. The tears were too close to escaping. She never cried, especially in front of others.

Charlie's awareness of the struggle increased.

"Cait…" He leaned closer to her. "Cait… it's okay," and he reached out and took her by the shoulder.

And then she broke.

Cait's strength gave way and she erupted into a storm of tears. She spilled out the entire story of what had happened. She told him about the case, about what they'd found. Cait told him about Scott, how he'd gone after *them*, about how they'd took him and killed him. She told him about walking up onto his body laid out on the front steps of the station. Tears flowed as the revelation struck deeper that the police would do nothing to help. Something was off about the whole thing. She explained they'd put her on leave and ordered her not to interfere, but she couldn't help it. She told him her captain showed he'd look the other way so she could continue the investigation. She had the van's description, and the license number, but she couldn't use police resources to track it, so it would be next to impossible unless she ran into it. She wanted to... she *needed* to finish this. For Scott. It was the least she could do for him. For his family.

She felt stuck. At least, that's how it seemed. That's what she told Charlie.

"The only thing I've got is what Scott wrote... about *you*."

She paused as Charlie squirmed.

Charlie took another step back. It was a lot to take in—Cait's story. Let alone his involvement in it.

Besides, her presence there now added weight to a lingering feeling. There was more to this. But what?

"W-what..." His words fumbled. "What did *he* write?"

Cait gulped. It looked painful. Then, feeling she'd made the wrong choice, she looked over at Charlie.

"Look, I'm sorry to have bothered you at all. This—it's... I..." She paused and turned away. "I can manage on my own."

Charlie's insides squirmed as she took her burden back, leaving nothing but the empty void which his own worries would soon replace.

"No!" He burst out.

Cait turned, unsure what to think.

"Can you," he said, calmer than before, "can you tell me what he wrote? Let's see if we can make sense of it."

Cait took a deep, more confident breath. Charlie could

feel the weight of the moment redistribute itself. It brought him peace.

After a slight pause, Cait spoke.

"*He* thought you knew more than you were letting on."

Charlie's face grimaced somewhat, and Cait jumped in as if to qualify or better frame her statement.

"I mean—I don't know what he meant—I don't think he thought you were lying. I didn't think you were lying, he just..." she trailed off.

Charlie, once again, stopped short.

Being one familiar with how intuition can help you read people, Scott's summation didn't shock him. What shocked him was how it had captured how he felt. That there was more to *all* this. But what? He couldn't figure that out; this gnawed at him.

He sensed Cait's embarrassment that she'd overstepped her bounds and rushed to console her.

"It's... it's okay."

He could feel the urgency in her and the weight she carried —for he carried it too now. He felt the fear in her. He wondered if she knew how well-hidden she kept it. Then there was her isolation. That lonely road one walks by choice. He wondered at why that was the path she had chosen. Were they similar to his own reasons? He didn't know.

Cait looked back up at him, his expression sturdier than before. As he stood there with her, she felt her burdens lift. It was as if she wasn't alone. It was a burden they could share, providing them both with a sense of strength and purpose. An end seemed possible.

Her confidence returned somewhat. "Do you have any idea what he might've meant?"

Charlie tried thinking through all the many scattered thoughts in his head.

"Maybe..."

He was all for helping her, but still lived in fear of letting another person into his experiences. No one needed extra weight added to their lives.

"Maybe how?"

Charlie took a deep breath as the pull latched onto him once more. It was always there, but strengthened then. Straining his consciousness.

"A feeling."

Cait grew more intrigued and took an unconscious step closer towards him.

Charlie didn't back away.

Cait stood there, poised to listen.

"It's..." Charlie tried to speak.

Cait leaned in closer.

A level of comfort trickled in; it felt so foreign to him. A sense of safety.

"It's like there's this veil..." He pulled away, and his eyes narrowed as he spoke. "... and on the other side is... is..."

Feeling foolish, he stopped.

It was her turn to console him. She grew intrigued.

"It's okay, Charlie. What is it?"

Charlie looked up at her as an assured warmth fell upon him.

"I dunno, *really*." He thought about it. "It's like there's this truth that's hidden from me."

Cait watched him as he seemed to disappear within himself.

"What truth?"

A genuine interest rose at his wondering.

Charlie looked up, shaking his head that he didn't know.

Cait could see in his eyes that he was telling the truth.

For a moment, they let the quiet speak for them; they basked in the lightness of sharing space without words.

Out of nowhere, Charlie did something that surprised

even him. He smiled. Maybe it was easier to compose himself while wearing Cait's problems instead of his own. His smile widened, followed by an awkward chuckle. Before he had even thought about saying anything, a single word escaped.

"*Funny...*"

Cait's head tilted, a little surprised.

"What's funny?"

Charlie squirmed at the need to explain himself.

"Oh—ah... well, you mentioned a van when you told your story..."

Cait's eyes refocused and her stare bore into Charlie as if on a desperate search; her determined glare spoke of her relentless nature to not let anything stand in her way.

The smile faded from his expression.

"Yeah? What about it?"

The two questions shot out of her, almost entwined.

His instinct was to back away, but he feared further upsetting the moment.

"Well, uh... last night," he began. "I was... I was... walking home and... sort of got clipped by a van."

Cait's expression collapsed, ending up somewhere between intrigue and concern.

"Jesus, Charlie. Are you- Did you get hurt? Are you okay?"

The flood of questions sent Charlie nearer to the edge. The peace was escaping, and he was on the verge of crumbling.

He took a step back then, his hands raised, feigning involuntary defense.

Cait couldn't help but notice.

"Sorry, Charlie. I–It's just..." She hesitated. "With everything going on... It can't be the *same* van. That would be impossible."

Charlie's arms settled back down at his sides.

"You are okay, though, aren't you?"

Charlie shot her a glance, unsure. More worried than before.

"I mean, did you see a doctor or anything?"

"No. I'm okay," he said, far too quick. "Really."

Cait shrugged.

"What did it look like, anyway?"

"What?"

"The van. And where were you?"

Charlie scrunched his forehead as he reached back with his strained mind to remember.

"Uh... It was one of those big work vans, you know?"

Cait nodded, assuming this was an odd coincidence.

"A sort of grayish color...."

She stood up a little straighter. Her thoughts spun in concentric swirls, along with the rising butterflies in her stomach.

"... with several big dents on the back above one tire and on the bumper."

Cait didn't realize it, but she was holding her breath, working to keep herself steady.

When Charlie looked up, it caught him off guard by how lost Cait looked in her own thoughts.

"Cait?" He waited a second for her to respond. "Cait? Are–Are *you* okay?"

"Huh? Uh, yeah, sorry. That's... that's the exact description of the van we're looking for."

Charlie's already turgid insides did several flips as he caught on to the connection.

Keeping her tone gentle, she pressed him a bit.

"Charlie?"

"Yeah?"

"Did you catch the license number?"

Charlie nodded he had.

"B... V... N..." she began.

"…2… 8… 3," he finished.

A rush of freezing wind punctuated the moment; it sucked the breath right out of both of them.

"*Scott*?" Cait said. The name escaped in a faint whisper. She spoke it with such fragility, it was a wonder it didn't fall to the ground and shatter.

Charlie held his breath as his overtaxed mind worked to catch up.

"Wait—" Charlie broke in. "What does this mean?"

"It means… Wait, Charlie, where did this happen? Did you see where they went?" They were assertions more than questions, and Charlie backpedaled more.

"Yeah, I can—I mean… yeah." He pointed down 3rd Street. "Just down that way by Union Station."

Cait was near tears—angry tears. Furious.

"Can you take me there? Now?"

Before considering it, Charlie nodded he could. His exhaustion screamed out. To go back to his room. To rest, but he told himself that could wait. He felt purposeful, and that felt good.

He *wasn't* thinking about himself.

Cait couldn't help but grab him by the shoulder.

"Where? Which way?"

"Just this way." Charlie turned to move, but stopped. It was fear that halted him. Immediate memories flooded into his mind of the last time he'd been there. He saw the van. The men who piled out of it. Followed by all the memories that invaded his thoughts the night before.

He wanted to help Cait and forced a slow step forward, but a terror crept in the closer they got. Building and building with each step.

Maybe he could just take her close, he wondered.

"Charlie?" she pushed, led more by a frantic urge than consideration.

"Yeah, sorry," he said, still fastened to the concrete, dragging to get one foot in front of the next.

Cait moved closer, a pleading look formed on her.

"Charlie?"

"It's just down the street. Can I give you directions? I-I'm afraid I'm so tired–" then he stopped himself. He saw the look as it formed itself on Cait. That desperate need not to be alone, which Charlie knew all too well. Nothing in him wanted to go. But neither did he want Cait going there alone. There was something wrong with that place. Something *off*.

"Please?" she said again. The word hit Charlie's resolve like a torpedo. In that moment, he remembered the versions of his past selves. He remembered the person who would always help someone in need. The person who always puts others first. That's all he'd ever wanted. To help people. And here stood Cait, a person who needed help. What was Charlie not to offer his help?

Swallowing the growing knot welling up inside him, he decided that Cait's need outweighed his own.

"Okay," he said, feeling tired but burgeoned with a strange sense of purpose.

Cait didn't look pleased by his response, nor did she jump with any sort of ecstatic joy. The look on her face spoke of nothing but a deep thankfulness. She knew she was asking too much of Charlie. She knew, somehow, that this would cause an immense amount of grief for him. Thankfulness welled up in her. She only hoped at some point she could make it up to him.

"Where to?"

"I'll show you."

He turned then, and she followed him up 3rd Street—in the one direction Charlie's insides were screaming at him not to go.

Eleven

A fearful silence overtook the laboratory when Mr. Blackwell exited the elevator and made his way to the observation room. His pace was quick, but still the moments lingered on forever.

"Mr. Blackwell, sir?" Dr. Grenier's words spilled out, mumbling, unsure of what to expect. "W-wonderful to have you h-here."

Mr. Blackwell's response ignored the fact that anyone else was there.

"When can we begin? Are we ready?"

To his shame, Dr. Grenier took a deep gulp and cowered at the questions. The man before him was a danger; or so he thought. A shadow of the man he respected. A danger to everyone present. To the project. Everything.

An urge built in the doctor to put an end to it. But he didn't follow through. He couldn't. His actions, too trained.

Instead of shutting it down—or standing up to this madman—he turned, facing the glass, and fell to obedience.

"Right away, sir."

"Good. Let us waste no more time."

The room gasped and grew quiet, as if something had knocked the wind out of everyone present—everyone except for Mr. Blackwell.

Dr. Grenier turned to his men, all of whom shared the same blank expression. At his nod, everyone went to work. Not for the looming presence hanging over them that struck fear. They worked for the brightness that lived and worked with them day by day. For the man they trusted. The man who knew them.

It was a procession as they went about their preparations, symphonic in its rhythm.

The doctor slid the main lever into place, and each man twisted their corresponding knobs and spun their dials. The surrounding walls came to life; engines turned beyond their view, and the piercing hisses of otherworldly fumes flowed.

Mr. Blackwell's eyes gleamed with a rueful and horrid excitement.

Even the others couldn't help their hopeful excitement.

All save Dr. Grenier, who'd never felt so low in all his life.

The wall behind the chamber slid open and, once more, another helpless subject collapsed forward; thrust from the invasive dark into the cell, screaming.

Dr. Grenier looked back and forth between this poor man and the man he'd once been proud to call his leader. The last dregs of his humanity tugged at his withered conscience. His heart hurt, but he was unsure of what to do.

Mr. Blackwell took another two eager steps forward and placed his hands on the glass before him. No man stood before him; helpless or not. He saw a nameless test subject, a path to triumph. *His* own path. His own rightful place etched into the cosmos. Victory at any cost. This thrilled him more than anything; his heartbeat faster as a comforting warmth flooded through him.

Everyone else stood silent and eager, each caught somewhere on the spectrum between these opposing men.

The subject himself slashed his arms back and forth against the glass. Tears flooded out from the corners of his eyes and his screams echoed off the inside of the glass, causing them to seem fuller and more robust.

All the while, the putrid fumes flowed, filling the chamber. This man's prison. Soon, they would envelop his entire body and he would disappear.

———

"Here it is," Charlie said, almost daunted. His shoulders sagged, having grown heavy, and his thoughts were thick with worry. The lingering agitation returned to him, becoming sturdier with each step he took. Charlie did his best to suppress its onset in front of Cait. He was thankful that her own worried preoccupation prevented her from noticing him at first.

Cait looked back and forth, confused.

"Here?" She looked back at Charlie. "I don't get it. These are just apartment buildings."

Charlie looked around as well, confused. Then swooned and collapsed forward where he'd stood.

He hadn't the time to consider it.

Cait dove toward him, reaching out and catching his arm. "Charlie!"

He caught himself somewhat, too, before falling.

It was then Cait looked at Charlie—a *proper* look—and saw his state.

She'd asked too much of him, she thought. In frustration, she cursed her selfishness for dragging him along. He might've needed a hospital more than just a good night's sleep.

"Jesus, Charlie. Are you okay?"

Leaning down, he blinked several times, attempting to clear his vision. Then he looked up at her, the pressure building all around him. It was so similar to last time; that thought itself ratcheting his fear.

Even Cait sensed something else, pulling her attention from Charlie. Whatever it was, things were amiss. It didn't fit this neo-urban landscape. So strange and surreal.

In the commotion, Cait failed to catch sight of a group of men standing on the opposite street, each wearing thick winter jackets and smoking cigarettes. When she noticed their quiet stares, she held her breath. Reaching out, she took hold of Charlie, as if to protect him from their not-so-subtle curiosity.

"Charlie?" she pressed. He'd yet to answer her from before.

His awareness was growing fainter and fainter; the pull in him was pulsing and building. He was much too concerned with his rising heart rate and the involuntary flexing of what remained of his muscles.

Vague thoughts penetrated the moment, sending him haunting reminders he shouldn't have gone back to that spot. It was too late, though. He was there. Done.

Worry spiked, mounting itself, emboldened by the flood of fear coursing through him and the debilitating lack of sleep. He knew what was coming; that any second, he'd slip into that free fall and lose himself once more.

Dizziness gathered itself within him, causing him to stumble again.

If Cait hadn't still been holding his arm, he would have tumbled over.

"Charlie! Shit. Are you–Are you alright?"

Again, he made no response, but his face scrunched up in pain.

Cait couldn't take her eyes away from his half-shaking

body. His safety seemed to be taking the most immediate precedence in the case.

"Charlie? Charlie, can you hear me?"

She circled around to face him and spoke slow and direct.

Cait felt torn. Looking around, she said, "Look, I can... I *should* get you back, okay? You need to rest."

For several long seconds, Charlie stood, rigid and shaking; Cait's mind went blank, at a loss for solutions.

At last, something in him settled. Cait sensed it too; like some far-away force let go. But what was it? She'd seen nothing like this.

As if a wave had curled over, crashed, and settled itself upon the shore, Charlie's eyes opened with a slow and strained movement.

"C-Cait?"

"Charlie! Wh–what happened? What's wrong?"

"I-I dunno. I'm–"

He couldn't finish his thought. The physical impact of his lack of sleep was overtaking him.

"It's okay, Charlie. I'm going to get you out of here, okay?"

Keeping quiet, he nodded he understood. Something of a smile worked to form itself upon him.

"It's okay, Charlie," Cait said, more of a reminder to herself. "It's gonna be okay. I'm gonna get you back. Okay?" She paused and looked back and forth. "I'll come back alone, check things out."

Charlie stood up at that, as much as he could manage, somewhat in shock. He tried to shake his head and, at last, could expel a weathered mumble.

"N-n-no."

Cait took him over her shoulder and turning walked him to the sidewalk.

"What do you mean?"

Clearing his throat, Charlie said, "... can't let you go in there... alone."

A flood of warmth struck her. She found herself thankful for the sentiment, but knew Charlie was in no shape to assist her, and neither could she wait.

"It's okay, Charlie. I'll be alright. Let's just get you back–"

A bullish voice erupted behind her, cutting her off.

"Who the fuck are *you*?"

Cait swung around—never letting go of Charlie—to find several men surrounding them. The same men from the corner before. Three of them with pistols at their sides.

Cait shifted where she stood, positioning herself somewhat in front of Charlie. She grew both more fearful and more determined.

"Say," said the same voice. "Isn't this the partner of that other cop we caught snooping around? Never learn, do they?"

What? Cait thought. Her head cocked to the side as her stomach squirmed. She was about to address him when he cut back in.

"And from what we've heard, right? She ain't even a cop no more." He looked right at Cait then. "Are you? You're all alone out here, except for this lump of–" the man stopped, somewhat shocked. "Is this the kid from last night?"

The other looked up, squinting.

"Looks like 'im," one of them said.

The other nodded his head in agreement.

A spike of fear shot up and pierced Cait. She didn't want Charlie involved. At *all*!

She took deep breaths to project a calm and collected look; far from how she felt.

Glancing back, she noticed Charlie ebbing back to the real world again.

"Cai–"

She cut him off in a sharp whisper.

"Shh, Charlie. Don't talk right now."

The first man chimed up again.

"What the fuck are you two doing here, anyway?"

The man's voice had somehow grown even more gruff and stern.

Cait made no move to respond.

Raising his pistol up at Cait, the man posed the question again.

"*What* are you doing here?"

Cait couldn't believe it. It was broad daylight in the middle of a residential area. That level of audacity was terrifying. She leaned in, held Charlie closer, and said nothing.

"Fuck it," the man said, keeping the pistol raised. "Grab 'em. Let's see if they'll answer to *him*."

The other men stood there for a second in hesitant alarm.

"I said grab 'em!"

The men scrambled forward at the burst, a pack of wolves circling in on their prey.

Cait sucked in a breath and held tight to Charlie, even closer than before. She wouldn't let him go. For the slightest of moments, her hand moved toward her own pistol, but she knew better. They would've gunned her down before she got a shot off. There was no use fighting; *then*, at least.

The men drew themselves around them.

For reasons Charlie couldn't understand, he was growing more conscious of the moment. Looking up, he flailed; an odd sense of strength shot through him.

"Cait—"

But it was too late. For them both.

The last thing either of them remembered were arms rising and coming down onto them, quick and hard. Then everything went dark. Neither of them heard or felt the sounds of them being lifted from the ground and dragged inside those strange and ominous triune towers.

———

"This had better work," Mr. Blackwell said, in a low, deriding bark. "For the sake of everyone here."

Dr. Grenier choked over his incoming breath and looked anywhere but in the man's direction, whose presence loomed over the entire operation. Neither would he look to the chamber, then half-filled with the sickly and putrid fumes.

Unchanged for the moment, the subject wailed. Though his screams settled some. The plaintive banging of his fists against the glass weakened; he was giving in as the situation sunk in around him. The futility of fighting. That there was nothing he could do to stop it; no one would come to rescue him.

Mr. Blackwell's cutting voice broke the observation room's quiet, startling most.

"Vitals?"

He spoke with an almost pained nonchalance—especially given the moment.

Dr. Grenier nodded to the man next to him, who muttered his response. "Stable, sir."

The expression on Mr. Blackwell's face settled somewhat.

The room was electric. The anticipation was palpable. Everyone save Dr. Grenier held tight to their longing for hope of what might be.

Mr. Blackwell leaned in as far as he could to the observation glass, which fogged up from his whispered breath. "I feel it, Doctor... I feel our triumph is near at hand." His eyes lit up in a wild and untamed frenzy. Dr. Grenier knew he would stop at nothing to achieve his ends.

The doctor's insides seemed to shatter; his ribcage acting as a vessel for the shards of organs that used to feel whole.

Looking up at their leader, he wasn't sure he wanted to succeed anymore.

Cait came to, gasping for breath, her mind addled with a headache. Dizziness came at her from all sides; that and confusion from the abrupt change of scenery. She jumped.

Once she realized the musty ceiling and stone walls had replaced the sky and streets, Cait reeled around, desperate to know that Charlie was okay.

He was there, lying still on the floor next to her.

She kneeled down next to him. The only light being the hallway's faint fluorescent glow; creeping in from the cracked door.

There was no natural light at all. No windows. Not even a bulb in the room.

Cait leaned toward Charlie, nudging him and whispering.

"Charlie? Can you hear me?"

He didn't budge.

She whispered again, shaking him a bit.

"Charlie?"

Voices came in, gentle echoes from outside the door.

Cait looked up, squinting. Hoping for a glimpse into the hall. She couldn't see much.

Accompanying the voices were a series of boot scrapes and taps.

Cait listened, trying to put the pieces together.

Her heart raced. She had to find a way out. She had to. That much, she thought, she owed Charlie. In her mind, it was her fault he was there.

She spoke his name a little louder, nudging him harder with each word.

"Charlie? Charlie!" She shook him. "Charlie, wake up! Wake up! We gotta—"

And he moaned, causing to her to wait.

She went to say his name again, but someone cut her off.

"Char—"

"Well," said a coarse and familiar voice. It was the man from outside. "Look who's awake."

Cait looked up; her anger burned.

Stay calm, she told herself as worry grew inside her. *Stay focused.*

His silhouette in the doorway bored into her mind. An image she wouldn't long forget.

Cait knew she had to project the strength to fend them off. Then she thought of Scott, and her strength faltered. She wondered if this was where they kept him. She wondered what sort of fight he'd put up and dwelled on how alone he'd been at the end. She wondered what he'd say to her if he were there.

Think, boss. What d'ya do next? he would say.

A word came to her then, a word Scott had spoken to her countless times before. It was a reminder Cait had often needed... still needed.

Patience, he would always say to her. *A good detective's patient. They let others make the mistake and then they make their move.*

A fragile hope welled up in Cait. It wasn't much, but enough. She'd have to wait it out; see what would come.

"Oh, don't worry, love," said the silhouette in the doorway. The tone in his voice at that last word filled Cait with disgust. "*He'll* be down to see you soon."

Gritting herself to show no sign of letting up, Cait kept on staring the man down. Beneath that veneer, she couldn't help but wonder who *he* was and what he wanted with Charlie and herself.

———

"Vitals still holding, sir..." the same technician said again. This time, his voice maintained a sturdy balance despite the level of excitement he attempted to hold back.

"And the process, Doctor? Compared to previous attempt–"

"Further than all subjects before except—"

"It's working," Mr. Blackwell broke in again. "It's–It's *actually* going to work!"

Both men couldn't help being swept up in the building excitement. Even Dr. Grenier couldn't help the giddy smile stretching itself out across his face. Yet, one question—one word—kept swirling itself about his mind: *How?* He couldn't fathom *how* it was working again.

The man's wretched screams tore through the hum of the machines, and the echoes of his body's transformation chimed: bones and muscles breaking down to reform themselves into their new horrid shape.

Mr. Blackwell's expression shifted somewhat at the sounds. A hint of worry appeared in the corner of his eyes and his smile waned somewhat.

"This seems very... very rapid, Doctor," he said, desperate to hide his own sense of awe and misunderstanding. "Is this... *normal*?"

"There's nothing normal about any of this, sir... but..." The Doctor couldn't help but let his excitement flow. "... but this? *This* is incredible... unprecedented, sir." He glanced down at the screens. "Even compared to last time..." He hesitated. "... but *why*?"

These last words he spoke in hushed overtones to himself.

Mr. Blackwell shot a glance over to the lead scientist. A brief flash of frustration rested upon his brow.

"But it is working?" His tone deemphasized the question, an attempt to hide his own shock. That even he might not have believed it would work. Something he couldn't afford to let others see.

"Yes... sir," said the doctor, in awe. It was now he who couldn't tear his eyes away from the procedure. "It's... working."

The subject's voice shot out again, a terrible yell induced by a horrible domino of cracking bones. Nearing its end, the shriek gave way to a shrill, inhuman cry, and *something* large slammed up against the chamber glass. Not an arm or a hand. It wasn't human at all. Long and reaching, uninhibited by the structure bones would provide. Its membrane pulsed, a similar hue to the filth and gaseous fumes that swirled around it. Covered in some slimy residue, it appeared as if it had reached up out of a strange, murky pool. From some faraway swampland, well beyond the normal haunts of man.

It screamed again before peeling its appendage back off the glass. Like a tidal wave being rewound, moving in reverse, it filled each man present with wild bouts of both thrill and fear.

Mr. Blackwell was standing there in awe, at the very precipice of what he deemed his triumph, when the lab door burst open behind him.

"Sir! We've—" The man in question stopped as he caught the slightest glimpse of something almost slithering on the gas-filled chamber's glass. "What the hell..."

Mr. Blackwell swung around to find the member of the security team. His mess of clothes and dark jeans and jacket were quite the contrast to the sterile lab and its normal patrons.

"What—" Mr. Blackwell said, constrained by his rising fury. "Who–Who the hell are you? Who let you in here?"

In fear, this intruder leaped where he stood. Then found himself unable to peel himself away from his present position. Or away from *what* he'd found. His mind seized; unsure how to reconcile what he could and couldn't see beyond the glass.

The screams were clear enough, though, and would haunt him forevermore, cutting through the defenseless silence.

The man found he couldn't speak.

"God dammit!" Mr. Blackwell boomed.

Everyone else stood in fearful awe, wondering where this intrusion would lead.

"No one outside lab personnel's allowed in *here*. Ever! What is it?"

Still, the man did not speak.

Mr. Blackwell strode up to him and stood just before him, speaking through gritted teeth.

"What... is... it?"

With his view blocked, the man shook himself back to his conceived reality and Mr. Blackwell came into focus.

"Um... sir... it's–"

"It's what? God dammit, speak!"

"We found something... *someone*?"

"What... who?"

"Another cop... and some... some kid."

"When?" A worried look now replaced the one of anger on Mr. Blackwell. "Where?"

"Just now, sir... Outside the complex."

Mr. Blackwell's expression morphed, juggling too much at once.

The intruder chimed in once more.

"I was told you'd want to see them, sir. It just... seems urgent, given... well... everything that's going on."

"Everything, huh?" Mr. Blackwell's expression flooded with fury. "What do you know about *everything*?"

The man dropped his chin and his glance fell to the tiles on the floor.

"Unbelievable," Mr. Blackwell said to himself. Then turned back to the intruder. "Come here."

In fearful stumbles, he did what he was told.

Mr. Blackwell pointed.

"You see that?"

Everyone looked up at whatever was squirming from behind the gas-filled chamber. Whatever stood hidden behind the fumes, its screams lessened, as if calming.

The man nodded.

Mr. Blackwell turned to his lead technician.

"Dr. Grenier?"

"Yes, sir?"

"Is the procedure almost finished?"

The doctor looked down at his monitors.

"Yes, sir. And still stable."

"Good. Now, son," said Mr. Blackwell, placing his attention once again on the member of his security team. "*You* were not supposed to see this. No one outside this room, even. So," he paused. "The question becomes: *What* do we do with you?"

The man went stiff with terror.

"*No one* can know about this."

Mr. Blackwell looked around the room; making eye contact with each man present before returning to the man standing stiff in front of him.

"*No one.* Is that clear?"

The man cowered.

"I-I won't tell anyone."

"I know you won't."

Mr. Blackwell reached into his jacket, pulled out a pistol, raised his hand, and pulled the trigger.

The man collapsed onto the floor; a splattering of blood sprayed across the white tile.

The room went still with shock. Its only sound was the echoing of the blast bouncing off each wall.

A monstrous screech rang out, cutting beneath it; more controlled this time. More contained.

Dr. Grenier leaped back in terror. Everyone else froze, and Mr. Blackwell's eyes widened once again. That fire in him had returned, unsettling everyone else around him.

"Doctor?" Mr. Blackwell said.

"Yes, sir?"

"Is this completed here?"

"Yes, sir. A second successful test."

"Good. Prep the next subject. I want to know why it worked and see that we can replicate it. Do you understand?"

"Yes, sir."

Mr. Blackwell paused for a second, losing himself in the rhythmic swells of the small chamber's fumes.

"And Doctor?"

"Yes, sir?"

"Have your men clean up this mess. I'm going to go down and check on our new guests."

"Very well, sir. Right away."

"Good."

With that, Mr. Blackwell turned. He made his way to the elevator, feeling he'd reaffirmed his grip on the situation. They were back on track, he mused; perhaps it might work out, after all.

As he disappeared into the elevator, the newly formed creature let loose another violent and raucous roar. It filled the men with terror, but as the elevator's doors were closing, one could have seen that it only made Mr. Blackwell's grin stretch further.

The elevator doors closed, and the other technicians all looked at Dr. Grenier. To see what he would do.

He took a deep breath before turning to his men.

"You heard him. Let's get this mess cleaned up. Then get back to it."

Everybody went to work.

Charlie reeled and shot up from the floor, his eyes stretched open almost too wide. He couldn't steady his breathing. He lay there, charged and alert. As if a bolt of lightning had struck him, awakening something bold within. The force of something beyond him flowed through the very fibers of his being.

Cait burst out.

"Charlie!"

He went to speak but found himself unable. Too preoccupied by what he felt surging through him.

Catching a brief sight of Cait's worried look, he ventured to call out to her but still couldn't. The room. Their surroundings. It all seemed so far away.

His mind drifted; to that far-off place; with those *same* feelings returning; feelings he didn't quite understand, but knew from before.

Cait faded from view as he shook. Remnant echoes of her voice called out to him, then disappeared.

Cait grew more frantic, but equal in determination.

"Charlie? Charlie! What's wrong?" She glared up as both guards entered the room. "What the hell is going on? What's wrong with him?"

Both men stood with blank stares.

"I-I dunno," one of them said.

"Can you... Do something!" She flailed, unsure herself what to do.

At that moment, Charlie screamed. It was a horrid and fear-filled screech. Inhuman. It pierced and hung in the air, unsettling every bit of dust that had gone untouched.

Cait and both men stood there, helpless. No one knew what was going on. No one knew what to do.

"Charlie!" She shook him, hoping to wake him from his deep and terrible sleep. "Charlie! Charlie!"

After a time of him not responding, Cait slid into a monotonous whisper, quiet and desperate. For herself more than him.

"It's gonna be okay, Charlie... It's gonna be okay..."

The two guards stood there, perplexed. Neither knew what was happening. Their hands hovered over their pistol handles just in case.

Without warning, Charlie's body went rigid; it froze, as if left outside for months in the unforgiving cold, shaking with increased meter and intensity.

"Charlie?" Cait shouted out to him again. "Come on, Charlie. Wake up!"

Charlie only shook more, with greater violence and intensity; his face scrunched, compressing inward, fighting off agonizing pain. Then, he screamed; it started deep and slow but grew with quickness. It built as if by some otherworldly force into a piercing, painful wail; stretching out, moment to moment; filling even the darkest corners of those shadows.

Cait and the guards all backed away in fear. None of them had ever seen anything like it.

Charlie's body shot forward then stretched out across the floor and shook back and forth, convulsing. It seemed he could've burst at any moment.

Cait wondered what could happen to him, what they had stumbled upon. Looking to the man nearest to her, never losing that determined glare, she exploded.

"What the fuck is going on? What's—what's wrong with him?"

Each man stood wearing the same blank expression somewhere between fear and awe. They shook their heads, never removing their eyes from Charlie.

Charlie's yell built and built, his body shaking even more wildly than before. Cait felt helpless, almost as helpless as when she'd stumbled upon Scott's body before. But intention drove her now. Even though they had the guns, Cait turned to the guards, screaming.

"You better figure out what the hell's going on—"

And then it stopped.

Charlie's screaming, his body shaking back and forth, everything came to an alarming halt.

Her own fear combined with the guard's fear settled onto Cait's shoulders. An eerie quiet once more pierced the space. The silence she found more unsettling than Charlie's wails.

She took a breath, then looked down at Charlie's body. It was limp, still lying flat.

The guards looked at each other, neither saying a word.

At last, Cait gave a gentle press.

"Charlie?"

But Charlie gave no response. As still and silent as a corpse, if it weren't for his pained expression, she would've believed him already dead. A worry she hadn't even realized had crept into her veins.

She took a timid step closer to him, then another. Then kneeled beside him. He looked to be breathing, though it was faint. He was alive, she thought. For the time being. Cait took what relief she could.

Reaching out, she wanted to call to Charlie, but a strange noise cut her off. The familiar clanging of an elevator sounded down the hall.

Cait shot up straight and hovered over Charlie, holding her breath. Keeping as quiet as she could.

"He's here," one guard said, both smiling. Each looked down upon their victims.

Cait's heart beat a little faster, as one recursive thought kept running through her: protect Charlie no matter what.

The elevator doors opened and they could hear footsteps tapping their way towards them, growing louder with each step.

Both guards repositioned their pistols in front of them and walked to either side of the door, ready. Then, the door burst open, and each guard stood up, standing as tall as they could.

"These are the two in question?" A quiet voice chimed. A voice void of any genuine feeling, let alone warmth or compassion.

Cait's heart raced.

The guard nearest the man nodded.

Stepping into the room, causing the light to illuminate his silhouette all the more finely, he directed his attention first to Cait, making the mistake in assuming that the man laid out on the dirty floor was inconsequential.

Cait was doing her best to maintain whatever exterior of strength she could. It didn't feel like much, but even she was unaware of how deep her anger ran; or how she wore it. She wanted them to know that she wouldn't give in.

The man standing over them grinned. In the lack of light, he appeared wicked and cruel. Not far off from the truth.

"You've interrupted something of great importance, *miss*," the man said. "And we don't take kindly to interruptions."

Cait let her glare speak for itself.

"And for what?" he pressed her. "What could you have hoped to accomplish, coming here alone?" He was near laughter and stepped forward again. The sharpness of his suit and hair surprised Cait.

The man drew closer still. Cait's only thought was to keep his attention on her instead of Charlie. Her stare grew sharp as she shifted her position to put herself between Charlie and the imposing man who stood before them.

Looking down at Cait and Charlie, a smug smile to formed on his face.

"Very bold... but *stupid*."

He zeroed in on Cait.

"I am..." he said, "... Weyland Blackwell."

Both guards straightened, shocked at the revelation. They'd always been told, no matter what, to never mention him by name.

Cait seemed unaffected; her sole concern was to keep the man's focus on her.

"And you are?" he pressed, approaching what could've passed for politeness.

Still, Cait refused to speak.

"Come now," he ventured again, pressing a harder. "It's impolite not to reciprocate."

Cait didn't budge. Not even sure why; only that she didn't want to give in to his threats.

At that point, Mr. Blackwell grew angry. Whatever facade of nicety he'd constructed fell away, and he pressed her a third time about who she was.

"I asked you who you are, dammit! What are you doing here? What do you think you've found?"

He swept in closer, crouching down near the cement. Drops of spittle from his last few words sprayed out, landing on Cait's hair as she ducked away.

Recovering, Cait worked to reassert her defiant position to the man who'd taken a stark and wild turn. The flare in his eyes now seemed contrary to his fashionable sense. He seemed off kilter and without balance, telling Cait that she was winning.

Next, he stood and turned his back to her. Snapping his fingers and pointing behind him, he signaled to the guard who'd been standing on his right. The man walked forward, reached into his jacket for his pistol, and swung, striking Cait across her jaw.

She let out a yelp and collapsed to the ground, leaving Charlie unguarded. Blood flew across the room, splattering the floor and wall. The burst shocked her and her split lip seared with pain, but she worked to hold her ground by pushing herself back up, attempting to cut off his view from Charlie, whether conscious of the fact.

"I'll ask you *one... more... time*," Mr. Blackwell said. His tone was dark, filled with enmity. "Who are you? And why did you come here?"

Cait's entire head throbbed. A shattering pain shot from her jaw down through her neck. She looked up, and in defiance shook her head.

Mr. Blackwell's eyes burned with fiery disappointment. He signaled to the guard.

"Again."

"It won't matter," Cait said, her defiance causing Mr. Blackwell to cock his head, sizing her up. He noted her posture and her position, then smiled.

"Alright." And to the guard he said, "Bring the *boy* forward."

Cait's stomach clenched.

"Shoot *him*."

Her mind spun. She had to do something, but what? Anything to prevent Charlie from being injured.

Her body shook as she screamed out.

"No!"

Mr. Blackwell's grin grew wide as her yelps rang out.

"Please... please don't!"

He lived for these simple lines of power.

"It's quite simple, young lady," he said to her. "You tell me what I want to know, and you delay your impending doom."

Cait took a deep breath.

"Tell me who you are. What you know. And who else knows it. Then, we'll get *it* over with quick. Fast. *Humane*. No pain." A wicked grin formed then. "Keep holding out, and... I don't think you quite understand the various hells we could put you through." At the last word, he smiled.

For one prone to resilience and strength, the shivers brought on by Mr. Blackwell's tone of voice were a new, unsettling experience for Cait.

Her countenance fell. Her chin rubbed against the front of her shirt, and Cait gave an exhale that spoke of the very ground eroding beneath you as you walked. Keeping in front of Charlie and making sure not to make eye contact as she spoke, she said, "Detective Cait Lane, Portland Police Department."

Mr. Blackwell's eyebrows rose with delight. "Detective La —" he said, unable to contain a burst of laughter. "Ah, yes. I believe they warned me about you, *detective*. Though you're not a detective anymore, are you?"

Cait looked up, shocked. It had only been hours since that had taken place. They couldn't even have filed the paperwork yet. How did this man know that?

Sensing both her dismay and her confusion, Mr. Blackwell leaned in to speak again. In a low drawl, he said, "Not to worry, my dear. *We* have people everywhere... who tell us *everything*." His smile curled on the ends, like they had placed wicked little rivulets on the corners of his mouth. "One of our many industrious informers may have mentioned that they relieved you from duty just this morning, no?"

For a moment, Cait's thoughts seemed to be stranded, just beyond reach. Before she could even gather herself, the man continued.

"Word is you have quite the temper on you, *Miss* Lane, and that this morning, you might have overstepped your bounds."

Cait worked to stay calm and still as he provoked her.

"Not too different from that partner of yours, I imagine." He could feel by the subtle shift in Cait's posture he'd struck a chord.

Cait's expression grew grave as even the mention of Scott,

let alone by this man, revived the anger she'd been feeling. Focus set in.

"It was a pity what happened to him." Mr. Blackwell spoke with a feigned contrition. In what Cait's anger took for a false and shallow empathy. "I understand he was a good man." He watched the fury wash over Cait just to stir the fire more. "You know, he needn't have died. Especially in such a way. He should have just waited like the rest of you."

Cait straightened her posture at this, as well as grew more confused.

"Neither did you need to die, or this whelp you brought with you."

Just then, Charlie's moans became more apparent. Cait worried she wouldn't be able to shield him for much longer.

"Don't talk to him!" she blasted.

Mr. Blackwell stood up and lifted his hands into the air, laughing off Cait's outburst.

"Ah! There's that golden temper. That's the spirit!"

She was shaking by then.

"So, what? You and your friend, here, followed the bread-crumbs... you came here to, *what*? Storm the building?"

"You won't win," she said to him with an assured conviction.

Mr. Blackwell laughed.

"You think so?"

He then squatted down to where he could see Cait eye to eye. She leaned away as he whispered.

"Darling, we have already won. *I* have already won. You don't understand what's going on," he said, working to hold back that arrogant smile. "But you will, eventually."

"Who is this poor person you've brought along with you, anyway?"

He stood up, turning away from them.

"Stay away from him!"

He swung back to face her.

"Ah, testy, aren't we, *detective?*"

Cait's hands clenched into fists. She wanted to leap out; to unleash her fury upon him; but she knew the guards wouldn't let her.

"Just like your partner," he mocked.

Cait almost sprung.

"You know, if you're not careful, it'll lead you to the same fate, I'm afraid."

Charlie's moans echoed out into the stale open space around them. Mr. Blackwell looked around, in comic awe of what he saw. "In all seriousness, who is this *person* you saw fit to bring along? I mean, where did you find him? He doesn't look like much."

Angry tears built up behind Cait's stone and near featureless expression.

"Leave him alone," she said. It was a weak demand. So pained, she looked away in order to keep speaking. "H-he wasn't s-supposed to… to be here. They grabbed us before I could get him away—It was…"

And she stopped.

Mr. Blackwell focused in, trying for a clearer picture of the boy in the dark. He looked at Cait as he spoke but pointed to *the boy.*

"But who is *he?*"

The room grew heavy; he looked at Charlie then back.

"I get *you* and why you're here. But our intelligence shows this boy's not a police officer. How's he involved, though? *Really?* I'm quite intrigued about who he is and why he's here."

The guard on Mr. Blackwell's left squirmed a bit and fidgeted with his pistol before standing up straight again.

Cait said nothing. Not looking up for a time, as if her own attention would detract the man from his goals.

Mr. Blackwell leaned in closer. He signaled for the guard to come forward again.

"Who... is... the... *boy*?"

His tone showed it would be the last time he would ask the question.

Noticing the guards stepping closer, pistol in hand, Cait leaned away, lifting her hand to protect herself. She stayed silent, only shaking her head in her desire not to share.

The more he pressed, the more resistant Cait became. Only proving to increase Mr. Blackwell's desire to know who Charlie was. He did not know the gift that sat before him. No idea of the link Charlie had already been to their success. But the more Cait held her ground, the more apparent something became in Mr. Blackwell: this boy was important.

Mr. Blackwell erupted.

"Who is he, dammit!"

Cait shuddered.

"I-I... I can't—"

Mr. Blackwell was about to yell out again when the guard interrupted him.

"Sir?"

Mr. Blackwell spun on the man, infuriated by the break in protocol.

"*What*, damn you?"

The edge to his voice was sharp.

"Um... this is the same kid, who..."

"Who what? God dammit, just say it!"

The man continued to stutter.

"What is it, man? Speak!"

"The other night... I mean, *last* night..."

"Speak dammit! Out with it!"

"We—we ran into *this* guy..."

"What do you mean ran into?"

"With the van–"

"You what—you *hit* him with the van last night? When you had Det—"

Cait shot him a glare he saw out of the corner of his eye, stopping him dead. A wave of realization flowed over him.

Everyone there stopped and hung upon that moment in wonder.

"Wait," Mr. Blackwell said, holding steady to think. "Last night, you say?" He was calmer. His tone more thoughtful a wicked brightness gleamed within his eyes.

The guard nodded.

Mr. Blackwell looked back toward Charlie.

"And he's here *now*, again, and..."

No one knew what Mr. Blackwell was guessing at. Even he wasn't sure.

"What time last night?"

The man squinted, trying to remember.

"Uh, a little after midnight, I think."

"You think? Well, are you sure? Are you certain?" Mr. Blackwell's hands shook in a frenzy as he pressed for details.

The guard, flustered by the stream of questions, stammered back.

"Yeah... um... yeah, yeah. I-I'm sure."

Mr. Blackwell fired a glance back to where Charlie lay, unable of much beyond his writhing squirms. He was quite taken by *something*, which seemed to confirm whatever suspicion Mr. Blackwell held.

"And you found him outside the building today?"

"Yes, sir."

"When?"

"Twenty minutes ago, sir."

"Twenty minutes..." Mr. Blackwell mused, thinking more to himself. "It can't... *be*..."

As he sidestepped Cait, she moved to cut him off. Mr.

Blackwell did not escape her; the guards stepped in and grabbed her.

He grinned as words fired out of Cait's mouth, blistering.

"No! N-no—" Near hyperventilating. "Stop it! He's innocent! He knows nothing!"

Mr. Blackwell leaned in close. "Is he now?" He looked down to catch a better glimpse of Charlie's features; still, the shadows prevented him from confirming his restless hopes.

"Is it *really* you?" he mused again.

Then Cait who cried out.

"Leave him alone, dammit! Leave him be!"

With a grace and calm that had disintegrated since the conversation began, Mr. Blackwell turned once more to Cait and asked one simple, blunt question.

"What is his name?"

Cait froze and stopped struggling. She couldn't understand who Charlie was to these men. He was a nobody. He shouldn't matter. Why did this man care at all?

"What is his name?" Mr. Blackwell put forth again.

Cait shook her head to show she wouldn't talk, and Mr. Blackwell showed to the guards again.

One reached up to grab Cait's arms—his grip harsh—and held them behind her back.

She fought back and kicked, but it was no use.

The other stepped up before her, raising his pistol once again.

Cait's insides flinched, but she could show no fear.

"I'll ask again," Mr. Blackwell said, each word almost levitating there in the musky damp. "What... is... the... boy's... name?"

Cait gritted her jaw for what she knew would come and shook her head.

Mr. Blackwell nodded as the pistol came down hard across Cait's head.

A sharp cry of pain fired out of her, but she stayed put as the guards held her.

Mr. Blackwell's cheeks flushed with an angry crimson hue. He lost it again.

"Who is he, god dammit? What's his name?"

Near tears, Cait shook her head again, and again Mr. Blackwell called upon his guard.

The second hit came harder. A splatter of blood flew from her mouth onto the ground, where it lay still and quiet.

Cait couldn't help it—she cried. But she knew it wasn't a sign of giving in. She held to the strength she needed to press on.

Mr. Blackwell nodded to the guard once more, whose pistol-clad hand struck down again.

Again, Cait yelped.

Mr. Blackwell held up his hand to halt the proceedings. Then leaned in looking into her. He thought he could see a falter in the facade she clung to.

She couldn't help but glance back over to Charlie, and Mr. Blackwell smiled.

He himself stepped toward Charlie and picked him up from off the ground.

Charlie groaned, and his head rolled back with the movement.

"N-no..."

Cait struggled to speak at all, confirming Mr. Blackwell's assumption.

Mr. Blackwell signaled for the guard to bring the gun forward. He reached out to grab the pistol and clicked the safety off.

"Now," he said, louder this time. "Let's try this again." He aimed the pistol right at Charlie's head. "Who is this person? And why is he here with you?"

Cait couldn't help it. She'd vowed to keep Charlie safe, so

she caved. Tears fell from her cracked countenance, issuing forth in blurry streams.

"His name is... C-Cha—" She stopped, choking up. "... Charlie."

When the word escaped her at last, her head sunk. The weight of perceived betrayal was too much to bear.

Mr. Blackwell's eyes expanded in a strange and crazed reverie.

"Charlie what?" he said, his voice calm and low.

"West," Cait said. "Charlie... West."

Mr. Blackwell looked back to Charlie. It seemed so impossible to him.

"That's why... That's why it worked. You made it work, Charlie."

Cait understood nothing he was saying, but she sensed the wild shift in the air.

Mr. Blackwell spun where he stood and barked an order to the guard.

"Bring him upstairs with me."

Cait screamed out.

"No! You can't!"

Turning, Mr. Blackwell gave her a glare that might have even pierced the shadows. "You don't seem to understand your situation, *young lady*."

Cait backed off, but with a slight resurgence in the strength she felt.

"You," he said to the guard still holding her, "keep a close watch on this one. We might need her yet."

"Yes, sir."

Before leaving, Mr. Blackwell turned back to Cait once more.

"How much do you *know* about him? *Detective*?" He hesitated, letting it sink in. "Huh? Where he's been? Or what he's done? Hm?"

Cait said nothing.

"Bring the boy, *now*," he said to the guard holding Charlie. The man nodded that he would.

"Come along then," Mr. Blackwell barked as he disappeared into the hallway, followed by Charlie being led by the guard.

To Cait, something was being torn away. She didn't know Charlie well, but this was bad. She couldn't let this happen; what could she do?

Her mind ran blank, but deep down, her purpose was clear. She had to get to Charlie. To get free and get to him. *Somehow*. She had to try.

Too shaken by yet another upending turn of events, Cait knew she needed to gather herself first. Then, she could focus and think. Even those thoughts the guard interrupted.

"Sit the fuck down, a'ight? Now! And don't try noth'n."

It startled her, but for Cait, only proved to awaken that propulsive drive within her. The more anger she could channel, the more she could push back. That much she knew.

In the meantime, Cait made her slow way to the icy concrete floor where she would bide her time. She couldn't take too long, though; she needed to move! The *how*, she knew, would come. She needed patience right then. She needed to think.

All the while, one continuous image circled itself through her mind: Charlie in his weak, exhausted state. It only made her more determined.

I'm coming, Charlie, she thought, needing to spur herself on. *I'm coming.*

Twelve

The elevator door opened, and Mr. Blackwell stepped out into his office. The dark cherry wood was a stark contrast to the eerie and discomforting off-white floors of the sub basements.

"Put him in the chair over here. Then leave us," Mr. Blackwell said to the guard.

The man did as he was told.

The entire ride up the elevator, Charlie settled further and further back toward consciousness. He was returning to the world, reluctant though he was given how desperately his body clung to its need for sleep.

Mr. Blackwell watched as he stirred; his body moved in subtle shifts, stretching itself, waking back to the world around it.

Charlie blinked, struggling to take in his surroundings. He could just make out dark wood paneling and the stunted brightness stemming from the wall of windows. A large desk rested before him, of a similar type of wood, where over it stood a looming shadow.

Shivering from the haunting visions that still plagued him, Charlie looked up. At last, garnering a clear picture of the man stood before him.

"Look at you," said Mr. Blackwell, awestruck. "At last..."

Charlie drew back in confusion.

"You know, Charlie, we searched for you. For ages."

Charlie's mind curled back, confused. His brow furrowed. Within him, a desperate hope fluttered that the man's words were some strange, wild mistake. That they were lies, or that he was talking about someone else entirely. Why would they've been searching for him? On the surface, it made little sense; yet, deep down, an odd remembrance lingered. A warning; a long-forgotten truth.

"W-where? *W-what...*" He struggled to start. "What did you do to me? Today and—"

"And yesterday, right?" Mr. Blackwell grew excited. "Yesterday, when you were on the premises, you had a similar fit?"

The man couldn't possibly have known that, Charlie thought.

"Oh, Charlie!" Mr. Blackwell's excitement grew. Standing from the desk, he clasped his hands together. He couldn't help but let himself move about the room. "We have so much to talk about. So much to catch up on. So much to share. Ever since—" He stopped and turned back to where Charlie sat, still in shock. "Well, since what some would call a great tragedy, I suppose. I think of it as the preceding step to our great triumph."

Lost, Charlie just stood there, his head ringing with the deep pangs and echoes of his pain.

"Uh... look... Mister–"

"Blackwell," Mr. Blackwell said, filling in the gap for him. He took several eager steps back over to Charlie to shake his hand. "Forgive me for the improper introductions. I'm Weyland Blackwell of Portland's Sect of The Order."

He spoke as if it should mean something to Charlie, causing a slight shudder to pass through him. It was perplexing, for reasons he couldn't explain. There was *something* about it. It made a strange amount of sense.

Mr. Blackwell continued his eager stare at Charlie, who, in his confusion, wasn't sure what to say.

"It's just baffling," Mr. Blackwell said in a haunting whisper.

Charlie looked up at him again.

"Huh?"

"You," he shrugged. "Here. Now? I mean, no wonder the procedure worked yesterday, then didn't, then worked again today. It's just that—well, we were so sure you were gone, but now..." Mr. Blackwell trailed off, unable to control the excitement rising in him. He couldn't stop himself from grinning. "Now, we'll be able to complete our task, Charlie." He looked up through his hopeful and determined eyes. "With your help, we will at last bring things to an end."

"What things?" Charlie ventured.

After a moment's thought, Mr. Blackwell gave a cryptic reply. "*Everything*, my boy." His expression hung, burdened, overcome by a desperate and solemn quiet.

Charlie sensed the weight and pressure Mr. Blackwell carried; he looked like a man ready to unload whatever excess he'd accumulated. Ready to rupture and burst.

This brought no comfort to Charlie. Quite the opposite. It only added to the weight he himself already felt. Yet, lost to this, a bold nudge struck him. A rarity, and he saw no reason to hold the question back.

"Um..." he began.

Mr. Blackwell looked up again.

"Yes, Charlie?"

"You... You seem to know a lot about me..."

Mr. Blackwell nodded along.

"And... you keep mentioning this... plan?"

"Yes?"

Charlie took a few careful moments to consider his words.

"Look, I don't know what's happening here, but..."

Mr. Blackwell's face reconfigured itself to show his confusion

"All I know is last night..."

Mr. Blackwell watched as Charlie shuddered at the thought.

"... something *really* weird happened."

The older man leaned in closer, burning to understand whatever connection Charlie had.

Charlie grew more tired as he spoke, as if even just thinking about what happened strained him.

"It was so strange," Charlie said.

"Yes?"

"And... there were these flashes... and..."

Mr. Blackwell's expression lit up.

"And what, Charlie?"

Charlie looked up at the man. He seemed almost to understand what Charlie was feeling. As if he were inviting trust, but to Charlie, trust was a weary road.

"Well, they felt like memories, but that's impossible, right?"

"What did you see?"

Charlie froze as the image re-entered his mind. It was everything he'd been trying to avoid. He looked away.

"Look, Charlie, I don't know if we can help you with these memories or dreams or whatever they are, but if you join us together, we can finish what you began in Astoria."

Every alarm within him fired at the word.

What he'd started? Charlie's thoughts somersaulted.

As he remembered, *it* had robbed him of his new life in Astoria. Whatever *it* was. His hopes, stolen, replaced by the guilt-ridden excuse for an existence he'd been living since he woke up in that desolate field of dust. He passed through each day. Through time. Spectating but never engaging. He'd learned to keep a distance. A safe distance. Never moving on.

"What do you mean?"

Mr. Blackwell cocked his head again.

"With what happened, Charlie. I mean, it pained me that Wilkes found you first. Plucked from *my* backyard, at that. But you touched the heavens, son, and that breakthrough, *your* breakthrough, has led to such discoveries. We are on the verge now. With you, we can finish this. Write the last chapter, if you will. Have it all over with. We—" Mr. Blackwell's excitement only grew, but he stopped, surprised by Charlie's blank look. "What's wrong, son?" he pressed.

Still taken by his pained confusion, Charlie shook his head back and forth.

"No, this doesn't make—I-I don't know..."

Mr. Blackwell's whole tone shifted back to one tainted by threads of worry.

"That's why—" He paused. "That's why you came back. Isn't it, Charlie? Last night and today? What makes little sense is why you stayed away. Why didn't you just come to us when you returned? Why didn't you come here? This is your home, Charlie West. Where you belong."

Images fired through Charlie's mind again of the strange library and hand-carved underground tunnels. He saw, again, men in black suits standing like shadows around a fire. The silhouette of the wild-haired man cast over them all, reaching high up onto the library wall.

Charlie shook his head to rid himself of these thoughts.

This wasn't helping. Charlie felt further from the truth than he did before. He grew frustrated and more panic-stricken.

Mr. Blackwell reached out to him.

"Charlie–"

"Don't touch me!" Charlie burst.

Mr. Blackwell pulled his hand back right away, knowing something wasn't right.

"What did Charlie?" He pressed. "What is it that haunts you so?"

Charlie looked away.

"Let *us* help you. We *can* help you."

"I don't even know who the fuck you are, okay?"

Mr. Blackwell stood up.

"I don't know what's what. Okay?" Charlie's breathing grew heavy. "I don't—I don't understand any of this. Any of —what's going on? I don't know what happened. I-I don't—I don't know what *any* of this means, okay? I just know—"

He stopped himself; his thoughts running wild again.

Something dawned on Mr. Blackwell then. He looked at Charlie, seeing the strain resting upon him. The weight of his confusion.

"Charlie, what do you remember about Astoria? About that night?"

Charlie thought about it hard, the images flashing in his mind once more. He pursed his lips and wrenched his eyes shut and spoke.

"*Nothing*," was all he said.

Mr. Blackwell stood there, watching as Charlie's chin lowered. Falling against the zipper of his jacket.

"Interesting," Mr. Blackwell said after a while.

For one long, drawn out moment, neither of them spoke. Then Charlie's voice chimed—frail, too fragile for the cold.

"What did you mean when you said I was gone? Gone where?"

Mr. Blackwell turned back to Charlie again, somewhat stunned. His grave stare at Charlie lingered. "No one thought you lived through Astoria's devastation."

Charlie, taken aback, stood there in awe.

"Even against the odds, we searched for you and found nothing. There was no sign or trace. We monitored your mother's home, watched over the bank, seizing and selling off her goods upon her death, and you were gone."

Both sat there upon this tension. The revelation that Charlie knew far less that he'd expected shocked Mr. Blackwell. This filled Mr. Blackwell with a slight and consequential dread he had to muster what strength he could to push it away.

"We were able, though..." Mr. Blackwell paused, drawing Charlie further in. "... to recover certain artifacts from Astoria's ground zero to use in our research here. We've been so close, Charlie! For months. But it wasn't until last night. When *you* showed up, that we succeeded."

Mr. Blackwell grew giddy as Charlie squirmed in his chair.

"And at last, my boy, with *you*, *we* can move forward."

Charlie sat, aghast, with his jaw wide open.

"What are you talking about? I still don't know what you're doing. O-or how my being here benefits you."

Mr. Blackwell nodded his head up and down as Charlie spoke. An awkward calm settled over him.

"Something I hadn't foreseen, but let's be frank, no one could have predicted your return... but I think we can remedy that."

Mr. Blackwell stood, a renewed vigor in his step.

Charlie stared up at him with that same helpless feeling of being pulled along.

"Come, Charlie," Mr. Blackwell said, making his way toward the elevator once more, a wild grin still plastered on his face. Charlie's anger flared again at not knowing what was going on.

"What? Wait. Where?"

Mr. Blackwell pressed the button on the elevator, and Charlie at last stood up from his chair.

"Where are we going?" Charlie pressed, confused.

"Even if I explained our plan to you, step by step, if you do not know of our purpose, you would never fully grasp the gravity of our goals. So, instead, I think I'll just show you."

"Show me?" Charlie responded. His stomach sank with the ominous and unnerving prospect of what would come.

"Yes, Charlie," Mr. Blackwell said, as his grin grew wider. "Call it your legacy, if you will. One we've worked tirelessly to carry forth."

Charlie's eyes widened as fear spread its way throughout his entire body—a burbling warmth that emanated, desperate to escape, leaving his skin with that horrible feeling that something was crawling underneath it.

The elevator door chimed and slid open.

Mr. Blackwell stood there, gesturing with his arms for Charlie to enter, his smile well-constructed; as if it built, never to fade.

Knowing there was no other choice, Charlie stepped into the elevator. Mr. Blackwell stepped in after him and, when the doors closed, they began their descent.

———

A musty vapor hung in the air where Cait was being held. It spoke of decay. Of the forgotten things of the world.

Even as the darkness tugged at her, Cait pushed. She fought back against the mounting despair, not willing to let herself sink. The more pressure that pushed against her, the more strength she gathered. That was Cait; she fought back. Whatever the adversity was that faced her—which was much because she'd always chosen to live so far from convention— she always met it with equal strength.

Soon after they'd taken Charlie, clarity returned. Her mind focused and her training kicked in. When it did, she considered what she knew. It wasn't much: one guard with her, one with Charlie; and they had taken Charlie to the asshole's office, wherever that was.

It was clear she had no clue what she was up against. Including who these men were. What they wanted. Or how many there were.

Fuck... she thought, in a sharp lament.

Scott's note about Charlie seemed to have proven true, given how enthralled the man became when he figured out who Charlie was. Yet Charlie didn't seem to understand why, either. Cait wondered how that could be.

Dwelling on that was fruitless, so she refocused herself. She put all her energy into what would be productive: getting out. There was only one guard, after all. She could manage that, she knew.

Cait looked for anything that could help. There wasn't much. The room was empty save for a single shelf hanging on the back wall. It was empty as well.

Drawing a blank, she wondered how Scott would push her were he there. He was always so good at leading her to any necessary developments.

Find the facts, boss, she could hear him say. It was something he often said to her when first entering a crime scene. He always followed it up with, *And weigh out your options.*

Cait smiled. It was a fragile gesture, something she hoped to keep clear of the elements to preserve it. She took a deep breath prior to assessing the space around her once again.

Closing her eyes, Cait let her senses reach out to survey the space. Sometimes, what a person saw could distract them from the relevant details. She'd learned that if you can distance yourself from the moment you arrived at a richer, clearer picture of the scene.

Her ability to operate with such sensitivity always impressed Scott. This thought filled her with a comfort, allowing her to further relax, thus enabling a deeper perception. Scott had always pushed her and coached her to hone this ability. She understood each room had a rhythm to it. A voice or tangible feel. She'd learned that if you listened, it would speak to you and spill all of its secrets. Cait hoped to find that voice now.

Breathing in and out, slowing and steadying herself, Cait's focus tightened. She let go, taking in the surrounding data in doing so.

Closing her eyes for a moment, she visualized herself stripping away the layers of murk and distraction. She focused and let her senses reach out. Droplets of water fell, breaking apart, being absorbed into one of several puddles on the floor. A rustling scrape cut through the space. Cait took it in, assimilating it into the growing orchestra of sounds. The scrapes moved back and forth as something's weight shifted. *The guard*, she thought. Then squeaking stretches of leather echoed. *His jacket.*

Even the shadows trembled.

As her focus grew, Cait felt brief glimpses of movement every so often. From out in the hallway. Stale breezes snuck in, filling her with the wildest hopes. Reminding her both of her direction and purpose. That was the way out.

Sitting there on the ground, Cait shifted her body to a more ready position. Her joints were stiff, a result of both the temperature and her inaction.

The cold had reached itself up through the ground and gripped her feet and calves. Its reach then grew—she could feel it in her arms and chest as well. Maybe it was the environment; maybe she was just tired and worn, but it grew difficult to breathe.

She looked back. The guard had his back to her. Staring out into the hall.

To Cait, it seemed stupid of him to take his eyes off her. But... there was a good ten feet between them. He had plenty of time to turn; get a shot off.

How do I get past you? she wondered.

A multitude of ideas flew through her mind. Most of which were far-fetched—things she'd seen in films. Faking sickness. Needing the toilet. She figured the guards' sympathy only went so far. Feigning any sort of helplessness would only prove to worsen her situation, she feared. For one desperate moment, she even considered flirting with him. It might've worked, but she didn't think she could sustain the act in her current state.

Going through every scenario her mind could fathom only made her despair grow.

Always keep to your strengths, rook, she heard Scott's voice say again. It spurred in her a certain comfort and warmth.

My strengths, she thought. Her mind flooded with all the people who'd underestimated her, especially in physical situations.

That could work, she thought. The idea took root and began to form.

With a deep, steadying breath, Cait sat up, readying herself. Careful to keep quiet.

One shoe scraped against the concrete. The sound was nonexistent, but in her mind, plates fell and shattered.

The guard coughed and turned somewhat, causing Cait to freeze. For several moments her lungs refused to take in any air at all, but her heartbeat raced.

The man turned, facing forward once more.

Cait exhaled and put all her weight on her heels to push herself up to standing without making a sound.

Waiting a second to be sure he wasn't about to turn, Cait

hoisted herself up from where she'd been sitting. Her shoes made the slightest of scratching noises against the floor—what Cait was hoping would not happen.

Shit!

Panic rose.

The guard turned, but only his head, not his shoulders. This would work to Cait's advantage.

"Hey!" he called out, then turning his whole body. But it was too late.

Go! Cait yelled to herself as she let the rising anxiety fuel her. She took two bounding leaps and dove low.

The guard had just been raising his pistol when she slammed into him. Aside from the crash of their bodies hitting the cold concrete, the only sound was of his breath leaving him. The pistol fell from his hand, landing not too far from them.

The man wheezed but could not breathe. In a fury to recover, he wrapped his arms around Cait and stood quick, lifting her off the ground.

Shit! She thought, knowing she'd lost the element of surprise.

It was no contest of strength. She'd have to outsmart him. But how?

Struggling to break free, the man gritted his teeth together and issued several grunts as he tried to lift her up over himself to slam her back down onto the hard ground.

Though fleeting, Cait kicked and flailed her legs to throw off his momentum.

Think, Cait! Think! It was difficult, though. Everything was happening so fast.

Then, the man seemed to lose balance, and he fell forward, still holding tight to his prisoner.

Cait landed feet first while the man's weight came forward

on top of her, but he recovered and struggled to pull her upward again.

That's when an idea struck her. Cait tucked her feet up off the ground, going with the momentum of his pull.

As her weight pulled them back down, Cait tucked her feet upward, hoping to get her body as low to the ground as she could. She felt more of a separation between herself and the guard's grip, and her feet touched down again. This time, as the guard's weight was coming down, she fired herself upward again, moving the force of her body against the guard's.

His torso and whole upper body came down hard as Cait's shoulder slammed upward into his neck and jaw. There was a slight crack.

The man choked, releasing his grip, and stumbled to the ground, holding his throat.

Cait looked over to see the man's jaw hanging loose from its joint. Even she cringed as he agonized in pain. Each scream only proving to further fuel the fire.

The next moment was one Cait knew she couldn't lose. She turned and spun, bringing her right foot upward, swift and sharp, where it connected with the man's already fragile jaw. A discomforting crunch echoed, flailing from a somewhat muffled yelp.

The man collapsed to the floor, unconscious—more from pain than the hit itself.

For several moments, Cait just watched the body. Making sure it didn't move or get back up. She had to be ready in case it sprang back to life.

It didn't.

So she stood, panting, adrenaline coursing through her. Looking around, Cait caught sight of the dim shine of hall light reflecting off the pistol barrel.

Hurrying over, she picked it up. Clicking the safety was off, she turned to leave.

Something else struck her, and she turned, walking back to where the guard lay on the floor unconscious. He was breathing, that much she could tell, but it was strained and rough. Other than that, he made no noise. Holding the pistol by the barrel; with the safety on, Cait reached up and brought its handle down—hard—upon the back of his skull.

The crack was severe; she felt it in herself, and his whole body jolted before going still again. The weight of his head came down upon the crooked jaw that caught it, keeping propped at an awkward angle. A large gash formed above his temple, with blood spilling out onto the floor and pooling. Cait showed no sign of shock or remorse.

Only then did the room return to its silent state.

Checking his pulse, she knew he was still alive. Incapacitated. Somewhere within her, she felt this should have made her feel better, but it didn't.

Confident he wouldn't follow her, Cait hurried to the door. Only one thought crossed her mind: *Charlie*. She needed to get to Charlie. If possible, get out of there. But she had to get to him. It was her fault he was there. At least, that's what she told herself. *Hell*, he wanted to go home. He'd only come knowing she would've been alone, isolated. It was now time for her to return the favor.

The hallway hovered, opaque, empty, and unhelpful. Cait jogged to its other end, the pistol gripped firm-in-hand.

The elevator she'd heard stood before her, and a utility stairwell. The stairs would be safer, she thought. Who knew where the elevator lead? Or what she'd find.

Cait did not know what to expect.

Taking a moment to gather herself, conviction settled in her once more. She would let that carry her forward and beyond whatever waited for her up those stairs. Whatever it was, she knew she would face it. *What else is there to do?* she thought. It was that or sit there, waiting to be caught and killed. She'd never allow that to happen.

So, after another deep breath to calm her nerves, Cait took the first stair, one string of thoughts still repeating itself over and over in her mind: *I'm coming, Charlie. I'm coming.*

THIRTEEN

The elevator doors slid open, allowing for Mr. Blackwell to come forth again and usher Charlie out through the cold and dismal confines of the dim-lit lab.

Charlie's first impression was its austere feel, well-hidden from the warmth of light. Its sterile hues stemming from the ceiling, floor, and walls were nothing but a feeble attempt at a more credible facade. The whitewashing of their grim work whatever that was.

Unnerved, Charlie gulped, finding even breathing an arduous task.

Mr. Blackwell seemed to be almost carried forward by the tangible level of excitement within him. He was a child on Christmas, with the mischievous bend to open his presents before his parents woke.

With no other choice, Charlie followed him down the lab's central hall to the room on the end, filled with bustling men in white coats. It was all odd and quite detached from what he'd been expecting.

Dizziness had crept its way back through him, starting the

moment the elevator descended. It grew stronger with every floor they went, its grip fierce as he followed Mr. Blackwell through that hall.

Holding the door to the observation room open, Mr. Blackwell stood as Charlie stepped inside.

Every man present stopped what they were doing and turned to watch.

Mr. Blackwell then entered and addressed everyone, a smugness returning to him.

"Gentlemen!" The burst carried outward, drenched in confidence, falling upon everyone present. "Allow me to introduce to you a distinguished and honorable guest."

He took in the technicians' varied expressions. Dr. Grenier looked bewildered. The words 'distinguished' and 'honorable' didn't line up with the tattered, sleep-deprived specimen before them. He looked at his leader with distrust. The man's eyes hung open—wide and dangerous—and he was emitting a strange and impulsive energy, out of sync with the collected man he'd grown to know.

"Someone we *each* owe our lives and progress to, and our thanks." Mr. Blackwell's grin widened as his head made a slow turn around the room.

This did very little to stifle anyone's confusion, but Mr. Blackwell reveled in the power it gave him.

"This, gentlemen, is Charlie West."

The room froze. Everyone present gave a unified gasp, as if synchronized. Every particle of oxygen seemed to evaporate, as if removed.

Charlie went light-headed, as the walls spun, and everyone turned to him.

The weak lights flickered in the silence, disrupted by Mr. Blackwell's words—dripping with contempt.

"*You* faithless ingrates," he said. "*You* thought this boy was dead, gone. *You* all thought us destined to fail. For that *unbe-*

lief we would've, if not for providence. The universe seems bent on our success, for it has returned this precious child to us." Mr. Blackwell's eyes flickered as he spoke. They lost him to his passions at that point, unaware anybody else was there, even Charlie. "*The Nameless* call to us with this gesture! It confirms our direction and rite! Our triumphant declaration of victory over everything and everyone that stood or stands in our way—even the Head and those precious higher ups!" Everyone else's shoulders twinged at the flippant tossing out of their leaders' names. It was unheard of, let alone in the angry tones that accompanied them. Mr. Blackwell had strayed far from the man he once led them; or so his men thought. Yet, no one present would dare speak against him; it wouldn't be right. Each man stood, too broken by fear.

"But, brothers..." Mr. Blackwell slowed his speech and turned to look about. "... Charlie here seems to be less aware of our purpose than I would have foreseen. So, Dr. Grenier, if we are ready, I'd like to show him what his actions have allowed us to accomplish." Mr. Blackwell's pupils constricted, then flared, wild-eyed at his own pronouncement.

Each man maintained their stillness as they took his reprimand in stride.

Charlie fidgeted, uncomfortable, as that same, strange bubble of fog seemed to stretch and weave itself around him again.

In the silence, Mr. Blackwell leaned over to the technician nearest him and whispered something into his ear.

With a nod, the man in question rushed from the room, following whatever direction he'd received.

Mr. Blackwell then turned back towards Dr. Grenier.

"Now, Doctor, are we ready?"

The man took a moment to consider; still riled by all that was happening.

"Nearly, sir. Just a few more..."

His words trailed off as he hit various switches and turned dials in front of him. Everyone else went back to finishing their jobs as well.

"Very good," said Mr. Blackwell, before turning to Charlie, whose body swayed back-and-forth. He reached up and took him by the arm. "Come, Charlie. Let's ensure you have a good seat."

With no will of his own, Mr. Blackwell walked him forward to the front observation window, where a clear view of the procedure awaited them.

Charlie's curiosity crept forward, though his thoughts seemed too frayed to take it all in.

Every few moments, one of the other technicians present —even Dr. Grenier himself—would steal a glance at Charlie's impossible presence. They struggled to believe it *was* Charlie. How could it have been? No one could've survived the events in Astoria. The shell of a person standing before them especially. But Mr. Blackwell stood convinced, so there was no reason to argue. And no one did.

Besides, to them, Charlie was such a mythic character—a legend—of their Order, placed on a pedestal just underneath *The Nameless* themselves. He was more than a person. Yet the shell standing before them then didn't seem like much.

Amidst the bustle, Mr. Blackwell spoke to Charlie again in a hushed and thoughtful whisper.

"Now, Charlie, you will see and *feel* true, transformative power."

Charlie shook at the words. He shuddered, every second feeling more lost than the moment before. Taken by shadows, he thought he would collapse at any second.

The door swung open again, causing even Charlie to turn and see. The man who'd scurried out at Mr. Blackwell's instruction returned. A prize of some sort clutched in his hand; hidden beneath a veil of dark cloth.

Mr. Blackwell lit up with excitement. An almost hungry cheer.

"Ah, thank you," he said, taking the package from the man. His words of gratitude seeming as off-put as his smile. Words that never fell from his lips. He then turned back to the doctor. "Are we ready yet?"

"Just about, sir."

"Good."

Everyone looked with eagerness to glimpse what Mr. Blackwell held firm in his hand.

"As I mentioned before, Charlie," Mr. Blackwell said again, holding up the cloth pouch, "After the dreadful events in Astoria, we sent people in right away so they could procure certain goods for us. Objects that have since become instrumental in our efforts."

Mr. Blackwell untied the end of the pouch.

"These in particular."

With his grin stretching wide, the man reached and pulled out a strange object. Something Charlie was sure he'd never seen before. Yet still, his mind and body shivered with a strange and weary recognition. Though he felt no visual recognition of the object, he *knew* it. Every ounce of him whispered with a horrid familiarity. Something he couldn't explain and hoped he wouldn't have to.

The simple bronze medallion haunted him so. The chain that hung down over the side of Mr. Blackwell's hand, the deadened crimson jewel inset into its body... Something within it reached out to Charlie, and as soon as Charlie saw it, something seemed to tighten its grip around Charlie's mind. Those same pulls and strains set in, upending the slew of memories to return to him, as if released from whatever prison had kept them.

"These items, in particular, have been quite helpful." Mr. Blackwell's smile curled as he watched Charlie stumble, having to grab hold of the desk next to him to ensure he didn't fall over. "Very interesting indeed," he mused to himself. "I wondered at how connected you were to the process. It didn't occur to me how tethered you were to it until your friend described what happened to you, both last night and this morning."

Dr. Grenier shot a dumbfounded look towards Mr. Blackwell at these words.

"Yes, Doctor, young Charlie's presence is the apparent need for our procedure's success. Therefore, I stand corrected." Dr. Grenier couldn't believe these words, but with Charlie's presence there and their work about to be complete, Mr. Blackwell seemed to have no problem admitting any sort of wrong. He was too close to commanding his own dreams to wake and walk forth into the real world. "He was here—on the premises—when first we succeeded. And again this morning!" Mr. Blackwell clasped his hands together, almost bursting with excitement, as he went on. "And now he's here *again*! In time for this procedure! With him, we'll ensure our victory and the *Nameless'* return."

"We're ready now, sir," said Dr. Grenier.

Chills struck Mr. Blackwell at the words. He turned towards the doctor, poised like a greedy child. "At last. Let us begin."

He turned to Charlie then, holding the medallion out before him.

Charlie swayed again as Mr. Blackwell stepped closer.

"Know, Charlie, as members of The Order, we've access to many relics and objects of importance. These being numbered among them. But *these* items in particular..." He stopped for a moment. "Well, they have a special significance. Very special, indeed. Do you know why, Charlie?"

Charlie said nothing.

"*These*, Charlie, are the very medallions used last summer

in your great ascent. When *you* reached the heavens and shook the foundations of the world. *These* relics, my boy, *imbued* —*endowed*, really—" Mr. Blackwell couldn't help but let his excitement carry him away. The pace of his speech increased; he couldn't keep up with himself. "And, oh Charlie, just wait until you see that power! Wait until you see what you've helped us to create! It is time, Charlie West, for your true purpose to be revealed to you." Mr. Blackwell's eyes lit up with the remark.

Everyone else there watching, Charlie included, held their collective breath as Mr. Blackwell lifted the medallion and placed it around Charlie's neck.

Charlie's body grew still, then seized and shook, as if a current was surging through it. He clasped his mouth shut tight to keep from yelling, though he lacked the strength even to make a sound.

The medallion hung there, resting itself upon his chest, nothing more than a dead hunk of metal in that moment. But soon it would awaken, Mr. Blackwell knew. Soon, its purpose, too, would show itself.

At Charlie's bodily change, Mr. Blackwell let out a low bout of laughter. More like a giggle; a sound no one had expected to hear from him. No one dared mention it, though.

"Begin, Doctor!" Mr. Blackwell boomed, slapping his hand down on Charlie's shoulder. In fear, Dr. Grenier turned back to his instruments, flipped two switches, and repositioned the lever to its upright, *on* position. The surrounding machinery awakened. It had begun.

Dr. Grenier's expression grew nervous and worried. He did not know what Charlie's presence here might do, nor did he trust that Mr. Blackwell knew either.

Mr. Blackwell, all the while, leaned towards the observation glass, willing time forward, eager to witness what would come.

The door of the small chamber slid open, exposing the terrified new subject as they thrust him forward. As always, his screams went unheeded, and it only took moments for him to toss aside his modesty and begin hitting the chamber's front pane of glass with both fists.

Everyone ignored his wails and calls for help and continued watching. All except Charlie, whose mind seemed to be somewhere else.

Gears churned and pistons fired as soft fumes hissed through the multitude of a long, snaking pipe.

"Charlie, behold," Mr. Blackwell said, his hand still on Charlie's shoulder. "Your birthright is at hand."

Yielding to no one else's pace, the fumes poured in, filling the little chamber, increasing both the decibel and constancy of the subject's screams until they stopped short.

In unison, he and Charlie both went rigid. Driven by the same invisible force, both their bodies convulsed and shook.

Mr. Blackwell's head swiveled back and forth to take it in, growing giddier with each twist of their bodies. His hands clasped together again. From a certain angle, he looked to be praying.

Dr. Grenier looked on with a heavy heart. This *differed* from every time before. By this point, they'd lost each subject in feverish screams. Lost from *this* world, forced to cross over into the unknown land beyond. This man, they'd lost him. To what? No one knew. No one knew what to expect.

The doctor looked toward a smiling Mr. Blackwell to see his reaction.

"At last," said Mr. Blackwell to himself. In his enveloping ambition, he stood alone in the room. *"At last."*

In that moment, Dr. Grenier knew that everything they'd done was wrong.

Mr. Blackwell broke in, interrupting.

"Doctor?"

"Yes, sir?"

"Is the subject alright?"

The doctor looked to his right. To the man who'd reviewed the subject's vitals before. The man nodded back.

"It appears so, sir."

Something in the doctor's tone caught Mr. Blackwell.

"Doctor, are you not enthralled by your success here? We are on the verge of the most important step in human history."

"Of course, sir," the doctor feigned, forcing a weak smile upon his face.

Both Charlie and the subject shook almost violently now. The subject bounced back and forth off the chamber glass, halfway filled with the churning, putrid smoke.

"Hold him up!" Mr. Blackwell came out in a half-shriek.

Two men ran over and took hold of his arms. At least now he wouldn't fall down.

Turning to his lead technician, Mr. Blackwell demanded an answer.

"What *exactly* is happening, Doctor?"

He failed to hide his rising concern. His own jaw dropped as he watched Charlie's eyes roll into the back of his head.

"Is—is he alright?"

No one dared respond. No one knew.

Dr. Grenier thought hard; he hadn't the slightest idea. This had never happened before.

"Doctor? God dammit! Is he—"

"There's no way of knowing, sir. *Really*. We've never done this before and haven't prepared adequate—"

Mr. Blackwell's glare silenced him. Turning, he placed his attention back on the small chamber in the next room. The gas continued to billow in.

"Oh, Charlie," he said, still to himself. "I only wish you could witness this, boy. After all, it's by your presence we will accomplish our goals. *This* creature. The second of *many* to follow..." He trailed off, lost to his own thrill. "When *enough* has changed... when *their* number is complete, we'll unleash a terror unlike anything this wicked world has ever seen." Anger bled from every word he uttered. There was such fierce conviction in him—such reckless hate and will. "And then, as the ancient texts have foretold, when enough devastation has occurred, *they* will finally hear us. The Nameless will come. Our salvation will come at last and wipe this earth clean..."

The technicians and Dr. Grenier all watched and listened. Fear sank in with every word. They'd always known the plan, but hearing it then from the mouth of this unraveling man brought with it a different gravity. But what could be done?

A sharp wail, which died down right away, broke everyone's attention. It came from the shoulder-high cloud of smoke within the chamber. The subject's two hands mashed up against the glass: still, at last.

Charlie's body, too, became still.

Whatever commotion had overcome them seemed to loosen its grip.

Mr. Blackwell grew more anxious.

"What's happening?"

"Sir, there's no way to—"

Then, both men broke out into piercing screams that tore through the open space.

One technician covered his ears from the horrid sound.

The screams built and built, growing stronger, rising at the same rate. Both men's bodies once more shook; both so pained and attached. Tethered to one another.

That's when the strange glow came.

Mr. Blackwell noticed it first emanating from within the gas-filled chamber. The crimson hues reached out, their shine blunted at first, but it grew sharper, especially as they noticed the same glow coming from the medallion around Charlie's neck. Soon, the entire room stood shrouded by its bloody lens.

While worry grew in most who were present, in Mr. Blackwell, only excitement grew.

"It's happening!" Mr. Blackwell burst out. "It's–It's going to work!" Like a child, his face pressed against the observation glass. He wasn't even watching Charlie at that point or worried about him.

Another scream tore through the room; but not from Charlie. It came from the chamber. Anything but human. It filled everyone with a surge of fear, Mr. Blackwell included. Yet he stood strong, smiling wider. That wild look returned to his eyes. His plans, he knew, were taking shape at last.

———

Cait breathed in and out, slow and with care, hoping that she would alert no one to her presence. She made it up the stairs and, to her relief, found the next hall at least finished. It had tiled floors and painted walls of a sterile and sickly white, not helped by the strained fluorescent bulbs, which created a sterile atmosphere that hung throughout the whole corridor.

To Cait, it was a welcome shift from the musty, cold cement, but did not improve her level of comfort.

Several steps down the hall, she heard a series of muffled back-and-forth voices, and froze. Her heart stopped as she searched for a place to hide, anticipating someone coming around the corner.

She was always going to run into someone, but hoped to prolong it.

The muffled voices grew louder, and Cait looked from left to right. Several doors lined both sides of the hall, and another stairwell beyond them.

Cait stood there, her feet somewhat frozen to the floor,

listening with intent. Soft echoes of a conversation carried down the hall to where she stood, this time with a hint of laughter. Her stomach tightened, shocked that a person could experience joy in this place.

She inferred they were coming from the last room on the left and, taking a deep breath, she exhaled—steady and slow—and braved another step forward. Cait removed her shoes so that her boot soles wouldn't make a noise against the tile. She checked each door she passed. Either with a glance or a jiggle of the handle, clearing the hall. She held the pistol, always before her, raised and ready.

She was less careful than she wanted to be. Feeling time slipping away, she needed to get to Charlie.

Cait stood back to the wall just outside the last room, listening. The pistol raised to eye level.

She took long, dragging breaths to help maintain a necessary calm.

Being so close, the voices carried much more clearly now, and Cait snuck a glance inside.

Two men sat before some sort of security station. Several screens lined the wall in front of them.

A flash of worry came over Cait. That they might've seen her. It faded as quickly as it had come. No alarms triggered; no one came for her; the men behind the desk were sleepy. Bored and distracted by the uneventful evening. She smiled, knowing she was about to remedy that.

The voices broke again.

Cait listened.

"Seriously, you know what's going on?"

"Hell no!" the other said. "You know they don't tell us anything. I've seen the same as you. These guys, whoever the fuck they are, all getting excited about *something*. But from what we've been hearing—those crazy screams... the noises—I think I'd rather not know. You heard 'em, huh?"

"Yeah, what the hell was that?"

"I d-dunno."

Cait heard the man's voice shake; sensing how on-edge he felt.

"You've been on a few of those runs, yeah? To dump the bodies?"

Cait didn't hear the man respond and snuck another glance, seeing him nod he had.

"Some crazy fucking shit going on here, you ask me."

The man nodded again, seeming to grow quiet as the conversation turned.

The other man continued his rambling.

Cait thought about how fear affected people in different ways.

"Can you believe Reggie got us into this shit? *He* doesn't even know, right? Whatever the hell's going on? This crazy Blackwell guy doesn't tell anyone anything."

"*Yeah...*" the other man and at last; his voice constricted by the haunting fear of what he'd heard. It was the strange rumors that stirred the most fear. "*Everyone's* on edge tonight, right? Spooked about something."

"You think it's that cop they found snooping around?"

Cait's lungs froze at her mention.

"Yeah, maybe, but I don't understand why they didn't just shoot her like the last one. Why take the chance?"

"Apparently, there was some kid with her. You saw Blackwell in the video, right? Got all fucking crazy about him."

"Weird shit. And it was right after–"

The man cut himself short, the look on his face grave and unsure.

"Yeah... almost *right* after."

Both men fell into a fearful silence. Cait almost felt she could commiserate with them.

The first man spoke again, flustered.

"And look at this shit!"

Cait watched as he pointed to the central monitor. It was the largest, and it was blank. "Always! They always turn the fucking cameras off in that room before the screaming starts! What are they doing in there? Why the—" He paused, exacerbated. "Why the fuck are *we* involved here?"

The other man shook his head again.

"What the hell was Reggie thinking?" the first man finished. "Place gives me the fucking creeps. Gets under my fucking skin."

The other man nodded again.

Cait shot another glance into the room. Keying in on the blank monitor, wondering if that's where Charlie was. Perhaps they'd take him there. She wasn't sure, but needed to move.

Scott's voice came to her again.

Hope doesn't have to be big, just present.

The words brought with them a tinge of comfort and the most subtle amount of confidence, reminding her she needed to act fast.

There were only two men, after all. Who didn't know she was coming?

The men carried on with their conversation as Cait made her plans.

A small island of cabinets stood at the room's center. The men sat in twin rotating chairs between it and the monitors. The island stood covered in a scattering of papers and files. Two mugs sat there, half full of coffee.

That could work, she thought, and she tucked herself down to move. Her socks slid across the tile, making no noise at all, and she was in position.

The men's conversation droned on, steering further away from the uncertainty of their present circumstances. They dreamed of what they'd rather be doing.

Scooting around to the far end, Cait leaned forward. The

left man was just before her. Her pulse raced. If he turned, he'd be looking right at her. But he didn't do that. The conversation kept him well distracted.

All she needed to do was move, but she sat there, waiting for several seconds. Seconds she didn't have, she thought. A rush of worry flutter through her with the thought that followed.

Seconds Charlie didn't have...

Closing her eyes, Cait breathed in and out.

Come on, Cait! she thought. *Move it! Now!*

Several options came as she considered her next move, but knowing herself, she settled on just diving in. Speed, surprise, and her anger would be effective enough. She would let that drive her forward without remorse. After all, she knew she reacted better in tense situations versus following any sort of plan. She knew Scott would have cautioned her against this, and even the thought of him chiding her brought her comfort. Enough comfort to move.

Fuck it! she thought at last and leaped up.

"What the hell—"

Cait cut the man's surprised flail short, bringing her pistol down—hard and fast—across his temple. With a strange gurgle, he collapsed back into the chair and fell limp and silent.

The second man leap out of his chair, reaching for his gun.

But Cait was quicker.

"Don't fucking move!"

Her voice bristled, and she kept the pistol trained right on the man's heart.

He froze, his hand hovering over the holster, everything in him telling him to go for it.

Cait sensed where this would lead.

The man faced her with an icy stare. It would be one or the other.

She'd never fired her weapon in the line of duty before,

let alone taken a life. But in the heat of that moment, she considered it with ease. She always figured it would be so difficult to make that choice. But there wasn't even a discussion. There was only one clear path. Either this man or Charlie, lost forever. Besides, these men had stained the city she loved so much. She would not hesitate if it came down to it.

"Hands up."

He raised them, but only just, intent on keeping them close just in case the opportunity struck.

Cait hoped she could take him without firing her pistol. Not wanting to announce herself any more than needed.

"How do I get to the main lab?" she said, her tone sharp and unforgiving. A question this man *would* answer.

The man said nothing at first.

"The main lab! How do I get there?"

The man twitched. His trigger hand lowered again—not subtle enough to go unnoticed.

"You'll never make it," he said to her. Almost a plea more than a promise.

Cait took a step forward, adjusting her grip on the pistol; she leaned in.

"Doesn't matter. Where the fuck is it?"

The man made no response; he only glared at her—his eyes like razors—considering something.

Cait adjusted her aim this time, right at the man's forehead, and leaned in toward the barrel, reaffirming her intent.

"Look, asshole! You're gonna to tell me right now, or you'll *wish* you had!"

He chuckled.

Cait's frustration flared.

"What are you going to do? There's a small army protecting this building. Even *if* you make it, what'll you do? Where'll you go?"

"That's my problem," she said to him, not letting the worrying realization settle into her. "Where is it, dammit?"

As she asked, he made his move.

The man's hand dropped to his gun, but Cait reacted first.

A concussion blast echoed through the tiny room, spilling out into the hallway.

The man's body went limp and crumpled to the floor, knocking over the chair with its fall. Blood trickled from the hole in his forehead and flowed into his hair. A tiny pool of it collected underneath his head from an exit wound.

For a moment, Cait froze, somewhat caught in shock. She'd never taken a life before. Her surprise came from not feeling as affected as she figured she would. This had seemed necessary. Justified.

She wondered if she'd feel the same the next day, *if* she made it out.

A scratchy voice over the radio brought her back to reality, and she jumped.

"Security 1, this is Operator, do you copy?"

Silence reigned as Cait gathered herself against what she knew was sure to come.

"Security 1, I repeat, this is Operator. Do you copy? We heard a shot fired. Is everything okay? Copy?"

Cait considered responding, but knew better. Then the voice returned, a flicker of worry making it more direct than before.

"Sub-level Team, do you copy?"

The response was instantaneous.

"This is Sub-level Leader. Copy."

"Did you read that? Security 1 is dark. We need you to run a sweep."

"Roger that. On our way."

"Keep us posted. Copy."

"Roger. We'll be down in two minutes."

Shit! Cait thought, worry flooding her entire self. *Two minutes? Shit! Shit! Shitshitshit!*

Fighting off the frantic, rising sense of dread, Cait looked up at the monitors. Each blacked out. The far-right corner screen showed a group of men gathered, sprinting in Cait's direction. Pulses of fear flared. She had no clue where they were coming from. Or how she could get away.

She turned, scouring the room for anything she could use. On the wall next to the door hung a map listing fire extinguishers, alarms, *emergency exits*. It also gave a rudimentary outline of the facility, each floor included. Somewhere in her mind, she was thankful that these men at least followed the fire code. Ripping it from the wall, she scanned it to get what bearings she could, glancing back and forth from monitor to monitor to map again, putting together what pieces she could.

Okay, she assured herself, her mind settling once more. Pressure had a tendency to focus her more—a trait she'd always felt thankful for. Especially in her line of work.

Cait grabbed a radio from the charging dock, and the pistol from the man she'd shot. It would take a lot to make it past what was coming.

There wasn't time to think. To wrap her head around everything. The situation was too big. Too strange. She couldn't think in strict terms of *the case*. What had happened? Any of it. She didn't think of Scott, or Stacey or the kids. She only told herself, *I've made it this far,* and placed her focus on what she needed to do next. If she made it past that, then she could take the next step. All of this raced through her mind in seconds, somewhere beneath consciousness.

Get to Charlie. Then get out of this hellhole.

A strength of conviction swelled within her, and she held the pistol tight within her grip. The odds weren't good, no. But Cait couldn't let that stop her from trying. She'd never been one to give up.

FOURTEEN

Charlie's body shook back and forth in harsh bursts, desperate to break free from the men who held him. Mr. Blackwell still paid him little mind; his attention he'd placed on the procedure to come.

The subject's continued screams overpowered every other noise, drowning out even the clanking of machinery and the hissing fumes of gas. Just beneath it, if you tried, you could make out the echoes of cracking bones as they snapped, the pulling and tearing of muscles as a man's body transformed into *that* abominable horror.

Charlie screamed out too, though his cries weakening the further the process dragged on. With each second, he slipped further and further away. Some place far removed from *this* world. A construct of the mind; difficult to reach. More difficult, yet, for a person to return from intact.

When this new-formed creature yelled out, Charlie's body reacted too. They were twins of a sort, connected through this dark and terrible rite.

In the chamber, *something* slashed through the rising plumes of smoke. Only ever revealing part of themselves. From their placement, they should've been hands. Cutting through the air as if it were water; the space filling itself in with immediacy, conquering what it could.

What had been skin, and pale and pinkish hues at that, stretched itself out over reconstructed joints. An almost scaly exterior. Greenish-grey, dripping with a horrid, almost amniotic ooze. The raw muscles tensed in perpetual flex. Whatever *it* was, it appeared weary of its new world.

The arms—or congruent appendages—flared upward, slamming down against the glass. At each end, no hands were present. With every slash, a clearer picture came. Fingers morphed into one singular curving protrusion, its inner edge arrayed with a series of suctions for grip. Like some ancient beast from the depths, come to terrorize the land. Something stemmed from each arm's new end; something murderous and terrifying. Just their presence seemed to threaten everyone there. A razor-sharp claw apiece. Protruding. Ready to dig into whatever person stood closest. They gnashed back and forth against the transparent surface of the glass with a futile fury, leaving no damage. Punctuated by the screams.

Even for the horrendous screams, the men watching—Dr. Grenier, the technicians, and Mr. Blackwell himself—couldn't peel their eyes away. They'd seen the finished product once before. Sure, but not like this. The procedure had never gone so well.

Nor had it filled them with such terror.

"Doctor?" panted Mr. Blackwell.

"Yes?" He'd forgotten the *sir* and hadn't even looked up.

"Is... is... this normal, Dr. Grenier?"

The doctor said nothing at first.

"I mean... does this *always* happen so... *quickly*?"

The doctor shook his head that this was *not* normal. He wasn't even sure if that term could apply to his world anymore. The terror of how quickly *this* creature changed.

The ease with which it took place. And how that would translate. The exponential change one such creature could trigger? And so on? In so many other beings? That was something horrible to behold. Or so Dr. Grenier thought then. He'd never considered it before, but nothing... nothing at all... could stop them.

The doctor's conviction faltered.

"Its... its vitals, then?" Mr. Blackwell said, again.

The doctor checked, then looked up again.

"Still stable... sir."

Everyone was quiet then, watching. Only the creature still stirred, still reeling, nearing the end of its transformation. Even Charlie calmed and quieted. If it weren't for those holding him, he would've collapsed long before.

Mr. Blackwell stared forward in relief, resting easier than he had in months. He couldn't help but imagine the looks on the Inner Circle's collective faces, especially the Head. Their doubts squashed. *They'd* done it, after all. *He'd* done it. And there's nothing they could do to stop him. Even if they came to shut down their operation. Even if they brought the full onslaught of the Inner Circle, their near-militarized force from the North. Once they saw the beauty of what *he'd* accomplished, how could they not let it move forward?

A strange peace settled in him—a feeling he was unfamiliar with.

Dr. Grenier's gut ballooned with dread. He looked around, seeing nothing save the doom he'd brought upon the world. A horrid end. *Yes*, the world was a wicked place. And *yes*, it deserved to be wiped clean. But *this?* He wondered. What stood before him? This abomination driven forth by the madness of selfish desire? *This was wrong*, he thought. *No one deserved such a pitiless—*

He supposed *extermination* was the only appropriate word.

He looked at Mr. Blackwell and saw a man he used to trust. A man he used to believe in.

Then, he glanced over to Charlie, who stood unconscious, held up by the bartered strength of others.

What had they done to him? Why did *this boy* deserve this?

He didn't. That was the doctor's conclusion.

A single thought plagued him then. That *he* was the one deserving of a wicked end. Muscles clenched around his heart, and his insides strained.

Two words came to mind. Words he'd never so much as thought of throughout his life; always one to push forward, no matter the cost, for the greater purpose. But when he looked upon Charlie, dwelling on his suffering, these words rang true with a painful clarity.

I'm sorry, he thought, and the creature growled again. Dr. Grenier shook in terror. *I'm sorry... for everything.*

———

Cait made it through an entire floor. Checking each room, ensuring no one could surprise her from behind. They were all empty, which seemed odd, given the facility's size.

She'd reached the top of the next stairwell when the first echoes of boots and voices made themselves known.

She stopped to listen; they were coming from the next floor up.

"Heads up!" she heard. The voice was bitter and determined. And closing in.

Her nerves tried to unravel. They tried to unsettle themselves and fall into a panic, but she wouldn't let them. She'd hold them together herself, one by one, if she had to. She was going to make it. No matter how determined anyone she was facing seemed, nothing would compare to her own resolve.

The voice still carried down the hall; quieter though.

"The shot came from two floors down. From here on, be ready for anything."

No response came from the order, save for the subtle continuation of boots skipping across tile.

Panic again tried to take hold, but Cait staved it off. There was no time for it. Her ability to manage such feelings was one of the few gifts her cold and distant father had passed down to her. Like him, she'd developed the ability to turn off how she felt.

Checking the few remaining rooms with haste, clearing the hall, Cait came to the base of the next stairwell. Right then, she *knew* her pursuers had made it to the top.

She felt their presence as much as heard it; and couldn't help the trickle of panic that crept in. It seemed understandable to her mind then. That in small doses, it would fuel a person. Keep them moving and alive.

Scott's voice returned.

Read the room, rook. Use what you have.

She smiled, and a certain, almost arrogant confidence returned to her. Cait channeled the fear and adrenaline into focus, pushing everything else to the side.

Right away, she noticed that this floor, compared to the others, had one unique architectural difference: a little alcove opposite the stairs to her left. The other floors had housed offices or closets in this space, depending. This space wrapped around, veering away from the hall and stairs, creating a blind spot Cait thought would prove useful.

A haunting whisper tore through the silence once again.

"Be ready for anything. Let's go."

They were almost upon her. She pointed the pistol upward, clasping it in front of her, and, using quick steps, backed her way up to the third stair. She had a clear view of anyone who'd come.

This, she knew, was stupid. Scott would have scolded her for even thinking it, but they would never see it coming.

She heard no orders. She heard no movement at all. Still, she felt them. All of them, and perceived the most subtle vibrations moving through the air.

Someone was coming.

And before her mind even registered it, two arms wearing the same navy-blue uniforms the men had in the security room had worn emerged, coming together where they held their own pistol out in front of them.

Cait waited half a second, holding her breath, until the man's head and torso emerged as well.

The man's eyes widened as he realized she was there; and Cait fired.

She wanted to be the one to give her presence away. To catch them off guard. Not him, and she succeeded.

The man's body crumbled, and almost folding over itself tumbled down the stairs; where it thudded to a stop on the landing and grew still.

Footsteps erupted as one voice shouted out.

"Suppressing fire!"

There was no need for secrecy anymore.

A barrage of bullets came showering down over the ledge.

Cait ducked below even before the body had hit the ground. She disappeared around the corner, hidden from sight.

The storm of bullets ceased, and another string of orders rang out. This time in a harsh whisper.

"Cover each other! *You*—take to the ledge. And *you*—down first! Check every corner!"

They're organized, Cait thought, holding to her conviction to survive.

She heard several quick steps above her, and a voice call out.

"Clear!"

Her heart winced.

Another set of footsteps echoed down the stairs; someone headed to the landing. Another voice called out.

"Clear!"

Everyone else followed then, making their way to her.

Covered, the entire troop pushed forward until they'd all reached the base of the stairs.

Shit! Cait thought. This was it. If she didn't make it, it was over. Done. They'd win, and she would've dragged Charlie into all this for nothing.

When she'd turned the corner, she'd found open space. In the corner, a closet waited, open and ready; just before the stairs stood a worktable. Littered with tools, and with a long blue painter's tarp hanging over the edge.

She worked with what she had and, making sure the door stood half-open, she ducked underneath the tarp. If she were religious, or even spiritual, she would have prayed. She was neither so cleared her head of any thought save making it through.

The tarp hung in such a way she couldn't see someone unless they were close. She listened, trying to discern as best as she could what was going on.

She counted the footfalls as they tapped their way onto the floor and spread out. Her best guess was that there were five men after her. Maybe more, but not less. That would've been a dangerous hope.

Cait's breath seemed to hold itself in. Her heart pounded, but she couldn't help but feel an overwhelming sense of calm and focus.

The footsteps tapped. Some closing in, while others faded in the distance.

Most crept down the hallway. The other way, she figured. That distance made them dangerous.

Her gut twinged.

She wanted to jump out; go after them. *Stupid*, she knew, so she stayed put. It took a lot to suppress that impulse.

Just then, she saw a boot round the corner to the alcove where she sat, hidden, followed by the entirety of its owner. His gun poised forward and ready.

Cait breathed in, slow, regimented, keeping herself steady.

The man took several small, slow steps forward.

She froze.

Coming to the table's edge, he looked down.

Cait watched as the side of his head showed in the tarp's gap. At the angle he stood, they'd just missed each other.

He didn't see her at all, and turned to keep walking.

Relief flooded her, building into a sigh; a sigh she then suppressed.

The man moved towards the closet, making it the distraction she hoped it would be.

He closed in on its half-open door, reaching it at last. Stepping inside, he halted, taking in his surroundings.

She wanted to leap out. To attack, make her stand, but heard another set of footsteps coming.

Shit! She swiveled her head to find a second man rounding the corner. That complicated things. Yet, she still felt she could still catch them off guard. It might help even the field.

She looked back as one man entered the closet. The second man then approached the table. He seemed to take a keener interest in it and closed in.

Gripping the pistol, Cait held it out before her, ready.

Like the first man, he looked down. Right into the tear in the tarp. Yet at that angle, he couldn't see her.

She held her breath, knowing he could see her at any moment, but made no move.

He drew closer still, then reached out his hand.

Cait's nerves sharpened somehow even more; her hand steadied.

The man's hand reached out; about to grasp hold of the tarp when it stopped.

All Cait saw were his eyes widening with realization as they locked with hers.

The action seemed to precede the thought. With no thinking necessary, she opened fire and heard the blast, followed by a man's grunt, while he collapsed to the ground before her.

One precise moment spanned out of where nothing happened. No one spoke or moved.

Then the scene erupted.

Cait swiveled and fired several bullets, blind behind the tarp, into the closet, a few missed. She recognized the pangs on metal canisters, concrete exploding, or the tearing of wood; but some of them hit their mark.

A second man groaned, then something heavy fell, knocking several objects to the ground before everything went still.

Another half-second of silence reigned, fading faster than before. Mounting echoes of footsteps were tearing down the hall.

Again, without thought, Cait burst out from beneath the tarp and faced the alcove's edge. In three quick steps, she'd backed against the wall next to the open hall. The stairwell was at her immediate right.

They were coming fast, but she also knew they would have a brief opportunity for cover.

Cait felt alive in that moment; more than she'd ever felt before. The situation allowed for her reckless self to emerge and thrive. That part of her that, for good reason, she'd always kept restrained.

Pistol raised and ready, Cait took a quick glance around

the corner. Three more men approached, and her insides fluttered. She'd been right. There'd been five.

Upon seeing her, the one closest raised his own weapon and began firing.

Cait pulled herself back just as two of the bullets slammed into the wall behind her, blowing chunks of paint-crusted drywall through the air. She felt each reverberation echo through the wall.

She stayed calm.

As soon as the firing stopped, Cait acted. It was second nature. Her body chose well before her mind had even processed the moment.

With ease, Cait rounded the corner again, committed.

Turning, she fired. Bullet after bullet flew. With her left hand, she retrieved a second gun she'd stashed away.

The men scrambled as she held both weapons poised, unloading in their direction.

One man dropped, crumbling to the floor where he lay still.

The next she tagged in both a leg and his waist. He collapsed to the ground, screaming.

Cait never stopped firing and never stopped pushing forward.

The third man dove toward the wall. He raised his own gun and managed a handful of shots before Cait could redirect her aim.

One bullet grazed her right shoulder, causing her to stumble and recoil. It knocked her back, and she yelled out. Her knee struck the ground, but she spun with her still-good arm. Raising the second pistol high, she fired one last shot and struck the man right in the neck.

Everything went silent save for the echo of his body flying backward and slamming into the floor. Followed by his desperate heaves for breath, he had little time left to live.

Cait stood up, watching the man lay there, bleeding out. A slight awareness of how much her shoulder hurt seeped in.

He held his throat as blood flowed out in steady streams.

For a few moments, he made eye contact as Cait looked down. She watched as his focus drifted away until the stare went blank.

His wheezing breaths slowed until they ceased at last. The grip upon his throat loosened, and his arm fell limp across his chest.

He was gone.

They all were.

Somehow, Cait made it out alive.

She stood there, looking over the bodies; an overwhelming sense of relief flooded her.

For a second, she wondered if these men would haunt her; if she'd see their eyes when she closed her own; if guilt would rise when the adrenaline faded. She wondered if her actions were justified.

These thoughts only slowed her down, so she shoved them to the side. She prepared herself for what might come.

Charlie's still up there, she thought. Somewhere. There was no time for celebration. God knows what they were doing to him.

She slid the action back on both pistols, realizing one was empty. She dropped it to the floor. Once it settled, she registered the faintest whimper coming from just in front of her.

It was the second man. Alive, but not for long.

Cait saw he was bleeding out. She walked up to him as he struggled for breath. He wouldn't make it, but life lingered in him with an unmerciful strain. She looked into him, considered how he'd used his life. What he'd tried to do to her. Part of her thought he deserved whatever slow demise was coming. She heard Scott's voice again, echoing through her thoughts.

We have *to believe everyone is reachable.* He'd often preach at her. *Otherwise, why even try holding the line?*

A sharp pain moved through her gut, shooting up toward her heart.

She looked down at the man, into his eyes. She saw that desperation hung there. It was a look close to remorse, and it was calling out for mercy.

Under the collision of that memory and that sight, Cait caved. Raising the other pistol, she pointed and held it out, then hesitated.

The man blinked once, then once more. It was slow and spoke of a hopeful peace. It was as if he was saying, *Please! Please do it now.*

He stared up at her with a permissive look of longing.

Cait pulled the trigger.

For several seconds, the bullet's reverberations expanded, ricocheting off the walls. They died out, leaving the room open in the eerie quiet's wake; somehow it felt emptier than before.

Cait tried to shake it off but felt its weight and strain. Forcing her attention back to the stairs, she readied herself to move again.

Her most consistent thought was *Keep going.*

She breathed in, then out again.

Get to Charlie... Keep going.

Coming to the body on the stairs, she picked up the man's pistol and checked its clip. *Full.* Ensuring the safety was off, she raced up the next flight of stairs.

Reaching the top, a hopelessness descended on her. It looked like every other floor before.

Was there no end?

Cait cleared her mind again and moved with continued swiftness. She checked each door with haste and moved on.

This floor, she found, was nothing like the ones before.

Two doors stood on the right, connected, fanning open to a garage. Her heart leaped, thinking she might've found an exit. At the opposite end stood a door leading to a boiler room of sorts. Her heart jumped again as several thoughts formed in her mind. But it looked old; filled with more outdated architecture than the rest of the building—it was strange. The builders had remodeled around old foundations; or fashioned a new body over whatever skeleton remained.

She'd heard of some of the Pearl District developers cutting corners like that when they remade this part of town.

Cait couldn't contain her growing excitement, and a certain sense of hope returned. She felt fuzzy plans forming in her, but that didn't quite matter yet. First, she needed to get to Charlie. Then she'd think about leaving.

———

The entire lab waited, masked within that horrid crimson glow. The strange, newborn monster's growl rose and settled in rhythmic, heaving breaths.

It did little to quell the collective rise of nerves. Everyone except Mr. Blackwell stood on edge. Yet even he could read the others and turned to his lead technician.

"*Doctor* Grenier, is everything alright?"

The doctor found himself incapable of answering. He had no words. Here they stood, victorious. Their goal achieved. And with unfathomable quickness at that. Yet, everything in him screamed to pick up the nearest stool and bash it into the controls before him; ensuring no other abominations would come forth. Into this world or any other. Everything about this was wrong. He let his glance fall on Charlie again and watched the boy twitch and shake. He had grown calmer than well, staying true to his connection to the creature.

The doctor's stomach twisted that he could condemn another person to such a fate.

Mr. Blackwell turned to face the room, his back to Charlie, having not even considered him since the procedure started.

"Well, gentlemen," he began, still bearing the look of over-confidence. "I believe congratulations are in order. Look what *we've* accomplished. And it looks as though you all get to keep your placements here."

Somehow, the room slipped into a deeper silence.

"Now," Mr. Blackwell turned to Dr. Grenier.

The doctor looked up.

"Doctor, I want you to prepare the next subject and bring him in right away!"

The doctor could not hide his astonishment.

"Will that be a problem, *Doctor*?"

The others each looked away. Some let their glances fall to the floor; each trying to remove themselves from the rise in tension.

"Sir..." he hesitated. "... that might take hours. W-we have to reset the machines, and–"

"So, you will not comply with the order, *Doctor*?"

The doctor grew more flustered.

"It–It's not that, sir.. W-we just need more..." He hesitated again, looking back and forth at Charlie. "We *need* more time."

He cowered under Mr. Blackwell's glare.

"W-we... we're not ready, Sir."

Mr. Blackwell took several slow steps toward the doctor, methodical and deep in thought.

"You know, I never thought you'd be one to hinder our project. What's wrong, Doctor?"

The doctor looked away as well, unable to maintain eye contact with his superior.

"Nothing, sir… it's just—I think–"

"Prepare…the next…subject…now, Doctor. Do I make myself clear?"

The doctor couldn't keep his jaw from rattling, nor his hands from shaking as he caved.

"Of course, sir," he said. "Right… Right away."

Mr. Blackwell stood there, a fierce and devilish look in his eyes. He went to speak again when another screech rang out, interrupting him.

Everyone's instinct led them to turn and face the chamber, but the swirling mist hung undisturbed; the yell was human, anyway.

The entire room's attention then fell to Charlie, whose body shook uncontrollably; out of nowhere, he went rigid; his eyes rolled back and forth till they settled, facing upward, in the back of his skull.

In that moment, worry struck, leveling Mr. Blackwell. Without Charlie, there was no plan. Their victory would fade.

He flailed out, screaming, sprinting to where they were holding Charlie up.

"Na-n-no! Charlie!" His body writhed. "Dammit, Grenier! Do something, now!"

The doctor raced to Charlie and followed his own instincts; he reached up to grab the medallion from around Charlie's neck, but Mr. Blackwell slapped his hand away and cut him off. Glaring down at the doctor, he screamed.

"Absolutely not!"

The doctor stepped back.

"But sir, we might kill him!"

Charlie's body fell into even more severe convulsions and painful screams ripped out of him again.

"We won't be deterred," Mr. Blackwell said, unsuccessful in calming himself. "No matter what, dammit!"

"But at what cost, sir? If he's gone, there is no plan anyway!"

At that point, Mr. Blackwell pushed everyone else away and grabbed Charlie by the collar of his jacket. His handling of Charlie was harsh and unforgiving, and his tone grew stretched as his eyes frayed with a disconnected wildness. He looked to be unraveling further yet. To counter this flooding feeling of failure, he tightened his grip and looked at Dr. Grenier. Taking charge.

"Get the next subject in there. *Right now*. Is that clear? We're pressing on!"

The burst silenced Dr. Greiner. He nodded his head and beckoned for the others to continue with their work.

The crimson glow maintained its reach over everyone as the men continued to bustle about their stations. Dr. Grenier couldn't hold himself together underneath the strain.

Through it all, Mr. Blackwell held tight to Charlie and glared down into the twitchy face of the boy he so desperately needed.

"Charlie? Charlie?" He called out, furious at the event's turn. "God dammit, can you hear me? Come back to us, Charlie West! Come back! Your work's not finished yet!"

But Charlie's shaking only grew more violent. The connection to the creature and breach had only strengthened his tie to the memories he'd worked so hard to hide from. The doors had been unlocked; with only one way through. Only one thing mattered. Did he—Charlie—have the strength to make it through?

FIFTEEN

By the time Charlie reached the laboratory, he was well beyond any natural state of exhaustion. He was ready to collapse. Every aspect of him—the physical, the mental, and the emotional, you name it. A vessel empty and void.

The elevator descended, having brought Charlie closer to that ancient artifact about to be presented to him. It was *that* hellish object which had been calling to him this whole time; the fated link to the *other side*. The further he collapsed inward, he found himself beneath the crushing depths of his own unconscious mind.

Charlie swam for his life as image after image fired through him, feeding his ever-growing fear; it was overbearing and impossible to hold back. All the images that had plagued his dreams these past months came rushing back. All the thoughts and would-be-memories planted deep, just beyond the state of sleep, keeping him from feeling rested, wore him thin.

As always, it started with his mother. Images of her from his childhood flew by—smiling, crying, holding herself in— the wails of a sustained and abused life, all followed by the image of her lying, cold, on her bedroom floor where Charlie found her body. Then he ran.

The images fired on with his drive over the pass; a mixture of sunlight and rainstorms baring down; the room he rented at night; the town itself, dazzling in the summer sun; Charlie saw a thousand faces from passersby, all smiling without restraint. His time there fast-forwarded, rocketing past him. He saw The Logger, meeting Trent, then Ellie—his heart shuddered—he saw the towering jetty waves and then himself strung out across his bed, unable to get up, quite detached from himself. Next, he was the passenger in a large, beat up, yellow truck; carrying him in a direction he didn't want to go; a finless animal caught in a current; it drove and drove and drove. There stood a house, tattered, fallen apart in shambles—and a second house; towering, overbearing in its structure and design; a mansion, dreary and oppressive, rising out of the rock on the forest's edge. Charlie knew this place; no specific recollection came, but without a doubt he *knew* it. He saw himself inside; he saw tons of men in black suits swarming around—a man sat at the center with wild, ghost-white hair sticking up everywhere; Charlie could feel his haunting laughter. Next thing he knew, he saw a dank, dark hallway, himself strapped to a chair being carried to a strange room; the sound of thunder boomed, and Charlie could feel his heart sink within; despite his dreaming state—these threads of thought were passing through the subconscious of his brain—he could still feel the assuming drops of pouring rain.

The dream always took him there. To this same place. The same clearing beneath that dark and brooding night sky augmented by the multitude of vast and far-reaching lightning strikes—hell-bent to tear the sky in two.

Charlie's body hovered for several moments before being spirited upward up into the broken heavens.

Carried upward, higher and higher, the wind grew fierce,

and the air grew thin. Exhausted, Charlie felt he could pass out at any minute—he tried reminding himself this was only a dream, but it didn't lessen the feelings of dread within.

The ground grew small beneath him, as the atmosphere expanded beyond him, expansive and wide; as always, mystery loomed all around him. A great shroud, cutting him off from the real world.

A branch of lightning shot down, as if with concise precision, and the sky beyond cracked and split. It tore itself at the seam, then spread towards the heavens and the earth.

Charlie's eyes clenched shut, as if with wills of their own. *This time*, though, *something* told him he'd go unprotected.

Most times when he woke, he'd shoot out of bed, eyes wrenched open. He'd throw on his boots and clothes and tear out of the room to march; trudge to forget.

But not this time. He was still immersed, lost to the dizzying dreams of exhaustion.

Eyes clamped shut, Charlie could feel the space before him being ripped open; he could sense that something monstrous and beyond him was emerging, reaching out to him, calling him forth. The sky tore open. The massive creature passed through. Charlie's fear couldn't help but rise—what else was there to do?

Charlie...

The voice in Charlie's mind felt calm and familiar, but brought no comfort.

He ignored it. Working to shrug it off, he wrenched his head to look away.

Charlie West, it chimed again. *It is time.*

Charlie caught himself wondering, *Time for what?* before he remembered he must keep fighting.

Charlie West, the voice boomed again. He felt a strange momentum moving against his body, moving his head back up to face the creature.

No! Charlie's thoughts yelled out.

It is time to face this. It is time to move on.

Charlie went to yank himself away again, to keep his glance faced down, but found he couldn't. He had no power anymore. Next thing he knew, his body went rigid, his jaw shot up, and before he could think, his eyes wrenched open—against his will. He hung, laid bare, before that horror hovering over that river beach and unprotected earth.

Words escaped him. He found no way to fathom, let alone describe, *this* wicked vision; his mind went blank. He held to a lingering unwillingness to settle with the past—with one faint thread of familiarity—that he'd experienced this before.

His whole body shuddered.

Charlie screamed. He shouted for his life. For anyone or anything to reach down and scoop him up and save him. That's what he felt he needed, but he lacked the strength to choose it himself. He needed saving. He needed a reprieve; a moment's peace from the heavy depths into which he had sunk.

Having reached the apex, his screams carried through the numb sky as he careened back down to the surface—though the ground below seemed somehow unfamiliar.

Different from before.

The beach stood long, stretching out well beyond the tiny cove he'd seen; forever in both directions, growing closer every second.

A deep fear was still present in him, but nothing compared to what he'd felt moments before.

The salty air seemed bent on pulling him down further, faster, and Charlie crashed down, plunging through the waves of whitewash. He tumbled underneath each small current's tiny pulls, tugged one way for a moment, only to be yanked in another direction seconds later. Just when he thought his breath might run out, he emerged. Soaked and sore, he found he could stand.

Right away, he recognized where he stood.

It was the same place he'd traveled to more often as of late.

Before him, just beyond the shore, stood the immensity of a towering wall. Stretching on forever in both directions, like the shore. Its height, as well, seemed to have no end.

Behind him, as he turned, waited an ocean, endless, like whatever lies beyond the reach of man.

Charlie stood there on the border between shaky thoughts of thankfulness and fear. Thankful to be out of the reach of whatever sought him. Fearful of what would come.

Out of habit, he put one mere footstep before the next and began walking toward the shore.

Drowsiness caught up to him, and his head swelled. His deepest yearnings were of sleep; sleep he *knew* would not come. *Then*, at least.

The steps of his damp shoes dug their way into the sand. Charlie looked up, feeling in infinite contrast between himself and the great wall's shadow. Keeping his focus down, not too far before him stood a door. Something he'd never noticed before.

Something urged him to go to that door and open it, but he froze. He didn't want to move. He wanted nothing to do with it, least of all to walk toward it.

Who knew what existed through the door?

Or what would happen if he opened it?

Charlie shook his head and looked away. He stole a glance in each direction when that same strange and familiar tug returned. The one that always called to him, and it took root, deep.

Unlike before, he heard nothing, but *something* reached up to him, *through* him. It was the strangest sensation: he felt his name being thought out to him from beyond the confines of where he stood.

He fought back, turning, facing the other direction; a small rebellion, but something he felt he could manage.

He hadn't noticed the heavy, darkened cloud cover moving overhead, settling itself right over the beach where these two worlds met.

The pull tugged even stronger, yet with what little strength he had, Charlie fought it. Fists clenched, his face scrunched together, he leaned his body into the winds.

The waves crashed hard with the welcomed force of the tides. They pounded on the shore in harsh bursts. Wide sprays of salt water reached out, soaking Charlie, carried further by the still-building wind.

The forces surrounding him coalesced; desiring to merge —bent on breaking his will.

If he could, he wouldn't have it, but he knew, deep down, that he couldn't outlast them all. He was tired of fighting, feeling weak and hollow. The whispers of giving in were growing stronger.

That's when he heard it again; the same voice from before.

His whole body sputtered as he rasped, a squandered half-breath in worried surprise. He knew that voice. It'd tormented his sleep for months, chased him to the edge of reason. Even here, it sought to find him.

Charlie, it said again, causing him to shiver.

He leaned his body further into the wind, hoping beyond rationality it would give him some reprieve, but he felt more naked and open.

Charlie West, the voice said again, echoing out over the ocean waves. *Charlie West, it is time.*

Those were the same words as before; Charlie shuddered as their cadence unfolded.

His body shook, but not from the cold. It was fear that

was taking him, and he clenched his eyes shut tighter, wanting nothing more than to prevent what his gut told him was coming.

What if? he thought. What if he just ran? Sprinted out into the waves, and when he couldn't run anymore, dove out and gave himself to the waves. He could swim until his strength gave out, then let the currents take him. His struggle would be over. His pain, like the waves themselves, would rise and break and fall. Recede back into the depths and fade. It would be one final push. Slice through the exhaustion and fog, all that crippling weight, and have it over. Let the rhythmic currents of the ocean's streams bury what had harmed him. He wanted nothing to do with it.

His heart wrenched as the voice cried out once more. Softer than before.

Charlie West, it is time.

Time for what? Charlie wondered, realizing the tears that were building up within him. His breathing grew faint as he worked hard to not give in; but there was nowhere else to run, save out toward the depths.

It is time, the voice said again.

Charlie lost it.

"What are you talking about?" he screamed and, turning to face the wall, he unleashed all that he'd been feeling, unsure where the anger was coming from. "Wh-what are you? Why are you doing this to me? God dammit! Just–Just leave me alone! All–*all* I want..." His burst ran out of steam as his tone dropped to more of a strained whimper. "...is...is...to rest...*to sleep*..."

The growing feeling in his gut ruptured, and the tears flowed. Charlie stood on the beach at the very end of himself, his journey's culmination, where his trail of choices had led. He didn't know what to do. All he knew then were his fears; what he'd spent his whole life running from. All the facts and abuses of his life pushed him toward what he assumed was the obvious answer, that quicker path to peace: the sweet and somber current of a grave. *Anything's better than facing those terrors,* He thought. *Right?* The ones that sought him so. Wherever that voice was leading him, nothing would come from it except for further pain. And Charlie'd had enough of pain.

No more, he decided as his tear-stained cheeks grew cold in the winds.

He knew the voice would call again. And soon. So he turned, sturdy upon conviction, and faced the sea. Trembling, his gut felt stretched like an old and tattered sheet. It wouldn't hold forever. It couldn't.

He couldn't.

His heart sank, and Charlie took a step. Just one, at first, into the sea's shallows. The smallest waves curled and broke over his shins as the tides moved back and forth, both pulling him and pushing back against his action.

He took another step, and something within seemed to crack. Both guilt and shame came like a set of waves and crashed over him, filling him with cruel remorse as the clarity of his choice grew.

He worked to bury that throb deep and let his steps carry him forward with rote precision when he heard another voice.

It was not the same dull drone as before, nor did it lack the warmth of the compassionate understanding of his situation.

Charlie recognized it right away, causing him more confusion. A voice he assumed he'd never hear again. A voice whose demise he felt ownership over. The warmth of churning shame within him swelled and grew as he stopped dead where he stood. The sea water lapping at him just above the knee.

Charlie? called the tender tones of his mother.

Shuddering and strained breaths struggled to escape his grip, unsettling him further.

It is time, Charlie. It's time to come back.

Charlie swung around, looking in all directions, believing he would find her standing there.

He found no one.

Silent for a moment, waiting, listening, Charlie hollered out to her.

"Mom? Is that you?"

The voice gave no response, but a rush of warm wind shot through his chest, confusing Charlie with an illusionary embrace.

He screamed out again.

"Mom?"

His thoughts flashed to when he'd first arrived back in Portland and found her lying lifeless on the floor. "I-I-I... Mom, I'm so sorry!" He burst into an almost violent sob, but the tears disappeared, fading into the falling rain. "I'm so sorry!"

A mix of shame and frustration flowed through him almost freely, but he held to the feeling. He clung to it, almost pinning it down, marking it as something he would never be free of.

"Charlie," the voice said, at last.

Charlie shot a glance up as the rain came tumbling down around him.

"It's time to let go, son. This burden was never yours to carry."

Tears continued to stream and pour. Even so, whatever he was holding onto, Charlie wouldn't release his grip.

"I'm just so sorry, mom, I–" his tears overwhelmed him. "For everything—"

"None of this was your fault, Charlie. Ever. None of this was yours to own. Come, please? Come to us now. Be free of it."

He heard the words, but he wasn't sure if he believed it. He felt like he'd never be able to be free.

Through a blurry lens of tears and rain, Charlie looked back as the far-reaching ocean waves wreaked havoc on one another. He sniffled and turned back once more. The impending and unforgiving stone wall stared back; the door seemed to have shrunk.

His insides pulsed and, confused, Charlie stood there in the pouring rain, unsure.

"Charlie," came the voice again. "It's time."

He shook as his previous conviction uprooted. He longed for that peace; but he felt sure that voice would lead him astray.

Should he trust it? he wondered. Was this just one more thing trying to lead him off to further pain?

Dammit! he thought as the storm brooded, growing around him. He'd never been closer to the end; yet never had he felt more lost.

A deafening blast came from far away, causing Charlie's confusion to mount. His mother's voice again stretched out over the wind and waves; not just hers, but others, too. He heard them streaming, reaching overhead; countless recognizable voices all calling to him.

His mother's voice reached him first, followed by Trent's, Oscar's, even Cait's—all people he had known; all people who had shown him care.

Each beckoned him forward, hoping to guide his will.

Still, he resisted.

They all shouted over each other, louder and louder, calling to him. Charlie felt somewhat overwhelmed when one cut through it all, sharp and clear.

Charlie, it said. It was Ellie's.

Charlie gasped. Even his tears slowed to listen. Her voice echoed softly through the windswept air.

None of this is your fault, Charlie. We're all accountable for our own choices. You burden yourself too much.

Charlie looked up at the door. Further away, it appeared somehow smaller than before.

It's time to let us go, Charlie, came his mother's voice. *All of us. Time for all this to end. Time for you to go back. To move forward.*

Charlie's tears broke once more, and he somehow only found the means to grip harder on all that he carried. The weight of it all. If he let it go, everything he'd ever known would leave him; everything that he'd thought was good. He would reel from the lack of it and lose all balance altogether. Then what would he have left? His guilt and shame? He didn't wish to fight anymore. Exhausted, tired, Charlie craved to give in.

Charlie, the initial voice chimed in again, arresting Charlie's attention. *The path to peace lies before you, not behind. Your fight is not yet over. But it will be soon, and you will have your rest.*

A flare of anger burst through him, but he welcomed it. It sheltered him from pain long enough to reason out what he deemed could be true.

He turned and faced the ocean, wondering at the worth of desperate hope.

Over the years, he'd reasoned that the harder roads were the right ones.

But this? He couldn't discern what was right or wrong.

Shit, he thought to himself, realizing he had already resigned himself to what he saw as the more difficult route. His rest would have to wait. It wouldn't be *a proper rest* anyway, he thought to himself. He couldn't rest. Not until it was *all* over. But what was *it*? And how would he proceed?

Come, Charlie West. It's time to remember.

Something shifted in him, like the contents of a shelf rearranging themselves. Charlie felt all at once unsteady, confused, scared, but also the faintest flicker that hope was possible.

The winds picked up, bringing with them wild sprays of seawater, colliding with that familiar pull. It's strength, the sheer gravity of it, harsher than he'd ever experienced before.

By some miracle, Charlie found himself standing before the door. The wall towering above him, reaching up into the indifferent sky overhead.

Time seemed to stop and the wooden frame before him creaked from the pressure, bent by whatever force laid behind it.

Then the winds died down, the pressure receded in exchange for a gentle breeze, and a familiar voice rode up its soft gusts.

It was Charlie's mother's once more, and it spoke with the softest reassurance he had ever known. Whatever resolve remained in him cracked and broke in two.

"I love you, son, but it's time. Time to let us go. Time for you to only carry your own burden. No one else's. It's time to move on."

Charlie wept. A dam had burst, and he felt himself caught up in its tumultuous wake.

I'm so sorry, mom, he thought, as the momentum of this release pushed him forward. Grasping the door's handle in his grip, he turned the knob and pulled.

A force greater than Charlie had ever known burst itself forth as a rush of water gave way and blasted out. It knocked him back—flailing—the current sweeping him out to sea.

He had no control at all. In the muffled swirl of underwater sounds, that familiar voice rang out again, speaking one word.

Remember.

Remember what? he thought. He did not know what he was supposed to remember. Either way, it felt too late.

Frigid waters flooded over him, too fast for his awareness. They kept coming. The pressure released by the tiny opening swelled, pushing against the door's edges. The immediate area bowed; the structure—the wall itself—leaned and sections gave way. Spidery cracks ruptured up in every direction from the small doorway. Its integrity would not last. Soon, it would fall in its entirety. Once the process started, it would unravel until the end.

The threads of his own mind followed suit to a breaking point, but he held tight; he felt himself fighting and flailing against the ebb and flow.

Then, something miraculous took place. Something he'd never felt before. Amidst the surrounding madness—chaos, real or not—Charlie *let go*. Body and mind, it was too much.

All control left him as his limp body hit the edge of the shallows and the rushing flow carried him further out from the shore.

That's when the images and visions, once again, flowed. Recreations of his childhood past flew by. The difficulties. The trials. The defining moments. His entire journey to Astoria and those first few days fired past. It all happened in a split second.

His body shot through every arching wave to well beyond the break itself, and still he kept going.

His mind and body racing along, he again settled back into a single moment. In the clearing along the river, just outside Astoria. Darkness hung, as it always did. A circle of little men in shadowy hoods stood around him, united by their haunting chant.

Charlie closed his eyes, hoping not to see what would come next. But it wasn't up to him anymore.

He saw his body shooting up into the embattled sky, the horizon filled with lightning and storm.

He knew his greatest horror was about to emerge.

The sky then ripped open and he tightened his eyes shut to keep from seeing, but could feel the heat.

He knew then what he'd been hiding from. And he knew its presence loomed, growing nearer and nearer. Instinct struck, telling him this time he wouldn't be able to hold it back. He wouldn't be able to resist it; it would force him to face his fear.

At last, the bursts of rushing water slowed, and Charlie found himself adrift, alone and far from shore.

In his vision, he hung before what he'd feared for so long.

That haunting voice spoke out again.

Charlie West...

He braced himself.

... remember.

Eyes still clenched shut, Charlie couldn't fathom what it was he should remember, but those pangs of guilt and shame bled out.

Remember, it said again.

This time, Charlie yelled out in response.

"What? Remember what?"

Only silence answered.

Then, the creature's voice came forth.

As you wish.

And Charlie remembered.

His eyes opened, and he looked upon the creature he'd spent so much time running from, but he only saw himself.

It all came rushing back, its fury unrestrained, and he remembered what he'd done. He remembered everything. The consuming anger. All that had taken place. The Order. Trent. Ellie, all of it. He remembered the destruction. It had been left up to him. Or so it felt. The decision had seemed placed in *his* hands. *His* choice. *He* had been the one to inflict that pain on to so many. *Right?*

The same pain that had been passed onto him, he thought.

Wasn't he just passing it on then? One more broken cog in a systemic world of hurt?

Anguish filled him.

Then he remembered the aftermath the next morning. His light and hope extinguished. All those lights that had gone out. And he knew the shame he wore, he had earned. And he didn't want it anymore.

He saw himself falling from the sky, tumbling back down to the world below. The wake of his destruction.

Charlie opened his eyes again and found himself surrounded by water, drifting in the currents of those great rolling waves.

His body shivered in the freezing cold. He welcomed it, that icy, numb embrace. *Wasn't this better?* he thought. Right where he wanted to be. The choice had become simple. He could *give* in. He could *rest*.

Hadn't the truth revealed itself at last? Wasn't it time for him to answer for what he'd done? To be free of it all?

As clarity formed, another voice called out. One that, for whatever reason, seemed more solid than the others. It stemmed from some place so real; or so it seemed. Though Charlie couldn't quite figure why. It ached with cruelty and vengeance, accompanied by laugher, though void of any mirth. It was unfamiliar to him, but still he recognized its icy tones. It came from the skies above him, well beyond where his mind dwelt in that moment, and it began pulling him toward his conscious self.

"Charlie!" the voice echoed. "Can you hear me in there? Come back! We're not *done* with you yet!"

As if answering some command, Charlie's body seized. As if lightning struck, far, far away; but it found him anyway, through strange and unseen roots.

Fury rode its way through him, and he wrenched and

reeled and fumed. His own yells turned into a sort of animal-istic growl. The creature joined him in the frenzy.

"There you are, Charlie! Thatta boy!" boomed Mr. Black-well, not taken to fear like the others standing by, watching.

Part of Charlie's mind was aware that he wanted to stop this, but another part altogether seemed more bent toward impending disaster.

A wayward laugh cut its way through the chaotic back and forth as Mr. Blackwell felt himself losing his grip on Charlie's jacket.

"Are we ready yet, Doctor?"

Dumbfounded, Dr. Grenier considered what he was seeing. He hadn't even heard whether the next subject was ready.

"Sir, you can't possibly—"

But he'd never finish that thought.

Charlie had stood, of his own strength, and knocked Mr. Blackwell's hands away. He glared down at the man who'd caused such strife.

"*You*!" Charlie said to Mr. Blackwell, rage swelling within him. "N-no more!"

"What do you mean *no more*, Charlie? Look how close we are. Look upon your legacy! Look upon the future!"

With that, Mr. Blackwell gestured to the chamber through the glass.

Charlie turned, taking in what he could.

His body shook, shuddering with the horror of what stood before him.

"There's no stopping what's coming, Charlie West. The past is set in stone, dictating what will come."

"No..." Charlie said again. "It can't be... No!"

"Yes, Charlie. Yes! There's no stopping it now."

Charlie's anger faltered and crumbled somewhat at his realization.

"All those people you hurt? All the pain you caused... We're here to end the pain, Charlie West! Are you not thankful for this deliverance? What has the world ever given you?"

There was a strange and weary logic to Mr. Blackwell's words.

Charlie looked around and saw no hope. How could he stop this? What could he do against this? Against them? How could he make it right? To fight? Wasn't this what he deserved, anyway? For the destruction he'd caused?

He loosened his grip on the man's well-kempt suit.

"That's right, Charlie. You have one choice: *give in.*"

Right then, the elevator doors chimed and slid open. Out stepped Cait, terror-struck by what she saw. Her pistol raised, ready. Not holding back, she screamed out.

"Charlie!"

Charlie turned to glimpse her familiar face.

Mr. Blackwell moved to break away from Charlie and yell out, but it was too late. The creature shrieked in the background, triggering the latent fear that laid within Cait. Without a second thought, she raised the pistol and unleashed upon the room. More out of desperation than anything else, paying sole attention to not hitting Charlie.

The room collapsed into chaos.

Sixteen

"Charlie, get down!"

Charlie heard Cait's voice call out as the bullets sprayed before he registered she was there. In shock and self-preservation, he dropped to the floor to avoid getting struck.

Shots sprayed through the room, hitting everything in sight. Computers, screens, and equipment, and three of the technicians, one of whom died right away. Another struck Dr. Grenier in the leg, and he collapsed to the floor, screaming. Mr. Blackwell, too, she hit in the shoulder, right next to his collarbone. He screamed out and fell to the floor, blubbering in feeble whimpers.

Two of her shots went wide of anyone, piercing the glass behind Mr. Blackwell after he fell. They ripped right through and continued on into the next chamber, where they struck against the case holding back the newborn creature.

Screams tore through the air once more, causing men to trip over themselves as they attempted their escape. A few made it. The rest would not be so lucky.

The bullets did not destroy the glass enclosing the creature, but several hairline cracks branched out in all directions from each hole. Its integrity wouldn't last.

Still, the creature screamed and beat against what remained of its inner cage.

Most everyone stayed low, laid out on the floor in panic, holding their wounds.

Cait sprinted up toward where Charlie lay, convulsing on the ground, still gripped by his connection with the creature.

"Charlie! Charlie! Are you...?"

But the sight of him cut her off. His body was writhing back and forth, still bathed in the horrid crimson glow emanating from around his neck.

A shattering sound rang out, followed by a series of yelps and gasps.

Cait looked up to see everyone in the observation room fumbling backward. The technicians, Dr. Grenier, Mr. Blackwell himself, everyone trembled.

"I-Its... its free!" someone yelled.

"Run! Go!"

Turning back, she saw the remnants of the encasement. Jagged chunks of glass either stood up from the floor or hung from the ceiling, from the casement's base and top. The putrid fumes cascaded over the remaining shards like fog pouring into a valley from the mountains before a storm.

It spread, reaching out to smother and fill every inch of space it could. Slowly, it seeped its way through the bullet-hole filled glass, further weakening its integrity.

More horrifying than that, though, was the creature standing there amidst it. Free. It's scratchy breathing hovering over the misty smoke.

Cait caught a clear sight of it, immediately wishing she hadn't after her mind registered what it saw.

It had more in common with some deep underwater creature than anything else, she thought, though it remained upright like a human, towering over everything. It stood there for a moment, its breath heaving back and forth, perhaps adjusting to its surroundings.

Cait froze for a second, just standing there, staring.

At last, the creature's scream broke the spell, and it reared itself to leap forward.

Cait's heart almost leaped from her own body, but she noticed something. *It* wore the same medallion as Charlie.

She had a thought.

As the room around her fell into panic, Cait reached down and tore the bronze artifact from around Charlie's neck. The change in his affect was instantaneous.

"Charlie!"

Cait couldn't hold back her own scream as the creature approached the observation glass, which, aside from a few bleeding holes from bullets, stood strong.

Charlie scrunched his eyes together and moved his head back and forth, moaning a little.

"Charlie! Wake up! We gotta go!"

Not waiting for his response, she just grabbed him by the arms and started dragging him out of the room.

Right then, Mr. Blackwell pushed himself back up from off the ground. He rounded on Cait.

"You! You've ruined everything, god dammit!"

But Cait turned away, flinching, having foreseen what was about to happen.

With the dagger-like clawed ends of the creature's appendages, it slammed against the still-cracking glass until it shattered, exploding all around the room.

It silenced everyone.

Mr. Blackwell stumbled, falling back to the ground, while Dr. Grenier and the few technicians remained cowered where they hid, fear-stricken and trapped.

"Come on, Charlie," Cait said; more to herself than to

Charlie. He showed no signs of returning to the conscious world.

The creature stepped over the sill, breaking off whatever glass remained, and touched down into the observation room. Its breathing rippled itself around the room. Its very presence seemed to suck all the warmth away.

At the sight of it, one technician panicked and tried to sprint away.

The creature threw one of its tentacles forward, catching the man right in the neck with its jagged claw. It punctured straight through and stuck, then reeled the man back towards itself. It seemed to examine him; like a mineralist seeking flaws in a gem. It held him up, and its arm shook. The sinewy membrane of its skin seemed to ungulate upward, pulsing away from its body, passing something from itself to the man whose body broke out into violent shakes. If not secured by the creature's arm, he would've fallen to the ground.

Cait was still dragging Charlie in a state beyond the point of comprehension. How could a person make sense of what she'd just seen?

"Come on! Come on, Charlie! We gotta–"

But then he spoke.

"Ca-Cait? Is that..."

"Charlie!"

His name spilled out of her mouth, coated in both relief and terror.

Seeing where he was and what was there, he shot forward in alarm.

"What the... What is that? Where... are we...?"

"I dunno what the fuck is going on, Charlie, but we have to leave! Now!"

He shook his head in agreement.

Mr. Blackwell stirred again and looked up at the creature,

both mesmerized and terrified. He would've preferred seeing the creature from a safer, more sterile, distance.

The creature retracted its claw, letting the man's limp body fall to the floor. His eyes rolled back, as if retreating into his skull. It then moved onto the next closest man, sticking its claw into him and lifting him from the ground.

Mr. Blackwell considered making a run for it, but was glad he didn't when he'd watched Dr. Grenier attempt to flee. The creature reached out with its other appendage, lodging itself into the doctor's neck as well—he made a similar guttural whelp before his eyes rolled back and it raised him, too, from the ground for whatever horrendous fate awaited these men.

Mr. Blackwell sprang up then and scampered out the observation room door. As he was leaving, he made momentary eye contact with Cait and Charlie. He didn't look terrified, but unhinged. Not even this disaster had wiped that stupid grin off his face. He disappeared behind a door in one of the floor's adjacent rooms.

"Let's g-go," Charlie struggled to say, and he labored to stand himself up and follow where Mr. Blackwell had gone.

"No! This way!" Cait stopped him. "I have a plan."

"A plan?"

"Well, I have *part* of a plan."

Charlie was in no place to argue. Either way, he trusted her —look at what she'd risked for him.

As soon as they were both to their feet, a sharp and piercing cry brought their attention back to the observation room.

They looked back just as two more fresh bodies hit the floor. What alarmed them most was what they witnessed rising behind the first creature. Reaching up first with its own arm, using its newly formed claw to dig its way into a nearby bay of computers and pull itself up from where it lay. Not yet fully transformed.

"It's not..." Cait halted. "That's... that's not possible—"

She turned to Charlie.

"We need to get out of here! Now!"

The second creature's scream reached out and pierced the air, planting a seed of genuine fear and dread in Cait and Charlie both. The first creature stood tall while the last remaining man hung from its grip, and the same rhythmic undulations pulsed through its arm, causing the limp man to shake.

Another turned, Cait thought.

Their numbers were growing—spreading like a disease.

A fear gripped Cait she'd never known before, but it fueled her.

"Holy hell..."

The words trickled from Charlie in a low whisper as remnants of Mr. Blackwell's plan formed in his mind. "This is —" The current seemed to stop. "We can't let *these* get out."

He and Cait stared at each other.

"It'll be—"

"We need a way out first, Charlie."

He nodded his head in agreement.

The elevator wasn't too far away.

Cait and Charlie sprinted towards it, mashing the down button over and over until the doors opened.

By the time they scrambled inside, Cait first and Charlie in tow, a third creature was already rising from the ground. The snapping of bones changing shape and of muscles reforming echoed through the empty room.

Inside, Cait mashed the button to the garage floor, panting the whole time.

"*Come on!*" she said over and over. "*Comeon-comeon-comeon!*"

The doors shut at last, as two more limp bodies dropped to the floor. Two *other* creatures had raised and were making their way forward. Their screams faded as the elevator doors shut, cutting Cait and Charlie off from being easy prey.

The elevator began its slow descent.

Cait turned, letting her near-panic lead her.

"Charlie!"

He didn't answer, but looked lost and deep in thought.

"Charlie?" she said again, shaking him this time.

"Huh? Wh–?"

He half turned, moaning.

"Charlie, what the fuck are those things? What the— what's going on?"

"We..." He started, then paused, exasperated. "Look... I don't really know, but—" Charlie stopped himself, remembering something.

"What? What is it?"

He looked up at Cait. She rescued him. Such a selfless act, but he wondered if it had been worth it.

Tears welled up in him, tears that he tried to push away. It was a welcome distraction, considering it shifted the way Cait had been looking at him.

"Hey, it's going to be alright. We—we could make it out..." she said.

The optimism in her tone surprised Charlie. Given what he'd just seen, he wasn't so sure. Besides, he wasn't sure he wanted to get out. Or deserved it.

"I-I'm... sorry," he said back, the words spilling out more in a plea.

"No. No, Charlie. You have nothing to be sorry about, okay?"

She reached out her hands again, and Charlie pulled away almost defensively.

"You don't understand," he said, anger rising in him again.

This lost her. She wondered what could've put a person in such a state?

His anger plunged once more and deflated into a somber puddle.

"*This*?" He motioned to their surroundings. "This is all *my* fault."

Shaking her head, all Cait wanted was to understand, but he wouldn't let her refute it.

"It's all my fault..." he kept saying.

Indifferent to the situation or his pleas, the elevator held to its descent, moving further and further underground.

"... It's all my fault..."

Cait leaned toward him and took him by the hand.

Surprised at first, Charlie looked up.

"Your fault or not, Charlie, we have to try getting outta here. And somehow *not* let those things loose. You saw what they did."

Charlie looked up at her. A soberness came as he wiped the tears from his cheeks.

"Imagine what they'll do to the city if they get out."

At this, Charlie tried to collect himself.

The elevator came to a stop and chimed, and the doors slid open.

As perplexed as Cait was by what plagued Charlie, Charlie was equally perplexed by Cait's forward drive. Everything in him told him to stop and let the wave crash over him. Then it would all be over.

But not her. She strove forward with passion and a need to reach something. It ignited a flicker of something Charlie knew he'd once felt.

Stepping out of the elevator, it was he who spoke first.

"So, what's *this plan*?"

Cait cracked a wild smirk.

"You're not gonna like it."

He pursed his lips together, trying to hide his rising sense of fear. He knew she was going to try it, no matter what. She wouldn't let him give in.

"And Charlie," she said, more gravely. "We might not make it out. I want that to be clear. I wanted to get you to safety. You're here because of me..." She felt the need to add. "... but we're..." She hesitated. "We're the only line here. The only defense against these... *things*..."

A strange comfort settled into him at those words. In that moment, he didn't feel the need to correct her he'd, in fact, brought himself there. No matter what, he would've ended up there. Somehow. If not then, then later. The Order would've found a way.

He looked at Cait then and spoke with an almost defiant twinge.

"Try me."

They were the most confident words he'd spoken in months.

Cait smiled again. This time, it was sincere and filled with thankfulness.

"Follow me," she said. Cait hurried to a door halfway down the hall and entered.

Charlie followed, the screams of the creatures reaching out from the floors above. They were coming, and Cait was counting on it. Hoping for it, even.

———

Bursting into his office, yelping from the force exerted by his injured, bleeding arm, Mr. Blackwell marched towards his desk, his assistant close in tow.

"How the hell did she get out?" He flailed. He was anything but steady. "This–This is an absolute disaster! This..." The words stopped; he crumbled even more, then.

The fault lines in his voice cracking and extending further. "... this was to be *my* triumph!"

His assistant looked away, avoiding the discomfort brought on by watching his superior cave. A man who'd once exuded the epitome of strength.

"P-perhaps we s-should phone the Head? See how they want us to proceed?"

"Absolutely not!"

"But sir–"

"I said no, dammit! I don't want them anywhere near this, do you understand?"

Like a disobedient dog, the man lowered his head to concede.

"They would take everything from me. Everything! It would be my end."

For a moment, neither man spoke. Mr. Blackwell seemed to consider something.

"Call up to the helipad."

"Sir?"

"I said call now! Tell them we need to leave in two minutes."

"Sir, that doesn't–"

"Two minutes, dammit!"

The assistant leaped back.

"Yes, sir. Right away." And he was gone.

As he strode off, Mr. Blackwell lumbered with a nervous stagger over to a screen built into the wall opposite his desk. He pinned several numbers in and said, "Blackwell, Weyland. 067214387."

A mechanical voice sounded off.

"Welcome, Weyland Blackwell."

"Initiate code 7 lockdown right away. Password *Breach*."

"Password accepted. Initiating code 7 lockdown now."

Part of his mind settled into an uneasy peace, but not all of it. *At least the sub-basement would stay secured*, he told himself. *Nothing would get out. The creatures or the gas.*

He took a deep breath.

They weren't ready yet. The plan just wasn't ready. This is just a setback, he tried convincing himself, though he knew otherwise.

He took several deep breaths, which failed to comfort him. Several unsure steps led him to a far wall where a painting hung. He tossed it aside, revealing a safe. His hands shook as he typed a password and placed his thumb upon a scanner. The safe clicked and opened. Inside was a copy of the borrowed ancient texts, one he'd pored over for hours on end. The other copy, they'd lost downstairs, somewhere in the lab's destruction. The chaos and disarray.

His assistant hustled back in, frantic.

"Just heard..." He Panted. "The helicopter said they'll try to be read—"

"Make sure that they are. We're leaving."

"Yes, sir."

A series of distant rumbles set up beneath them, an unsettling sound and feeling given their proximity.

"Let's get outta here," Mr. Blackwell said, still unwilling to admit to failure.

"And where are we headed, sir?"

Mr. Blackwell looked over to the man. He didn't know, but couldn't admit that.

"Anywhere but here," was all he said.

His assistant knew not to question him.

Seventeen

"What is this place?"

Charlie's voice bounced off the walls, echoing through the hollow space around them.

Cait looked around, following his dead stare.

"It's an old boiler room," she said.

Charlie nodded, his jaw half ajar as he took it all in.

A series of gauges lined the wall on the left. Each with their own accompanied pipe that reached upward to the ceiling. They curved back towards the room's center where they converged; they bent downwards, inserting themselves into the giant monstrosity of a boiler standing before them.

"I found it on my way to find you. Thought it might serve a certain purpose if we got desperate."

"And we're..."

"Desperate."

Charlie worked to keep still and straight, finding it impossible to gulp.

"At first, I thought it might help us escape. Serve as a distraction. But now..."

She trailed off, and Charlie watched as her mind churned something over.

After a few seconds, he pressed her.

"But *now...*?"

Digesting whatever idea she had in mind seemed difficult, even for Cait.

"Whatever the hell these things are..."

She looked right into Charlie's eyes.

"... we can't let them escape." She paused. "We have to bury them."

They each turned then and faced the boiler while Cait kept talking.

"Get out if we can, but..."

Cait didn't finish the thought, but Charlie knew. And his preference for *that* end filled him with shame.

Charlie felt Cait letting go. Coming to terms with that potential reality. Knowing what might come gave him the push he needed to move forward.

Either way, her tenacious desire to act was infecting him. Scratching an itch he hadn't felt in several long months. Since he tried taking the reins of his own life and moving to Astoria.

Charlie shuddered and pushed the thoughts away.

Instead, he focused on helping Cait.

"So, what do we do?"

Cait grinned, extending something to him.

"Take this."

Charlie reached out and, before he knew it, was holding a bucket.

"Fill it with whatever flammable canisters you can find on that shelf over there."

With that, Cait sprinted off, gathering what they'd need. To his surprise, there was a shelf he'd overlooked, filled with cleaning and painting supplies, most of which were flammable.

"What do I do with it?"

He still didn't quite understand the plan.

Cait responded without looking at him.

"Dump it in the middle there. Then get more."

Charlie turned to where the boiler stood, waiting. It stared right back at him. Shrugging his shoulders, he got to work gathering what he could.

Cait disappeared into a closet in the corner. Echoing sounds of her investigations trickled out of the shadows. She rummaged through boxes, and shelves, and whatever she could find.

"Yes!" he heard Cait call out from the shadows.

"What is it?"

She didn't respond right away.

Charlie dumped the second load of canisters in the room's center and Cait called out again. This time to him.

"Charlie, come help me with these."

Before he even took a step, Cait had already exited the closet doorway, dragging a large wooden crate filled with an assortment of whatever she'd found inside.

"What is that? What's this all for?"

"No time! Just come help!"

Together, they dragged it to the center of the room, and they both stood up to catch their breath.

"Okay," Cait said, canvasing the room again. "Here, help me with these."

The order rushed out of Cait but came gentle enough. Easy to follow. Charlie's tired mind struggled to keep up, but the time spent in his unconscious dream state had him some semblance of rest to carry him on.

Cait's eyes were electric as she grasped hold of the little metal wheel before her. "You get that one," she said to Charlie, and she started turning. She was halfway through rotating the first wheel, closing off the valve, when Charlie reached his. As it turned, a sharp hissing noise droned from above them. The first of many.

"I think this'll work, Charlie."

Cait did not hide the excitement in her voice.

At last, Charlie completed the gauge. Though he struggled with it at first, he turned the handle until it wouldn't budge anymore. The piercing hiss increased as pressure built, and he moved on to the next.

Cait had already made it past her second and third valve and was onto her fourth.

Together, they'd finish in no time.

Once completed, the room wheezed. The air seemed to retreat as the surrounding space filled with a mounting chorus. A pressure, desperate, in need of release. Machine parts clanked, fighting to follow the routine tasks for which were built—this level of pressure not being one of them.

Cait was counting on that.

Shooting across the room, Cait called to Charlie again.

"Here, help me with this thing."

Jogging to catch up, Charlie's head felt light again. Detached. He watched in wonder as Cait dragged a huge iron barrel to the center of the room.

Exhaustion crept its way back up through Charlie, battling the adrenaline as it made its slow way toward his mind, but he stepped in to assist Cait. He still hadn't the slightest idea what her plan was. Together, they rolled it right to a spot where it rested in front of the boiler's main tank.

"This is all old, right? Run down for this modern a building?"

Cait shrugged.

Often one for silence, Charlie was unsure why he felt the need to fill the moment with unnecessary chatter, but he couldn't help it.

"Just doesn't make any sense."

"Yeah, it's weird," she said at last as she opened one bottle they'd collected and dumped it into the barrel. Without looking up at him, she said, "Here, start dumping. Anything that's flammable."

He jumped to it, picking up the first bottle he could find, unscrewing the lid, and pouring it out.

Echoes of liquid trickling filled the silence, and Cait broke in at last. Though with a certain amount of reluctance.

"I think it's the rich guys who run these projects."

Charlie looked up. Cait wanted to say more; that much was clear.

"The outside is always so polished. *Spare no expense*, as they say, but with the inside—spare *every* expense."

He could see he'd struck a nerve. For a time, neither of them spoke. They just kept opening and emptying bottles until the barrel was full. The fumes carried themselves upward, mixing with the heat emanating off the then-shaking pipes hanging down from the ceiling.

"How do you know so much about—"

"My dad was a developer," Cait said, cutting him off. "Never cared much for starting from scratch. Just come in. Put on a new face. And move on. That was his way."

"*Was*? I'm sorry."

Cait picked up the last bottle, looking up at Charlie. She sensed herself growing frustrated, but knew it had nothing to do with him. Given their end might be imminent, she hoped to leave in peace.

"Thanks," she said to him. "That was a long time ago, though. Let's just get this done."

Charlie shook his head in agreement, and they left it at that.

They'd both tossed their last empty bottles to the ground, except for the one Cait held under her arm.

Charlie looked up, a little lost.

"What now?"

Cait's smile grew wide as she pulled out a box of matches from her pocket.

"Found these in the closet."

Charlie's jaw fell open.

"You're going to–"

"What'd you think the plan was here, Charlie?"

He stared at her.

"And *I'm* not. We are," she said, matter of fact.

"But–but that will–"

"We don't know want it's gonna do. Fact is, I don't have the slightest clue how this'll work. All I know is it's the only idea I had, and—"

She stopped herself for a second. She was defending herself again, a painful habit she'd rather not punctuate the end with.

Charlie gathered himself and nodded his head.

"*Okay*," he said, shaking.

"Those things are coming, and *this*..." In desperation, Cait pointed to the boiler. "... might cause enough damage to take 'em out, or at least bury 'em."

Following her every word, Charlie only had one more question.

"And us?"

Cait looked up, unsure how to respond.

"I don't know. At first, I needed to get here. To this place. Then it changed. I had to get to you. Get you outta here, right? But *now*..."

She'd begun rambling, not something she was used to.

Charlie felt he knew. She didn't have to answer. If this were the end? So be it. No big deal. At least his struggle would be over.

"We don't even know what we're dealing with. What those creatures are. Or what's happening."

Charlie's mind raced. He wished he had time to fill Cait in more. Knowing there wasn't, he just nodded his head to agree.

"Let's just—"

Cait stopped, her words cut short by the wrenching screams of their nameless pursuers echoing from up the stairwell.

"Shit! They're here, Charlie. We gotta go!"

Panic struck again, rocketing its way through them both, but watching Cait stay so calm and focused led Charlie down a path he was unfamiliar with. It was as if his body had a choice, and he'd chosen to let it roll over him. The feelings still existed, but he'd pushed to the side. Somehow. Making him feel more awake.

Cait slid off the last bottle's lid and emptied it, making a trail from the barrel to where she stood.

Then, holding up the box of matches, Cait grit her jaw and, looking up at Charlie, spoke through a jack-o'-lanterns grin.

"I'm just glad whoever worked down here was a smoker."

Cait thought it was something Scott would've said, bringing her comfort and filling her with pride.

Charlie cocked his head and couldn't help but smile.

"We have no clue what's going to happen?"

"None."

"Okay."

"Okay."

And Cait struck the match. Sparks crackled as faint sulfuric hues dissipated into the air. Cupped in Cait's hand, the little flame woofed outward, settling itself into a tiny beacon within the warm glow of her fingers, though it was pale and weak given the shadowed spaces within the room.

As she was about to drop it, Charlie hollered.

"Hey!"

She paused. "Yeah?"

"Thanks for coming for me," he said. There was a sincere closure in his tone.

Cait turned to him one last time.

"Thanks for not wanting me to come here alone. Turns out you were right."

Charlie gave a weak grin, thankful even for the slightest flicker of hope.

"Get ready to run like hell," Cait said as a final warning.

A chorus of screams echoed through the halls once more, ricocheting towards them. They were drawing nearer.

After a nervous exhale—the flame flickering in her hand—Cait let go.

Charlie held his breath as he watched the little flame fall, but Cait had already turned and gripped the door handle.

"Come on, Charlie!"

She grabbed him by the shoulder and pulled.

The match hit the puddle by their feet and went up in a faint burst as the chemicals ignited, filling the musty air with a blizzard of unfamiliar smells.

It was like watching liquid dominos tumble as the trail went up in one fiery shot, determined to find more to consume.

Cait had the door pulled open, tugging Charlie from where he stood.

"Run, Charlie! Go! Go!"

One step into the hall, Charlie stumbled, surprised by the fresh and furious flood of screams that made their way towards them. A strange and terrifying tentacle-like appendage touched down, and his eyes went wide with alarm. The first of many to appear.

Charlie froze.

"Run!"

Cait's shrill voice rang out as she continued her charge

forward. The garage was just ahead. Across the hall and on the right.

Cait had only one thought: to keep moving. Reaching back again, she yanked Charlie forward. In only a handful of frantic steps, they reached the door, Cait first, Charlie in tow, as the wild, inhuman shrieks pierced the heavy air.

Fumbling with the door, Cait mumbled to herself.

"Come on! Come on! Comeon-comeon-comeon!"

Charlie looked up. The creatures were halfway down the hall, almost to them. He screamed.

At last, the door opened.

"Come on, Charlie!"

They'd made it into the vast concrete understructure and garage when the first of several explosions struck. It knocked Cait and Charlie both to the ground, and dust fired off the wall behind them.

"Get up, Charlie!"

She reached down to give him a hand. He did his best, but exhaustion slowed his ability to move at the proper speed.

"Come on!"

A line of vehicles stood not too far ahead.

They sprinted on as a rabid thump hit the door behind them and a series of muffled shrieks sounded off.

A second, much larger blast erupted, blowing right through the wall behind them. It knocked Charlie to the cold concrete floor.

Several of the creatures, too, flung through the debris, almost tossed into the garage.

Cait kept her feet, but her heart sank. Panic-stricken, she dragged Charlie behind her.

"Come on! Come on! Come on!" Cait said. An almost brainless mantra; there was no time to think.

One creature stood up at last and, leaning forward,

bellowed and sprinted. One by one, the others gathered themselves and followed suit.

Their movements were strange. Foreign to the eyes. Quicker than Cait would've predicted.

She made it to the first truck, which she found locked.

"Fuck!" She was unable to hold the outburst back, but pushing on, she sprinted around to the other side, grabbing hold of Charlie's shirt. "Come on!"

The creatures were closing in.

The second truck, too, they found locked.

"Shit! Shit! *Shit*!"

If one of these vehicles wasn't unlocked, they were done. Everyone would be lost.

And *her* explosion, as far as she'd seen, hadn't done quite what she'd hoped.

"Come on, Charlie! Come on, Charlie!" Cait said. More so encouraging herself to keep moving.

A piercing fear rose in her, the starkest Cait had ever known. Still, she knew the risk of failure. The consequences of those creatures getting free. Overrunning the city.

It seemed a wild thing to consider, but kept her convictions clear.

Cait stole a glance, and *they* were almost upon them, their snarling screams echoing off the concrete, their wild limbs lashing through the darkness. Sometimes sparks shot out where the jagged claw at the end of their arms pierced itself through and dug into the ground, leaving substantial scars behind. They were gaining ground, their shrieks growing only louder and fiercer.

Just then, the loudest concussion yet struck. The floors shook. Cait would have sworn she'd heard entire floors of concrete crack as a wave of force thundered through the underground, bringing plumes of dust and debris with it.

The blast flung the beasts to the side a dozen feet, shocking them, while Cait and Charlie braced themselves against the truck. This gave them time enough to reach the next vehicle. It was an old, beat-up van, but it just needed to run.

To Cait's exasperated wonder, it was unlocked, and the keys were in the cupholder on the center console.

Cait gasped with hope.

"Charlie! Get in!"

She pushed him in through the driver's side and he spilled over into the passenger seat. Cait climbed in and took the wheel. The keys rattling in her hand, she overcame her nerves, found the ignition, and turned it over.

The van roared to life. It was the most beautiful sound Cait had ever heard. The hope of making it out flickered through Cait, though she didn't dare hold too tight.

So, they made it out? She thought. *What then? Wouldn't the creatures too?*

Cait's stomach sank.

The tires screeched as they spun against the near-frozen flooring before catching, and they were off.

As they took off, something sharp and jagged pierced the van's side paneling. It halted the rising momentum, almost causing the van to stall.

A gash ripped through the metal where the back doors attached, revealing a gleaming set of putrid, yellowish eyes. A second puncture broke through and a force unimaginable tore upward, creating a hole. Flaps of metal peeled away like aluminum foil to reveal a creature, its viscous upper torso and face—if you could call it such—illuminated by the van's faint light. It let loose a screech that pierced deep into both Cait and Charlie, supplanting what fear they already felt. Its tentacles rippled forward like a flag flapping in the wind at the force of its shriek.

Cait slammed on the gas, but it was too late. A wild

thump echoed as *something* crashed down on the van; followed by another, and another.

Claws, one after another, began digging their way in through the metal.

The van tore around each bend on the path before them in a desperate search for the surface, and though Cait feared it was too late, she kept going, never taking her foot off the pedal.

Since seeing the band of creatures collected at the base of the stairwell, Charlie was slipping inward again. He couldn't help it—plagued by the visions he understood at last. Each shriek was nothing more to him than a reminder of what he'd done, and a blanket of guilt, uncomfortable and warm, wrapped itself around him. It clung tight. Suffocating. So far from reason, Charlie's mind struggled to cope with the developments.

Without thinking, Cait took the pistol from where she'd stowed it and tossed it to Charlie. It landed in his lap, awkward and foreign.

He gave her a feeble look.

"W-what do I do with this?"

Cait screamed back, keeping her focus forward.

"Use it!"

But Charlie sat there, frozen, taken by the weight of each wild thread of thoughts. Crippled.

"Charlie! Fucking shoot them!"

But Charlie couldn't move. He just sat there, staring down at the weapon in his lap.

Cait drove, challenging him to act, to do anything at all.

Jagged claws tore through the back of the van. Piercing, screeching, and snarling, seeking their prey. They'd be through in a matter of seconds.

"Charlie!" Cait screamed again, her voice somewhat lost in

the cacophony of sounds. Charlie wouldn't have heard her, anyway, as he sunk inward.

———

The explosion's initial blast had been large, shaking the surrounding walls; but not what she'd intended. A deep pit formed in her gut as she looked back to find, despite substantial damage, the walls and dominant structure of the building still standing.

It only delayed the creatures.

However, the ruptured boiler worked to set off a series of generator shutdowns, causing much of the digital systems within the building to power down. One of these systems had been what powered the piping between the laboratory chamber and the machine The Order had built to reach between worlds. Triggered by the bursts, the fumes flowed again.

Unobstructed, the gas streamed, making its way to any exit it could find. It caught fire from one of the many bursts that erupted in the basement, and those flames ate their hungry way in both directions along the pipe's given path.

In mere seconds, they found their unimpeded way to an exit, spilling into and flooding the shattered remains of the transformation chamber and lab. The flames flared as long as the gas flowed to fuel them, spreading to consume everything it could, as if bent on wiping away any stain of wickedness that remained.

In the other direction, the fire's guided path led deeper underground to recesses of the building known only to the most informed members of the Portland Order. The flames ripped through the walls, consuming their way down to the lowest rooms beneath the surface. A machine sat there resting, unrecognizable to the average person. An engine whose design stemmed from the *beyond*, twisted by the schemes of wicked men. It almost looked alive, as if breathing. It lit up, shining with every inhale that it took. A transfigured collection of accursed science and ancient lore; a horrid link between old and new. Built from breadcrumbs left by an ancient people, brought to fruition by those deemed maligned and lost.

It was with this device they harnessed power from beyond the veils of time and space; the tainted and otherworldly fumes to transform beings and call the Nameless back.

The flames filled this room, lighting up the darkness, consuming all it could.

Almost sentient, one might've heard the engine cry out before the end. With little power itself to temp whatever fate would fall, it ruptured. A massive explosion erupted of such force, nothing could contain the blast.

And the world shook once more.

———

"Charlie!"

Cait's shrill voice ripped through the frantic scene.

"Use it!"

She flung her hand towards him, slamming it hard into his chest.

His eyes widened. The smack ignited something in him. Reawakening his tired consciousness, even if just for that moment.

Caught between the tightrope of control, Cait hung there, on the verge of tears.

"Come on, Charlie!" She pleaded.

The creature's wails spoke of their proximity. One tentacle had disregarded the metal frame and was reaching itself forward then. It made a desperate grasp for Charlie's chair, the claw at its end scraping and tearing into the cushion, but it never took hold.

They took another turn at high speed. Cait leaned into it with the wheel.

She and Charlie held on as the van straightened back out.

It pushed forward.

"Charlie!" Her words, this time, flowed, lined with both weary hope and surprise. "Look!"

Charlie, his mind fading to a growing fog, glanced up.

An exit stood there, waiting. They were almost out, but a slight problem presented itself.

Each rotation of the van's wheels brought them closer and closer to their assumed salvation, only the closer they got, the closer the two massive steel doors drew together, sliding shut before them.

"No!" Her panic crept. "*Nonononononono!*"

She pushed up with her foot, lifting herself off the driver's seat, and leaned back, as if that allowed her to apply even more pressure to the pedal.

A fresh scream burst out as another of the creatures broke through. The other had pulled itself deeper into the van, and its razor claw, at last, pierced and embedded itself into Charlie's seat.

Charlie, all the while, sat statue-like throughout the entire wild ride.

Cait yelled out, tugging at the wheel and barreling on toward the emergency doors continued to close.

The van's speed had topped out.

We're not gonna make it, Cait thought. It was one of the last realizations she thought she'd ever make.

Still, she was proud they'd never given in.

"Char—"

The largest explosion yet shook the entire structure, cutting her off as they neared the still closing blast doors.

The otherworldly engine had ruptured.

Throughout the facility, pipes burst, foundations cracked and ruptured. The pulse of the engine spread its destructive reach in all directions, and all three buildings kneeled at once, as if they, too, were hiding in fear of whatever horrid torment awaited them.

Hungry flames consumed anything that was left, everything that was in their path.

Splits and cracks formed in what remained of the building's structures, preparing them for the fall.

Everything came crashing down.

The explosion rang outward, emitting a blast more furious than Cait had never known. The van fired forward, propelled beyond their control.

Flames erupted forward. A bright light stretched out in all directions. For a moment, the whole earth stilled. The concussive blast drowned out even the creature's frantic shrieks, and then everything went silent.

All Cait or Charlie would remember later was the heat. Though far from direct contact, even with the blast's extremity, their skin felt aflame. For those few terrible seconds, they screamed.

The light reached out—a mind to cleanse—wrapping itself around the van's rear side but making it no further.

The creatures clinging to the weak metal burned up in an instant, as if evaporating in the wild heat, and were gone.

In the van, Cait and Charlie fired through the door's gap just before it closed. What remained of the van's back paneling scraped against the door's steel, bending as it closed.

But it got through.

Cait's body seized, cinching herself back, bracing for the still-expected, inevitable end.

They fired up the exit ramp and took off through the air, landing some feet forward in the parking lot. The ground continued to shake beneath them. Cait lost complete control of the steering as the concrete rippled and curled upward like a rising wave dead set to break. There was nothing to do but let this current carry them forward.

As the pulse pushed outward in all directions, the wave of cement crashed behind them and disappeared into the growing crater that was emerging. The ground behind them gave way as Cait and Charlie continued onward in the current.

Crossing the threshold of the parking lot, a second great pulse shot outward from deep beneath the earth. A wave of pressure burst, towering upward. It climbed the side of each building. Each pane of glass shattered along in its wake. Shards tumbled downward; their freefall interrupted only by the flames rising to catch them. What remained of the entire city block crumbled and sank beneath the surface.

The upward force rammed the corner of the van into the street's curb, flipping it over. As it rolled, it flung Cait's body against the windshield and went limp. Charlie had strapped himself in, still frozen within a chrysalis of dread and fear. They careened forward across the street, nearing the river's edge.

One frantic thought took hold in Charlie's mind: that this van would be his tomb.

His ironic wish would come true. The frigid waters of the Willamette would wrap their icy arms around him and carry him on from his pain. This thought soothed him.

He saw Cait out of the corner of his eye. Cait? He wondered. She deserved more than this.

There was very little he could control; he told himself. Very little indeed.

These were Charlie's thoughts as the van hit the rail at the river's edge and tumbled over the embankment.

Toward what Charlie was sure would be their grave.

Eighteen

Given the altitude's stormy winds and the propeller's drag, Mr. Blackwell and his assistant had to work to make their way across the roof. Mr. Blackwell hugged the carrier bag filled with the remaining few objects that were precious to him.

"Sir!" The assistant's words faded into the wild winds and did not reach Mr. Blackwell. He tried again, but to no avail. "Sir!"

Mr. Blackwell kept walking, never looking up. His only goal was to close the distance to the chopper.

"Sir!" he said once more, and Mr. Blackwell at last stopped. He swung around to face the lesser man, breathing his annoyance.

"What? What is it?"

"Um... sir? I... where are... w-we going to g-go?"

Mr. Blackwell only shook his head and quickened his pace, ignoring the man altogether.

"Sir?" his assistant said, almost pleading. "Sir! We are accountable to The Order, sir. Surely we must go north and report back to the Head himself and the–"

Mr. Blackwell barked. "Don't you dare mention them to me!"

"But sir?"

Just before the chopper, Mr. Blackwell stopped. He turned, glaring down at the man, contempt brimming.

"No," Mr. Blackwell said. "*We* are not accountable to them. Not anymore."

His assistant took a step back, shocked. He didn't know what to say. It didn't matter, as another blast ruptured beneath them.

Mr. Blackwell pulled out a pistol of his own. The assistant gasped, but it was no use. He fired two shots into the man's gut, causing him to keel over and collapse onto the ground, where he lay whimpering. His lamenting wails faded, intermixed with the raging winds.

The building shook as another blast erupted from the floors below, and Mr. Blackwell climbed into the helicopter, leaving the man behind. He spoke two words to the pilot, in a lifeless and sterile tone: "Let's go."

That was it. The helicopter lifted itself off the roof and began its ascent into the clouds.

———

The free fall had been just as Charlie had imagined. Time slowed and stretched out; a single moment bled into several. One long and gentle stream, it lulled Charlie closer toward his yearning sense of sleep. His thoughts appeared as if they might catch up.

Floating there, in those brief moments, a bitterness crept up in Charlie. Something he never imagined he'd feel. This end? It felt too soon. Too abrupt. Lost for so long, he'd just wanted it to end. Not anymore, though.

He realized; he was *still* lost. Not out of the forest yet. But he *wanted* to find his way. A strange comfort.

The waves had knocked him far off course. They'd carried him well beyond his means of getting back to shore.

Worst of all, it seemed too late.

The cold air and surrounding pressure enveloped him, forming a strange cocoon around him. One that would harden and remake him. Prepare him for his journey beyond.

His heart wretched and shook. Something flickered to his left, a light refracting off the water's surface.

He glimpsed the unconscious Cait—unaware of their coming end—and something ignited.

The van struck the river's surface then, flinging them forward. That sharp jolt of the impact pulled Charlie from his terrifying reverie.

He reached out at the last second but couldn't prevent the force of Cait's body flying forward against the windshield. If it wasn't for the wall of water building up beneath them, she would have flown straight through.

Icy water filled everything around them, grabbing hold of his feet and ankles first, then moving up his legs and waist and beyond.

The impact knocked his attention off course, returning it to his dreadful hope of rest. But a certain focus came, over-powering. It tightened, burning. He welcomed it. It awakened in him those parts of his mind that he'd allowed to stay so dormant, so lost to their wicked dreams... they could sleep no more.

The water continued rising as the van sank. Time slowed down, and a strange clarity came to Charlie. A feeling he almost couldn't remember. It seemed he should be worried, but he wasn't. It wasn't the end he would have chosen, that much he knew. His thoughts felt odd. Things seemed *unfin-ished*, in a way.

At last, the preceding months found their context in the

night's revelations. He understood the pain. He understood himself. He saw the reason for the heavy weight. The burden he'd carried. It didn't remove it, but it felt easier to bear.

Though he didn't think it was something he could carry much further.

As the water rose to his chest and neck, then to his chin, he had almost no time to hold his breath before the water covered him. The currents swelled, pulling at him. His thoughts screamed to let go. To let it end. Let the pain subside and for the waves to carry him down the river currents toward more peaceful shores. As he began letting go, Cait's limp hand brushed against his, jolting him back. She hung there in the water, trapped with him in the cab.

Torn and confused, content to let himself sink toward a fate that to him seemed well-earned, Charlie couldn't leave Cait to the same demise. What had she done to deserve that? Beyond the foolish mistake of coming after someone who'd committed such an atrocity. Or so he thought.

Those fateful words echoed through his mind once more: *As you wish.* Remembering them made him feel sick.

No...

Fighting against those droning calls for peace, Charlie *knew* what he had to do.

———

Stunned into silence, Mr. Blackwell gaped, despondent, with both his hands pressed against the helicopter's window. He watched as the building's last pieces of integrity snapped and gave way. He watched as all three towers crumbled into dust, their only remnant being a massive rising plume of what remained.

Mr. Blackwell didn't see it as mere stone and iron falling, but the reality of his hopes and dreams crumbling before him, crushed to dust and gone. All he'd hoped to build and to accomplish. All he'd hoped to overcome. There would be no recovery from this. That much he knew. Watching the building fall was like watching a premonition. He imaged the remaining sects of The Order converging on him, swift and harsh. He needed to hide. To get away. But where?

The pilot called out, interrupting his thoughts.

"Sir?"

Mr. Blackwell's response came in a desperate growl; his body shook with rising fear.

"What?"

"Sir, we're just holding here. Where should we go? North up to–"

Mr. Blackwell's heart seized at the notion, and his fury broke in to cut the man off.

"No, god damnit! Any–anywhere but there..." His words seemed to break down and lose steam as he spoke. "Anywhere else..."

After a moment's pause, the pilot chimed in again.

"But... where, sir?"

Mr. Blackwell couldn't think. He was so overcome with grief. But at last, he managed.

"South," he said, his attention lost somewhere outside the window. "Just fly south for now, and I'll figure something out."

"Very well, sir."

The helicopter rocked back then forth as the pilot turned, setting a course.

Mr. Blackwell turned himself to keep the building's rubble in view. The longer he stared, the harder it was to believe what had happened, that it was all gone. To think, by morning, everything he'd built would be nothing more than cooling ash, its temperature brought low by the oppressive winds. Frantic, Mr. Blackwell's mind shook, feeling unable to connect one thought to the next. A man used to always having the next several steps planned out. The struggle crushed him. He had no clue where to go. Or what to do. Was there anyone he could trust? He racked his brain but could think of nothing. Nothing at all.

For the immediate future, he'd tell the pilot to keep heading south. Anywhere but towards The Head or The Order's Inner Circle.

———

Charlie unbuckled his seat belt and, right away, floated up a little higher in the water. He reached over and grasped Cait's arm.

A part of him lamented the loss of what it saw as his chance to rest. Yet this action, this simple movement of his body, driven by conviction, awakened something in him. Something he had felt only traces of following Cait through the building. He wasn't in a conscious place to process this, anyway. Not yet. Getting Cait to the surface was all that mattered. If the slightest chance of getting her out existed—let alone alive—Charlie had to try.

And so he did.

The steady weight of both guilt and shame clung; his all-too-familiar companions these past months. Still, a strange freedom rose in him—a mere fragile early spring bud. Many such buds held that destiny, never to bloom; falling to frost's far reach.

Grasping hold of Cait's arm, Charlie planted his feet against the dashboard and pushed off with all the strength he could muster.

Holding tight to her, he aimed his body straight to the center, where the van's back doors used to be. The entire back had been torn away. seared off and ground down to the wheelwells. Blistered edges of metal still flickered against the water as they cooled.

It appeared they weren't moving at all, as what remained of the van kept its course, drifting down beneath them. What little air existed in their lungs held them, lifting them somewhat towards the surface.

What had been their tomb slipped further beneath the surface, descending to the river bottom in search of its own resting place. As soon as they were free of it, pressure returned to Charlie's chest—his body was desperate for a fresh breath of air.

Faster than Charlie realized, momentum carried them upward, cutting through the river's dark and murky depths. He swam as he could, holding tight to Cait, using his cupped hand to pull them through the water.

The distance seemed only to keep growing. He felt they'd never reach the end.

Seconds felt like hours, but at last, the Portland cityscape emerged above them. Taking shape, there at the edge of the Pearl.

Flickers of flames lit up the outskirts of the water's surface as the buildings came into view.

The need for air grew desperate as they continued to rise. He couldn't hold it much longer.

The light grew stronger as they rose upward, and the darkness disappeared beneath them. He just needed to reach the surface.

Unconsciousness readied itself to pull him back down into the depths, but the surface fought back.

To his shock and relief, Charlie burst through the barrier between water and sky, greeted by the crisp and harsh midnight air.

Charlie gasped for his first breath when Cait's body shot up then up then bobbed back down, pulling him back under.

He choked on an invading gush of frigid river water before he could release a series of frantic kicks and waves of his one free arm to pull and keep himself above the surface. Struggling for a second, he worked to gather what breath he could. He wouldn't be able to hold them out of the water for long.

He strained, holding her up, and could get a quick glance around. To his relief, they weren't far from the river's edge. One of the city's many utility docks floated not forty feet away.

It wasn't a question of *if* he could make it. He had to. So, Charlie swam.

There was nothing left in him, but still Charlie pushed his body to move forward. With every movement, each muscle screamed. There was one positive to this, though: he wasn't thinking. He'd stumbled upon some default part of his brain that was more reactive. Nothing in him was freezing. His body just knew what to do.

Making it to the dock, at last, brought about its own problem. How could he pull them up? They were soaked, frozen, and exhausted.

Again, Charlie's brain had no time to process the situation; he just started moving. Holding on to the edge of the dock, he used his free hand to hang the back of Cait's shirt against one of the many weathered pylon screws. It held her body up as it bobbed up and down in the water, keeping her just above the surface.

Charlie was free then and climbed out of the water. With one great heave, he hoisted Cait out of the water.

The night air was cold and unforgiving. Charlie shivered.

Cait's body lay still, unaffected by the temperature, and she wasn't breathing.

The outskirts of his mind leaned towards the usual paths of panic, but something in him blocked it. Something staved it off.

He felt free to do what *needed* to be done.

With gentleness, he repositioned Cait, so she was lying on her back, flat against the dock, then checked her pulse. There was none.

Stay calm, he assured himself. *You can do this, Charlie.*

Self-encouragement felt strange after living void of it for so long. A garment he hoped to continue wearing if it got him through this.

Then he got to work administering compressions as her body rose and fell according to his movements. He felt her sternum bend underneath the pressure he used, and around the fifteenth press, he felt and heard it pop. He knew that only meant he was getting somewhere.

Reaching what he'd thought was the right number, he leaned in, lifted her chin and plugged her nose, then breathed what life he could back into her. Two quick shots of it. Then he listened. There was still nothing.

He began again.

Compression after compression, he pressed down.

Cait's lifeless body jolted and twitched with every push.

A warmth settled itself into him, along with a conviction this wasn't the end.

At last, he reached the end of the count again and breathed what weariness he could into her fragile frame. Her chest rose as the oxygen entered her lungs, then collapsed back again after it exited.

She still wasn't breathing.

It was then that worry crept itself in again, faltering Charlie's newfound sense of confidence and purpose.

"Come on, Cait," he said, pleading. "Come on! Come back to me! You need—I need you to come back to me now, okay?"

Tears welled up behind his eyes.

He settled back into compressions once again, as it started sinking in that she was gone. But he couldn't give up. Not yet.

He lost his rhythm, and tears fell with an overbearing weight.

Come on, Cait! he thought. *Come on! Come on, damnit!*

He switched to breathing and still nothing.

Charlie fought away the onslaught of despair, attempting to pummel itself down onto him. That's when, as he raised his arms to begin the compressions again, he collapsed. He fell forward, wrapping his arms around Cait's limp body, and lifted her up.

"I-I'm sorry, Cait."

Nothing could stop the tears then.

"I-I'm sorry you had to get involved with this... with these men and *this* crazy..." His voice rose, sifting back and forth between anger and despair. He looked toward the city, to where it lit up the cloud filled sky. "I'm sorry for what—for my—I'm just so sorry."

It all came flooding out then. The pressure and weight of it all. Going back to Astoria and before. He thought of leaving his mother all alone to start his *new* life. "I'm so sorry," he said again, this one coming out in nothing more than a feeble whisper.

"It's all my fault," he said. His head fell, chin against his chest, lamenting the latest casualty to his strange odyssey.

The dock grew quiet, aside from Charlie's whimpers. Every few seconds, a gentle wave lapped against the dock before receding.

Then something stole Charlie's attention back again. A gurgling cough followed by a low, muttering voice.

"Charl—"

In shock, Charlie released his grip and opened up his arms. He looked down in wonder. A set of confused and tired eyes stared up.

"*Charlie*?" a faint voice said, weak but hopeful.

Charlie's whole body leaped.

"Cait!" He pulled her tight once more. "But how? But... you? And then—"

"I'm... okay," she said, groaning, grasping at her shoulder with her free hand. The bleeding had stopped, but it still throbbed where the bullet stuck. "Sore, but–" she paused as if to think, then wheezed in pain. "I'm dunno where we are. Or how we got here." She coughed. "But I know one thing."

Charlie looked up, not knowing what she'd say.

"*This* isn't your fault."

He gulped but couldn't rid himself of the knot in his throat, and his stomach churned as a series of sickly ripples moved through him.

"Cait, you don't under–"

"No, Charlie," she said to him. Her look was piercing; stern, but filled with understanding. "I don't know everything, okay? I don't know what happened. I dunno what those *things* were. Whether *this* is even over, Charlie..." She hesitated. "... you didn't cause this."

Charlie's lips quivered as the weight settled itself back onto his shoulders and brow, bent on not allowing him to get rid of it.

"*You* are a good person, Charlie West. I haven't known you that long, but I know that. I see it in you. They were using you and you stood up to them—and those things—"

"But I failed—I wouldn't have made it out—"

"But *we did*, Charlie! We did! And look around you!" She pointed to the dock. "You got *me* out, Charlie! Doesn't that sort of make you the hero here?"

The sickly feeling in him wouldn't accept the term. It wouldn't let him consider it, but Cait drawing such a line in the situation was helpful. The weight subsided somewhat as he thought.

"The way he talked about you?" Cait said. "That man? That they'd been searching for you for so long. And needed you for *this*? And for what happened in—"

She stopped.

"Astoria." Charlie said, finishing her thought. Guilt rose, but he felt an interesting wave of strength rise to combat it.

"But you didn't do that."

"They couldn't have done it without me, though," Charlie shot back. "Or this!" He burst, pointing up towards the fire-filled skies as angry tears worked to free themselves again.

Cait looked up at him, at last understanding his pain and the weight he wore.

"Have terrible things happened because of these situations, Charlie?"

Charlie shook his head that they had and then it hung low.

"Did *you* choose to take part in any of it?"

Charlie paused. His head rose, looking upon Cait once more. His head shook back and forth. He hadn't chosen to take part at all. This came as an unstable relief.

"These men, whoever they are, used you, Charlie. *Are* using you."

Charlie's shoulders lifted some.

"And am I wrong to guess this isn't over?"

Charlie shook his head again, this time in agreement.

"But tonight's over, right?"

Charlie nodded it was.

"And those strange creatures?"

"Gone *for now*."

It was Cait's turn to nod at Charlie's comment. She pushed herself up from the dock, reeling with the pain and trauma her body had just endured.

Charlie shot up and helped her.

"Thanks," she said, shaking.

"No, thank you," he rushed. "I mean, you came for me.

Who knows what would've happened if they'd been able to keep going?"

The scene flashed before Cait. Only a haunting memory now, one that didn't even seem real.

"Thanks for pulling me out," she said, pointing to the river. "How'd *we*...?"

"The van."

"Huh."

"That explosion you planned must've struck something big."

Cait couldn't hide how proud she felt her plan had worked.

"I knew it would," she said to Charlie.

"Oh, yeah?"

His joking tone of voice was unpracticed, but welcome.

As Cait and Charlie stood there together, the wind shifted, blowing the embers of what remained of those Pearl District high rises far upriver, away from the city.

Standing there next to Cait, Charlie felt a foundation reforming beneath him—at least it felt like maybe he could rebuild it. Hope blossomed. Something he almost couldn't remember.

As for Cait, she didn't know what it meant, but she felt purpose building. Untethered by the constraints, she couldn't understand why she'd worked so hard to be bound by them. Doing this with Charlie, stopping these men—it meant something. It wasn't something she was doing to prove someone wrong or to show her worth. It was just right, and it made her feel alive.

It was Cait who spoke first after a short period of silence.

"So, I guess the only question is, what's next?"

Charlie looked up at her, shocked.

"What do you mean?"

Cait looked at him, her head cocked.

"What do we do now?"

Charlie's shoulders lowered as he thought about it for a second.

"I have one idea, but it's vague. Blackwell mentioned an *Inner Circle*. Some place up north he didn't want to answer to anymore."

Cait looked on, her interest piqued.

"He also mentioned that they'd wanted him to shut this operation down to put all their resources into whatever *they* were planning."

Cait's eyes widened.

"Well, shit," she said. "Bigger than *this*?"

Charlie hunched his shoulders.

"I dunno," he said. "Honestly? I dunno much. Just fragments I picked up."

Cait's look grew grave for a moment, and she thought of Scott. She wondered what he would've said right then and smiled.

"Well," she said to him. "Looks like we've got some work ahead of us."

A weight settled over Charlie's shoulders, but standing there with Cait, it seemed bearable. He spoke then; with more confidence than before. More than he'd felt in months. It felt good.

"But first..."

"What?"

He looked up.

"First, we have to get up there." He pointed to where the street waited for them. "Before we turn to ice cubes."

It was his turn to let that grave stare construct itself across his face as he looked down at Cait's injured arm and bruised body. A trickle of blood ran from a slice in her forehead, a bruise already forming around it.

Cait looked up. The dock hung at the base of a thirty-foot

keeping wall. The river's edge lining Downtown's West Side, a ladder made up of metal rungs, lead to the top. But she only had one good arm.

"Shit…" She looked up and winced. A residual despair clung to her. "How are we going to do this?"

Charlie turned to her, then looked up. A brightness lined his eyes, an unfamiliar gleam.

"The same way we got through tonight."

Cait held her breath and looked up.

"Together, one step at a time," he said, and her jaw quivered just so. What she felt perplexed her. She wasn't used to being a part of anything. To stave back her own set of tears, she just nodded.

They turned together to face their next challenge.

It was a daunting sight as Cait looked up, but she readied her weak arm to hold what weight it could as she placed her other hand on the rung in front of her. Then, after taking a series of long, deep breaths, she placed her foot on the bottom-most step and spoke one word to herself, a rough whisper.

"*Together.*"

A hopeful grin formed on Charlie. Determination flooded as he watched Cait climb. He would be there if she fell. They'd reach the top, and they'd continue to be there for one another.

Something new was forming. They just had to keep going, *always*.

Cait made steady progress up—slow, but steady.

As for Charlie, he followed close behind her. Each step brought him closer to a world that he'd felt ready to abandon. Not anymore. Cait had triggered something. Charlie remembered who he'd always hoped to be. It fueled him, leaving a revelatory impression that he might make it, after all.

He knew—*then*—he at least had to try.

Epilogue

A gentle sprinkling of snow fell from a bright, cloudy mid-morning sky as an aged man stood in his kitchen cutting vegetables—some for dinner that night, but the others he would store and use in whatever meal he decided over the course of the next week.

The radio played in the background. He let each tune's movement carry him forward in his work.

He was methodical, precise. As soon as he finished a row of chopping, he lifted the cutting board and used the knife to push some of them into the skillet he had placed over the stove. The rest, he slid into a wide Tupperware container he had put on the counter.

Once the cutting board was empty, he would begin again; a ritual he'd come to appreciate about life in the mountains.

There wasn't much he missed about city life, nor the cut-throat pursuits the world of academia forced upon him. He missed people, but only those he was close to. Often, when he thought of his friends or family members, those he'd loved most, he only wished he could have explained why he had to disappear, and that it was for their safety more than his own.

Loneliness was his penance, he told himself whenever the thoughts arose. How would he have known what his discoveries would lead to? If it kept the people he loved safe, it was worth it.

In the end, life up in the most northern reaches of British Columbia's Cascade Range was quite peaceful, filled with time for reading and reflection. He could keep up with some aspects of his research that way. Still, it wasn't the same.

Even in the heavy winter they'd had, he'd got outdoors some. He treasured those moments.

He set three carrots in front of him and cut them each longways down the center before rearranging them into smaller chunks when a fright-filled voice interrupted the peaceful drone of the radio that had been filling the empty parts of his mind.

We interrupt your listening pleasure to deliver breaking news about an explosion in Portland, Oregon last night. The cause has not yet been determined; but crews are working round the clock to establish what happened. We will bring you updates as we receive them, but all we know right now is that a trio of subsidized apartment complexes taking up an entire city block in Portland's Pearl District is no longer standing. The city's devastated by the loss and filled with fear and confusion.

For one frightening moment, the old man's breath seemed to flee from him. The knife slipped from his hand, hit the cutting board, and slid far too close to his fingers. He shuttered and lost his balance. Grasping the counter with both hands, he was able to stay upright.

No threats have been made, nor has anyone come forth to claim responsibility. Still, the question of terrorism lingers. Authorities have ruled out the possibility of it being an accident. Authorities also registered no seismic activity in the area, and seeing that no other buildings were affected, they'll most likely rule out natural causes.

The city mourns this morning as it grapples to figure out exactly what happened, but stay tuned, and we'll keep you up to date. Our hearts and prayers go out to all affected by this tragedy. Stay safe out there, everyone.

In local news, three more hikers disappeared in the northern reaches of the Yukon Territory...

The old man had tuned it out. It took several seconds for him to catch his breath. Once he did, he hustled over to the phone, picked it up, and dialed the number he knew by heart. After a few rings, someone picked up.

"Hello? Liam—that you?" said the old man. "Yeah, yeah, it's me. *It's time.*"

Quiet settled as the old man listened.

"No, it's them. It's *them*, for sure, and I can't take any chances. I'd like to move ahead with the plan. I'll gather what I can from up here—can I meet you in Lower Post? Just at the junction there? Then—yeah, yeah. That sounds perfect. And remember, don't book it under my name. Please don't use—I know, I know. Sorry, this is just bringing out all my nerves. No, thank you. You've been a real help." He listened for another moment. "Yeah, yeah. Well, the less you know, the better. Trust me. If you can get me near Watson, I'll follow the trail north. No, I'd rather you not get more involved. You don't want any part of this madness. I promise you that. What? Yes. Yes. Thank you. Yes. I've a hunch, and I might need you close to the border soon. I'll keep you posted. Thanks. See you soon."

With that, Dr. James Lake hung up the phone and forced himself to take several deep breaths. Finding his resolve, he turned and scurried about the cabin, gathering what he'd need for the journey to come. All the while, a panic-stricken look shrouded his face. He'd forgotten what he'd been doing, and the scene in the kitchen sat frozen and untouched. The

Tupperware waited, half-full, the skillet unlit, while the vegetables sat, waiting to be chopped.

The End of Part Two

Charlie West and Cait Lane will return in
The Northwest Trilogy Part 3: The Mountains at the Edge of Madness

"This above all: to thine own self be true."

— William Shakespeare, *Hamlet*

Afterword

This book was as freeing to write as it was difficult. Threading Charlie's pain from page to page exercised my own. I learned a great deal about life and about myself while writing this book, not always expecting the dark corners and alleys it led me down.

At the start of writing this series, one question always hung in my mind. Can someone who struggles with severe anxiety and depression still be the hero of their own journey? Was their life destined for tragedy or was recovery possible? So, I toyed with the Elements of Story, seeing how the classic hero arc overlaid with various horror/suspense genre tropes, all the while through the lens of a character with extreme struggles.

For the first time in my life I see certain elements of my own life, the one's I kept hidden from as many people as possible (which only holds us back—as you can see with Charlie in the first half of this book), play out on the page.

When Doom came out, I received several messages asking whether I was familiar with The Hero's Journey. These questions always made me smile as, to me, they proved one of two things: Either they didn't understand what I was trying to achieve...or I didn't portray it well enough. Enough readers could comment on their understanding of what I was doing. I didn't think too much about their comments, but it caused me to reflect.

The hero is supposed to reject their path, only to be thrust into it early in the first act of the first arc. It's interesting to look back and cite Charlie doesn't do this. In fact, Charlie never engages in his own path with any direct intention (by choice) in the entire first book. To me, this is vital to his story. Taking it a step further, when writing this book, it intrigued me to find out when he would at last pick up his own mantle and move forward on his own accord, if ever. It came, but at the very end, as you saw. Six acts into a three-part story (according to classic models), but it felt so realistic and true to the experience of people who suffer.

The entire drive of this story to me (all three parts) cruxes on this question: Can we become the purveyors of our own stories? Considering it another way, are we the most alive when we are forging our own path? It breaks as well as warms me that Charlie has at last broken through the wall of whatever was holding him back. Writing book three has been an incredible exploration of how these elements continue to translate for such a character (it's unfortunate how many of us relate to this). I won't spoil what's coming, but I will say the back and forth of how Charlie (and now Cait) operates once making it onto that path has been an enriching experience.

My hope is that these books have challenged you as much as they did me. I hope they've inspired, created questions, discussion, thought, and made you consider or reconsider the nature of autonomy and what it means to forge your own path in this world.

Charlie has been my whole heart these past few years, and I cannot wait to share the final stage of his journey with you in The Mountains at the Edge of Madness, where we find out whether Charlie finds peace and can steer his own way along the road with confidence.

Thank you for reading. It means the world to me. Thank you for loving Charlie and caring enough to see his story through to the end.

Craig Randall
Corvallis, OR, August 2022

JOIN THE NEWSLETTER